Having worked for the *Daily Telegraph* and the *Express*, Tiffanie Darke is now an editor at the *Sunday Times*. Her first novel, *Marrow*, was shortlisted for the WHSmith Fresh Talent Award.

### Praise for MARROW

'Wickedly accurate' *The Times*

'An entertaining insight into the badness that goes on behind kitchen doors . . . if I were a commis chef again and came across this book, I'd be very afraid'
Allegra McEvedy, *Express*

'One stormy tale of out-of-control egos and shameless back-stabbing' *Company*

'A great cast and fab locations make it pure fun' *Shine*

'Tastily packed with sexy secrets of the restaurant biz'
*Cosmopolitan*

'Will make you laugh out loud' *New Woman*

'Comparable to Fiona Walker, Darke's first novel is frothier than a well-whipped cappuccino. Lap it up . . .' *Mirror*

# Strapline

Tiffanie Dark

POCKET
BOOKS

LONDON • SYDNEY • NEW YORK • TOKYO • SINGAPORE • TORONTO

First published in Great Britain by Pocket Books, 2002
An imprint of Simon & Schuster UK Ltd
A Viacom Company

1 3 5 7 9 10 8 6 4 2

Simon & Schuster UK Ltd
Africa House
64–78 Kingsway
London WC2B 6AH

www.simonsays.co.uk

Simon & Schuster Australia
Sydney

A CIP catalogue record for this book
is available from the British Library

ISBN 0-671-03755-2

Typeset in Garamond by M Rules
Printed and bound by
Cox & Wyman Ltd, Reading, Berks.

With thanks to all my family and friends
who have been unendingly supportive and encouraging

# chapter one

Charlotte Want settled back into the plush leather seat that ran along the back of her chauffeur-driven limo. Outside the rain splashed noisily; she inspected her stockinged feet carefully for mud splatters, but it appeared her stilettoes had been high enough to protect her. Just another thing that had gone right today, then. Firstly the call from Wella, followed by a grossly oversized bunch of flowers from London's most exclusive florist congratulating her on the success of the ad – sales, apparently, were up 5 per cent. Then the call from Chloe, informing her that one of the ten limited-edition print dresses she wanted had arrived and been put aside for her and, when her PA had finally brought her her post, a gilt-edged invitation from HRH the Prince of Wales and Donatella Versace to their Autumn Diamond Benefit next month had proclaimed her move from the D to the C list absolutely official.

Even Victor Power – Uncle Vic as he liked to refer to

himself – had telephoned to congratulate her, and had insisted she do another shoot for *Hiya!* magazine next month. Very satisfactory indeed, she mused, and allowed the sharp angles of her face to deepen into a smirk. Instinctively she put out a hand to smooth her pleasingly expensive leather miniskirt, then raised her perfectly manicured fingers to her lips, and tapped her violet nails against her teeth. Could this really be the end of bit-part TV, and the start of something really major league? Her agent Doug had seemed pretty convinced that 'she was on the verge of the big time', but then he had said that more often than she had been down Bond Street. Still, an invitation from Donatella Versace and Prince Charles – you didn't get more upwardly mobile than that. Surely a proper acting part or even a record deal had to follow now?

Charlotte's thoughts were moving fast. None of this would happen unless she could capitalize on her invitation. And the surest way to capitalize, surmised Charlotte, whose instinctive skills for the wants of tabloid newspapers had got her a long way already, was with a Dress, of course. What she required, what was, indeed, absolutely essential for the party was a Show Stopper – in fact not just a Show Stopper, but a real Front Page Hogger. One that had 'That Dress' written all over it. This party, she decided, was going to be her moment.

To date, Charlotte's career as an AMW – actress, model, whatever – had not exactly made her world famous, but had certainly conferred upon her, among the circle of magazine journalists, party organizers, model bookers and promotional experts who mattered, the status of a luke-warm celebrity.

Charlotte's parents had begun her ascent to fame within months of her conception. Before she was even born their daughter had become the instrument through which they decided they could live out their own frustrated hopes of stardom. So Charlotte had been brought up to believe she was destined for fame and fortune, by whatever means possible: her mummy and her daddy told her so.

When her parents had first met, her father Don had been on the verge of signing a major record deal with Arista. After playing every single pub in his home town, Cambridge, and then several years of touring every spit and sawdust watering hole in the south of England, Don Want's rock band Stainless Steel had eventually played to a particularly drunk A&R man one evening who had promised them untold riches. Following a night-long excessive celebration, Don had rather exuberantly decided to rubber stamp his love for Gloria – an over-zealous groupie who had been hanging round the band's mosh pit for most of that summer – with a Caribbean wedding holiday paid for out of a substantial part of his advance.

In the end, however, the record company were taken over, the deal was off and – needs must, needs be – Don had had to become a door-to-door salesman because his new wife was now pregnant and unable to do anything other than eat chocolate. Fortunately, he had prospered, and as the Fens took on the status of Britain's answer to Silicon Valley, his small software company, started with his winnings from selling the *Encyclopaedia Britannica*, had burgeoned. By the time Charlotte was sixteen the Want family were living in a mock-Tudor mansion in the countryside with two cars and a time share in Majorca. And Mrs Want had all the gold jewellery and hair appointments she could wish for.

So while Don spent his days flogging floppy disks, making his money in the Thatcher's Britain that his band had so fiercely sung anthems against, Gloria squared their devil's deal with capitalism by taking their daughter to every singing, music and dance class there was going. As Charlotte grew older, their hopes were buoyed by her appearance, for there was no denying that she was beauti-fully photogenic. With almond-shaped eyes, olive skin and dark (albeit enhanced) chocolate-coloured hair her small frame was prone to a little pudginess, but this was carefully controlled by rigorous diets imposed by Gloria to make Charlotte fit model-size clothes. Any imperfections were ironed out when her parents gave her a nose job for her seventeenth birthday. Her newly straightened nose did much to highlight her cheekbones, which were now so sharp they looked as though you could cut yourself on them, although they had the rather unfortunate propensity of making her appear as if she had swallowed a wasp every time she pursed her lips – something she did regularly, but never in front of camera.

After graduating from the prestigious Anna Scher stage school in London, Charlotte was cherry-picked to be the fourth 'sultry' member of a girl band which the manager promised would take over the world.

Three years on, however, the girl band had barely made an appearance in *Smash Hits* magazine. The group were disbanded and Charlotte was reduced to jobbing as a model. (She was once given a presenting slot in MTV, but she was sacked after two weeks for not being able to read the autocue.) Then Gloria found out that the one-time drummer of Stainless Steel, Doug Bowser, Deadly Doug as he was now known, ran a very successful East End showbiz agency, so she marched Charlotte along and demanded that Doug make her a star.

Now, Doug had a songwriter on his books who was unfortunately lens-crackingly ugly, so the two were paired together in a Manchester studio in what was hoped would be a wonderfully harmonious union of talent and looks. Three months and plenty of tantrums later, a single had been recorded, and Charlotte timed its release to coincide with a very public affair she was having with the latest Italian signing for Manchester United. The Italian and his team's other three strikers had chosen to take Charlotte and some of her pretty showbiz friends out for a night, and they had ended up in a jacuzzi in the city's flashest hotel. Somehow, the pictures had been blazoned across the *News of the World* the following day, making Charlotte a temporary star of the front page, and the Italian striker the devil of the back pages. The net result was that United's new £15 million signing was suspended for a month, and Charlotte's debut single went straight in at number one. While Don was horrified at the public nature of his daughter's antics and rang up Doug to complain, Doug himself rang up his showbiz journo mate and thanked him very much.

Unfortunately, the songwriter had by this stage stormed out, refusing to work 'with such tawdry trash'. Doug decided that as talent was not going to win the day for Charlotte, he would resort to the one sure-fire way of building on the small amount of tabloid currency Charlotte now had – Victor Power.

Victor Power was in the business of celebrity. His lucrative publishing empire had gained attention five years ago with the launch of the phenomenon that was *Hiya!* magazine – every week the promise of grizzly details about the latest Hollywood marriage, GMTV christening or Vanessa diet shifted half a million copies off the shelf. But the confessions of the celebs began to come at a price and the bigger the celebrity, the more expensive their interviews became. So Power had decided to grow his own stars.

As far as Doug could see, Charlotte was pretty much exactly what Power wanted – young, malleable, hungry and with just enough residual fame to give Victor something to build on. Late last year he had signed a contract with Power committing Charlotte to a certain number of shoots, and absolute exclusivity on anything that happened in her career and life. The contract was worth nothing to Charlotte financially, but it gave her exactly the exposure she needed. Power threw in a chauffeur and a PA (both helped create the illusion of her fame) and so far it seemed the plan was working well. Charlotte's omnipresence in *Hiya!* was fooling the ad agencies into hiring her, and the public into buying into her.

And now the invitation to a royal event. Nestled in her limousine, Charlotte could hardly wipe the smirk off her face, in fact it was only the panic at the thought of what it was she was going to wear that was keeping her from leaping up and down on her leather banquette. Little did she know, although if she had thought about it she might well have suspected, that the invitation had been a direct result of Power's influence rather any burning desire by the hosts for her presence. Power's most recent cheque to Elton had been hefty, ooh yes, very hefty, and he had intended to squeeze every favour out of the man he could in return. Exclusive pictures of Elton's new decorating job at his villa in the South of France were not quite going to suffice.

Charlotte, of course, preferred to think it was her own achievements that had merited the invitation, but she was also smart enough to know how those achievements had come about. She was an absolutely perfect match for Victor Power's needs, Doug had decided when he had put her up for the deal, because it wasn't riches Charlotte lusted after, she had, after all, never wanted for anything material, it was *fame*. And, it appeared, she would do almost anything to get it. When she had explained this to Power, he could not have heard anything sweeter even from the lips of an angel and, clasping her cheeks in both his perfectly manicured hands, he had planted a kiss full on her lips, to Gloria's slight discomfort and Charlotte's delight. Shoving a batch of papers across his desk he offered her his Mont Blanc fountain pen and begged her to sign.

'You haven't got a biro, have you? I'm not sure I can sign with a nib,' she said.

That had been just six months ago, and the fruits of the deal were already beginning to ripen – Doug had even begun to tentatively suggest they might go and see the record companies again soon. One more massive shoot for *Hiya!* and that should do it, he'd said. Charlotte was pleased, very pleased.

Inside her Vuitton bag one of her mobiles began to ring. It was her private line, which could only mean a booty call – or her mother. She checked the number calling – not specified, and picked it up.

'Hello, Charlotte speaking.'

'Darleeng. Are you still in London? I need to see you,' replied an urgent, gravelly voice in a thick Brazilian accent, just the one Charlotte had been expecting.

'On the motorway heading north, baby. Where are you?'

'Checking into ze nearest otel, right now. Ow long till you get to ze Malmaison?'

'Ninety minutes.'

'I'll see you in Room 101. I've got somesing sparkly for you, somesing I know you will luuurve.'

'Good.' Charlotte smirked with satisfaction.

'You will wear zose panties, won't you . . .?'

Charlotte laughed and clicked off. Lifting up her leather skirt she slipped out of her Calvin Klein thong, dropped it on the floor of the limo and fished a minute scrap of purple lace out of her handbag. She dangled it in front of her and examined the slit in the crotch for the second time that day. The panties had arrived by express delivery this morning, and she couldn't help feeling they were a touch tasteless, but Brazilian men were Brazilian men. And, she reasoned to herself, if there was one thing she enjoyed, then it was other people enjoying her body. That, after all, was why she was here, she thought with the mistaken satisfaction of utter selflessness. She slipped the panties on and adjusted the straps to something approaching comfortable. Then she pulled her lipstick out of her bag to apply one more coat of the thick, dark purple that was her current trademark. It was one of those uber-trendy urban makes, sent to her by the PR company in industrial quantities in the hope that she might popularize it. Idly she turned it over to check the name. Smug Bitch it said. How wonderfully appropriate, she thought, as she switched on the television and opened a half bottle of champagne. Sometimes life was just too, too easy.

## chapter two

Toby regarded Cas carefully as she bustled about the kitchen, cleaning, washing, straightening. Her hair, nearly dry from her morning shower, was curling coquettishly down her back – curls which she hated and which Toby loved. A frown of concentration across her face showed she was set into her tasks, but her mind, Toby knew, was elsewhere. The creases on her forehead punctured her expression, dragging her green eyes down with it, pushing up her bottom lip and dimpling her chin. It was an expression that gave her a misleading air of vulnerability and it was not an unusual one, especially recently, thought Toby.

At the age of twenty-nine Cas found, in the parlance of glossy women's magazines, that she 'had it all' – flat, job, man – but that nonetheless, she wasn't as happy as she was told she should be. She had never stopped to ask herself precisely why not, she was usually too busy. She placed a saucer of tuna on the floor for Sindy, her spoilt tabby, so called because Sindy had the kind of doll's life Cas longed for: plenty of cushions, plenty of stroking, plenty of sleep. She caressed Sindy's back as the cat entwined itself between her legs, then chucked the tin in the bin and threw the fork into the mounting pile in the sink.

She and Toby had been living together for nearly a year now, which wasn't a problem in itself, but Cas thought the imbalance of work was becoming one. It had been she who had urged Toby to give up his day job and concentrate on what he was good at full time, while she supported them both. Toby was a sculptor, and a talented one at that, but there wasn't much money to be made from sculpting, and neither did he have any of his own. His family were actually old-school English aristocracy, but in time-honoured tradition they had lost all their money and now lived an impoverished existence. Besides, Toby was something of a black sheep in the family – quite literally. His coffee-coloured skin, high cheekbones and coal-black eyes did not exactly fit in with the rest of the family's Anglo Saxon appearance and was proof of a family humiliation from great-grandmother's heyday during the Raj. Being plagued by debt was one thing, being plagued by great-grandmama's penchant for kaffir sex, was quite another. Unfortunately, great-grandmama's indiscretions with the servants had only chosen to manifest themselves three generations down the line and the eastern sultriness of Toby's appearance could no longer hide one of the family's less proud moments.

But Cas adored his looks, which thrilled Toby who had been brought up to believe his appearance was a disgrace. Even more, she adored his talent for art (his father had been horrified when he had chosen to sculpt. 'Art? Art is for nancy boys! Good God, don't tell me you're one of them too, are you?'). So when Toby and Cas had been looking for a flat together, and had found this place in the East End – a living space with a bedroom downstairs right next to a huge sky-lit garage, one that could easily be converted into a studio – Cas had known what they must do. By accepting the deputy editorship of a prestigious Sunday supplement, she had been able to pay the rent for both of them, leaving Toby free to make something of his talent and attend the lecture course at the Slade he had always wanted to.

But the job had not quite turned out to be the dream career move Cas had originally hoped. She had been employed by the editor of the newspaper – a cool, liberated feminist from the seventies who still believed journalism could be a morally responsible, socially enhancing tool. Susie Farlane ran a mid-market tabloid, the *Daily News*, but not for her the scandals of soap stars, kiss-and-tell football shaggers and lengthy witterings from It girls about parties they had been seen at. She had other ideas about what should be in a tabloid – investigative journalism that you invested time, money and staff in which exposed the realities beneath so much of the modern-day spin. In other words, what journalism used to be. She ran the paper as a seven day operation and had offered Cas a job on the Sunday magazine supplement because she was someone with a track record for serious journalism. Cas had been put in place to temper the frivolities of the magazine's fearsome editor, the Psychotic Bitch From Hell (PBfH), Tamara Yearbank, whose obsessions with the latest lipsticks and celebrity gossip had made the magazine somewhat 'lite' in Farlane's eyes. Yearbank, however, was less than enamoured with Cas's appointment and spent her days ritually abusing her and exploiting her authority as Cas's boss by completely ignoring her, regularly undermining her and, more recently, insulting her directly to her face. All the while making Cas do most of the work while she swanned around town lunching and shopping.

Cas found this very trying, but looked on it as something she had to live with. Every idea for a story she came up with, Tamara would tell her it was unworkable, and she would have to fight tooth and nail to get it commissioned. Every headline she wrote Tamara would reject, every picture she chose Tamara would overrule, every suggestion she came up with Tamara would sneer at. It took her days to persuade Tamara of anything, making the process bitter, difficult and always three times the work it should be.

Cas tried not to take her problems home, but Toby could see the day to day hell was beginning to take its toll. Toby, for his part, would stroke her hair and wonder if he was meant to feel guilty about her job, and in moments of doubt would ask her if it was his fault she was doing what she was doing.

'Of course not. No, I took this job because it was a good move. It was a prestigious thing to be offered. And I'm learning stuff from it. I'm certainly learning,' Cas would reply slowly.

'You know, if you hate it so much you should leave, find something else. Screw the money. We'll find a way.'

'Well, I can't leave just yet, I haven't been doing it long enough, it'll look like I've got no staying power.'

'Look like no staying power to who? Who cares Cas? Isn't it more important you're happy?'

But as far as Cas was concerned she had made commitments and now she had to stick by them.

This morning though, had brought fresh cause for concern. The business pages of *The Times* reported that the City expected Lord Paul, owner of the *Daily News*, to announce his intention to sell. There had been rumours to this effect flying around work for weeks, but yesterday she had heard something was definitely afoot and, since she had been unable to sleep, she had got up early to get the paper. Cas failed to see how a change of ownership could be a change for the better. If the paper was bought by someone else then there was no knowing who she might end up working for. This worry gnawed deeply at Cas, and she snapped the paper shut on the kitchen table. At the moment her job was bearable because it was worthwhile – she was proud of what they eventually achieved at the magazine, PBfH notwithstanding. Unfortunately however, their achievements were not proving too commercially successful: politicians it seemed, were not as interesting to the general public as actresses.

Despite her tiredness, despite the animation that had gone out of her movements, she looked beautiful this morning, Toby thought. The curves of her body at her hips and bust straining at her clothes lent an irresistible sexiness to her tired movements. She had woken up early, and he had listened to her pottering about the flat for the last hour. He had thought she might come back to bed and say hello, snuggle into him one last time before she got dressed, as she sometimes did. But she didn't, so he had got up to watch her instead. She had been at some function last night for work and had got in late, and she was going out again tonight. It was funny how you could live with someone and yet never see them, he thought.

Standing in the doorway, his long, lithe body naked beneath his dressing gown, his dark hair falling over his eyes, watching her, Toby was overcome with a powerful feeling of admiration and desire for this woman whom he loved with a passion he had never known before – one that overtook him, shocked him and shook him in a way that astonished him every day.

Her unhappiness sharpened Toby's love. He admired her industriousness: coming from a family that had done little for itself for centuries, simply resting on its laurels, her sense of responsibility and purpose was arresting. Stealing across the living room, he approached her from behind as she bent over the sink and, placing one of his strong hands on her buttocks, he reached up with the other to the curve of her breast.

'Mine, all mine,' he whispered into her ear. 'So beautiful, so sexy, such a woman,' he murmured. Moving his hand round to the curve of her tummy, he squeezed her into his warm, naked body, her head fitted perfectly under his chin, the roundness of her buttocks nuzzled his groin. Cas stopped shuffling the crockery in the sink, glad of a break from considering budget slashes, months of uncertainty, possible redundancy – all the likely outcomes from a new ownership of the paper.

Leaning into Toby, she allowed the pressure of his body to relax her. His right hand was working its way up underneath her shirt, his left hitching up her skirt to discover the top of the stockings she had only just put on.

'Do you have any idea how erotic it is watching you wash up?' he murmured again, feeling himself grow hard against the small of her back.

'Is that why you leave it for me to do then?' Cas bit back, instantly regretting it.

Toby ignored her, an argument – of which there seemed to have been a few recently – was not on his agenda. Instead he turned her round to face him, and cradled her face in his hands.

'Undress,' he whispered, while he planted lingering, light kisses on her lips and cheeks. 'Undress for me, Cas.'

Cas closed her eyes and shut out her day ahead. Suddenly it was just her and Toby, alone in a perfect world. Slowly a calming blanket of darkness descended on her cluttered mind and as she felt his kisses brushing lightly on her skin. She found her hands were beginning to undo her shirt, while his voice caressed her, comforting and reassuringly familiar. This, she thought, was the one thing it was all right to surrender to. She pulled her jumper over her head, her beautifully rounded breasts staring up at Toby, cradled in their lace bra. She watched his face as he took them in and noted his appreciation. Toby's enjoyment of her made her feel so good.

'Now your skirt,' Toby urged her, tearing his eyes away and looking back to her face. How easily he could forget everything, not care about anything but the present, she thought. He would never worry about a rent cheque. She allowed herself to swim with him on the moment, forcing her anxieties out of her mind again, drowning herself in his glazed eyes which looked on her with such desire.

She made a move to unzip her skirt, but now, with a curl of his lip, he had changed his mind and, grabbing it by the hem on either side, he hitched it up onto her hips, exposing the tops of her stockings, the flesh of her thighs and the black lace panties he had bought for her on her birthday. Her premiere lingerie armour. It must be war at work today, he thought, faintly amused and very pleased too.

'Turn round,' he ordered her, with a mischievous glint in his eye, 'and carry on washing up.'

Slowly turning her shoulders, then her waist, then her head, she began to enjoy herself, playing the game and following Toby's commands, feeling her own dampness as his hot breath warmed the back of her neck. His dressing gown had fallen open and she could feel the heat of his skin against her as his fingers began to trace the naked flesh at the tops of her inner thighs. She smiled, complicit in his game and groped in the sink for a plate, noticing with amusement she still had her yellow Marigolds on. Toby pressed against her harder now, and she could feel his skin on hers, the flesh of his torso warming her back, his hardness against her, becoming more insistent and stronger. His arm slid around her front and down between her thighs just as she picked up the dishcloth and began to wipe the plate.

Now he was murmuring his appreciation hypnotically in her ear, encouraging her to continue washing up and to fight her desire. She picked up a mug, but by now her eyes were half closed and she wasn't sure what her hands were doing any more. Every time she stopped he asked her to continue until it became an excruciating battle between her conscientious action and his manipulation of her body. She was now soaking wet, but she didn't know if it was her juices or water from the sink dripping down her legs, and she let out a long moan as he explored with his fingers gently, teasingly, between her legs.

'Keep going,' he said and she fished around in the bottom of the sink for an object – anything so long as he didn't stop what he was doing. Then she felt his hardness nudging into her and she arched her back to encourage him. He pushed her away – this was his game and not hers.

'Finish your washing up, young lady,' he said in answer to her body, every cell of which was urging him inside her, and gently pushed the small of her back until she was pressed right up against the sink and he could admire her shape, as he traced the curves of her buttock cheeks with his hands. When she picked up another plate he rewarded her by pushing into her. Each time she wiped the dish he pushed further and further until she dropped what she was holding and it clattered to the floor. Now he was pushing hard up inside her against the edge of the sink, pushing her off the floor, and the sweet ecstasy of the pleasure and the almost-pain of his forcefulness gripped her body. Toby pulled out suddenly and spun her around, lifting her up so that she sat on the edge of the sink, and then he entered her again. Distractedly Cas's eyes flicked open and she saw the urgency etched on his face.

Grasping her round her waist he pulled her into him again so her breasts pressed tight against his chest, the lace of her bra separating their skin. Behind her back he had expertly unclasped her bra, and as he pulled away from her again he pushed it off her shoulders to expose the round globes beneath. He took one erect nipple in his mouth and rolled his tongue around the hardness, pulling on it until Cas moaned aloud and he released her, and pushed into her again, this time harder, deeper, insistently, and the two were rocking together against the sink, water splashing everywhere until she cried out, and he allowed himself finally to let go inside her, so both gushed in spasms over each other as they clung tightly to each other.

'Okay, then,' she said after a while, when she had caught her breath. 'Maybe I don't mind washing up so much.'

He smiled at her, his dark eyes drowned in drunken ecstasy, and smoothed her cheek with his hand.

Suddenly Cas jerked awake.

'Oh my God! What time is it?'

Toby looked at her, slightly disappointed. He saw her mind had left him, she was back in her own world, and he pulled his hands away from her body and put them up in the air, giving in and stepping back. She moved round him looking for the oven clock.

'It's half past! I'm going to be late. Oh . . .' Cas looked down at the pile of her clothes that were now sitting in a washing-up-water puddle at her feet. 'Toby!' she said accusingly.

Toby stared at her in disbelief. 'Sorry,' he said, not sounding it.

Cas met his gaze for a second, but it was too late, her day ahead had already taken her from him. She looked away.

'Look, I've got to go.'

'Obviously,' he said, overcoming his own resentment, forcing himself to understand. 'Go.'

'Shit, my clothes are soaked!'

'Shhh, don't worry, I'll go and get you some clean ones.'

'I don't have anything clean. It's all still in the bottom of the laundry basket,' she said accusingly, displacing her dread with her resentment of his domestic inadequacy. If she earned the cash then the least he could do was the chores, she thought.

Toby shrugged and left her as she spun herself into a frenzy, pulling on her clothes and searching for her keys. She might not want to talk to him about her work, but she certainly let him know how she felt about it. She left without saying goodbye.

As she rushed out of the tube, Cas could feel the moistness between her legs from their moment together, the dampness of her hastily retrieved clothes and their misunderstanding. She knew she was doing wrong by him, but she felt unsupported. Sex was great, but it did not pay any bills. Was it too easy for him to depend on her? she wondered. She looked up as she emerged from the tube station, already sweltering in the late-summer heat, despite the early hour, and her heart dropped heavily into her shoes as the monstrous grey building that incarcerated her daily loomed into sight.

# chapter three

At the very top of the grey building, through the window that ran the length of one side of the building and dominated the penthouse office, could be seen Lord Paul, chairman of the board of directors and majority shareholder of the *Daily News*, who was taking a phone call his secretary had just patched through to him.

'Victor, how are you?' he said, after picking up the receiver.

'Always well, Richard. Always well. I see *The Times* is speculating.'

'You want to learn to ignore what they put in the papers, Victor.'

'That's where you're wrong, my friend. I want to have a hand in it. As you well know.' Victor Power's voice boomed down the telephone line, so that Lord Paul had to hold the receiver away from his ear. Power's voice exuded confidence, too much for Lord Paul's liking. But Power was a man who had never taken no for an answer.

Lord Paul was not overly fond of Power: he was not the sort of man it was easy to form an attachment to – he had his own agenda and wasn't interested in any one else's, and he made that quite clear from the moment you met him. But this, of course, was not a bad thing in business. No, Lord Paul's main problem with Power as a potential buyer of the newspaper was not his manner, but how he had come by his wealth. For although Power liked to keep quiet about it, it was well known Power Publishing had made most of its money from top-shelf magazines, and family newspaper proprietors did not normally associate themselves with pornographers. Lord Paul, however, was a greedy man at heart and was therefore quite willing to consider allowing a porn magnate to become the owner of one of the country's oldest newspapers, particularly since he was offering £5 million more for it than anyone else. Ethics, Lord Paul reminded himself, did not come into business. Ever.

'There is a board meeting this afternoon, at which I shall be discussing your proposition, but I have to tell you there are question marks over your suitability as a newspaper proprietor. As I am sure you are aware your . . . other interests may well be an issue for the rest of the board.'

Power gritted his teeth. It was precisely this attitude that had inspired him to make an offer for the newspaper in the first place. The snobbery of the English establishment had shut him out of everything he had tried to gain access to, just because he – Victor Power – hadn't been born with a silver spoon in his mouth, but had earned his money in a way that the bastards didn't approve of. He had poured enough of his profits into charity coffers to have merited several knighthoods by now (and a life peerage), but still he was shunned by the ruling elite. It infuriated Power, this po-faced attitude to sex. Hypocrites – that's what they all were. He'd seen them himself, kerb-crawling in King's Cross and Shepherd's Market. He bet that half of them bought his 'disapproved of' magazines as well. Well, if he owned the *Daily News*, then they would have to sit up and pay attention.

'Then I'll increase my offer,' he spat. Nothing was going to stop him taking over this paper, it had been too long in the planning for him to lose it now.

Lord Paul paused. 'By how much?'

'Five million.' Power knew his reputation wouldn't influence the decision, but his money would.

Lord Paul nodded. 'I should have an answer for you by Wednesday next week.'

'Not good enough. I want an answer by 9 a.m. Monday morning.'

'Very well, then,' replied Lord Paul tightly. He was going to have to close this deal soon anyway because he was finding it increasingly difficult to deal with Power without losing his temper.

'I look forward to it, Richard,' said Power, his tone instantaneously relaxed. 'And I'm sorry you don't find me a suitable candidate for your organ,' he continued, 'but I think you'll find I'll turn the *Daily News* into a top-selling paper, which is more than can be said for it at the moment.'

There the conversation ended, with little love lost between the two men.

Victor Power replaced the receiver in its cradle and steepled his fingertips together. Closing his eyes, he let the anger wash out of his body, in the way his therapist had taught him. Eventually, with his mind and body clear, he got up from his black leather Charles Eames chair and made his way over to the bar at the end of the room. His Timothy Everest suit clung to his still muscular fifty-something body beautifully: Everest was the only Savile Row tailor Power had been told he could trust with his measurements. Money had bought him many things, and one of the most valuable, he considered, was the guidance of his personal stylist: the redoubtable Adrian Fagge, the man who proved money *could* buy you taste. Power had very quickly realized that style was something he desperately needed if he was going to achieve his ascent to the ranks of the rich and famous. Fagge ensured his suits no longer came from Moss Bros, his house no longer had Mia Casa written on its helipad roof, his offices were decorated in beige and leather as opposed to crimson and leopardskin, and all his entertaining took place at the Ivy rather than at For Your Eyes Only. With these changes in place, Power found he could be utterly convincing as a player on the twenty-first-century social scene.

It's true, he had nearly failed to secure the picture rights to the latest Michael Douglas wedding when he had ordered egg and chips at Hollywood's Spago restaurant.

Nearly. Now Fagge had the menus sent to him in advance and instructed Power what to choose (and how to eat it). Since the launch of *Hiya!* magazine, Power had had to embark on a crash course in nu-celebrity manners. For the first time in his life he had been out of his depth, but part of his talent was that he recognized this.

Power poured himself his fourth black coffee of the morning and surveyed the view from the floor to ceiling window of his penthouse office. To the east the Docklands area of London stretched out before him, a futurescape of glass and steel buildings, each bidding to beat the other to reach furthest into the air, each a pinnacle of unrestrained urban ambition. Docklands was a burgeoning area of new build that in the last ten years had come to be recognized as the new business park of a city. Power, of course, with his shrewd eye for a deal, had seen that immediately, and most of the company's first year profits had gone into investment in the building in which he currently stood – Power Towers, as he sniggeringly liked to call it (much to Adrian Fagge's disgust). As he followed the snaking line of the river Thames down through the city, Power could make out Tower Bridge (rather smaller than his own towers) and, tucked just behind the bridge, the offices of the *Daily News*. Soon, they would be his. He sipped the black liquid slowly in celebration and enjoyed the burn as it slipped down the back of his throat.

A knock at the door disturbed his concentration.

'Come!'

In walked Mike Pitts, the executive editor of all of his

company's titles, a thickset man whose pockmarked face and closely shaven head ensured he did not look too dissimiliar from the great British bulldog. He had proved a very handy assistant to Power over the years, and his loyalty had been justly rewarded as Power's wealth had increased.

'Got some new models for you to look at Victor, with *Sport Beauty* in mind and that,' he announced.

'Models – ah!' replied Power. There was nothing he enjoyed more about his business than picking the models. Although he ran his own publishing company, Victor Power still liked to personally hand-pick the models for all his magazines' major stories. Even with a title base of over fifteen magazines, and plenty of other publishing interests, he was still very much in editorial control. The models themselves were crucial, he liked to say, to the look of his publications, and although he was forced to delegate most of the day-to-day editing, he could never bring himself to relinquish entirely the important decisions. Besides, twenty minutes of ogling at the slide projector every day was not exactly arduous. Long enough to smoke a fat Monte Cristo, in fact. As he settled back into his armchair for some mid-morning entertainment, he allowed himself just a little flush of smugness at the thought of his impending deal.

'Too small!' he pronounced as the first image lit up the screen. The slide projector whirred, and a new image replaced it.

'Too droopy!'

The image was summarily dismissed.

'Pig ugly!'

Another image quickly replaced it.

'Too big!'

'Too big?' Pitts said incredulously – he'd never heard that one before.

Power took a prudish puff of his cigar, the mound of dark hair that carpeted the top of his hand bristling from under his Paul Smith shirt cuff.

'They can be too big, you know. This has got to be a classier operation now, Pitts. There's gonna be some smartening up around here.'

Pitts sighed, and pressed the button for the next slide.

Deep in his armchair, after a couple of seconds thought, Power sniffed. 'Not blonde enough. Good arse, though.'

'She can be made blonder, sir.'

'Well, do it then, for Christ's sake. Blonde is always better than brunette. Next.'

There was a long pause after Pitts revealed the next image. In it the model was embracing the trunk of a palm tree with a strange contortion of limbs that managed to show off her swollen breasts, her taut stomach and rounded behind to excellent effect. Even the tree looked pleased. Her hair fell down her back in a wet tangled tumble, and with her microscopic white bikini she looked like a modern Ursula Andress.

'Now that's much more like it!' Power nodded from his armchair once he had lingered appreciatively over the image before him. 'Natural. Healthy. Wholesome, even.'

'That's Delia, sir. New signing.'

'Good signing. You see, Pitts, she's got what it takes.

You look at her and you think: "Yeah. I could have her. Definitely." If you'd have her yerself, then the punters will want to have her too. Got to look fresh, the birds now, especially for this new mag. Its launch is going to be very high profile. They got to look untouched. Trouble is with most of your lot, they look like they've been round the block ten times already.'

'That's cos they have, Victor.'

Victor Power had not yet taken his eyes off the blonde and the palm tree.

'Delia!' he said to himself, rolling the name in his mouth, as if she were a boiled sweet. 'I think I'd like to meet her. Bring her in. She might just get the job.'

*Sport Beauty*, his latest title, was a further step along the road to mainstreaming his titles or, in other words, bringing the majority of them down off the top shelf. Due to launch next month, *Sport Beauty* was a stylish, celebrity driven (well what wasn't nowadays?) magazine dedicated to body worship. The difficulty had been in persuading the supermodels to work for Power Publishing. Disappointed and, frankly, infuriated by the dismissive tone of certain fashion-model agencies, Power had decided to create his own stars, and had already booked in Charlotte Want for the cover story – she was, after all, vaguely known. The trouble was that nameless models just didn't cut it nowadays – the cult of the personality was all. But then Power should know all about that: he had invented it.

The cult of course, had found its purist definition in his own, self-launched *Hiya!* magazine, now so popular that it had a circulation of over 500,000 a week. But it was a little-known fact that *Hiya!* magazine made hardly any money at all, and some weeks actually lost money, such were the fees the celebrities were now demanding. Its amazing success was financially supported by the more anatomically graphic of Power's titles.

The sex industry was an area in which Power was well versed. He had been brought up in it. The son of a prostitute, he had seen a lot from an early age. His mother had been shipped over to England from Bombay to make a hard-core porn movie under the impression she was about to star in Bollywood's finest. Her life had been short and tragic – she had eventually died of her heroin habit when Victor was only ten. Consequently, little shocked Power now, and the rules he'd had to learn when young, the scenes he'd had to witness, had inured him to life's worst atrocities.

*Hiya!*, in fact, had been his first and very recent sortie into the 'straight' world, and he loved the entrée it gave him into that most English of snobberies – the social hierachy. He had the ear of people now who would have not have wiped their feet on him before. The experience was intoxicating for Power, and it left him with a taste for more. He craved a place among the British establishment, he craved a voice along the corridors of Westminster, and at the garden parties of the landed aristocracy. This was the last bastion of society Power had yet to conquer but, for a man with the roots he had, it was the most important. And this was where the *Daily News* came in.

Other than funding, the purchase of the *News* brought

with it one other problem: image. There was no denying that his company was heavily involved in porn, and he knew that would set him up for a public hiding. But Power was already making plans. He buzzed through to his secretary, Miss Wattle, a prim lady in her late fifties who had worked for him quietly, loyally and without complaint for many years.

Miss Wattle stood out among Power's female employees as one of the few who came with no silicone. Where most dressed in lycra and the briefest of skirts, Miss Wattle stuck to her uniform of buttoned-up white or cream chemises, occasionally decorated with the cameo brooch her mother had given her. She had no interest in the content of most of Power's magazines, although she had had no idea when she applied for the job just what it was that Power Publishing published. Her job was to organize Mr Power's diary. She took immense pleasure in it, and did it with such a degree of job-satisfying efficiency that by the time she discovered what Power Publishing was really about, she really no longer cared. In fact, Miss Wattle found she rather began to enjoy the 'frisson', as she called it, of her business. Until she had taken the job with Power, she had never done anything dangerous or risqué all of her life: she had been a schoolmistress at a girls' private boarding school for a while, until her mother became ill and she had to take care of her full time. Then she had moved into her mother's semi-detached in Hounslow, and five years later her mother had died leaving her the house and, finally, her freedom. Miss Wattle could not somehow face going back to teaching, so she decided she would find herself a secretarial job in the racy world of the City. Someone rather cheeky in the secretarial agency where she had signed up had decided it would be a great joke to set her up for the Power job, but Miss Wattle had taken to it like a koi to an ornamental carp pond, and had stayed there ever since.

Up until that point Miss Wattle's life had been singularly unadventurous, but she suddenly found she thoroughly enjoyed chatting away to celebrities and fending off ambitious young topless models. She took a keen interest in the business side of the company too – scrutinizing her boss's accounts and looking for gaps in the market. She watched and learned from Power's entrepreneurial spirit and had begun to dispense really rather good advice, thought both Power and Pitts. As a result, the very prim Miss Wattle had become something of a legend within the company. Power was not slow to reward her, and now handed her as much responsibility for the company's affairs as she had time for. Not only did she earn a very reasonable salary, but there were a number of perks to the job, not least a company hairdresser who came and set her greying barnet twice a week. Really, thought Miss Wattle, with such a wonderful salary, a Christmas bonus and free hairdressing, why on earth would she move somewhere more respectable?

'Miss Wattle?' Victor's voice came through the intercom to his secretary's desk outside.

'Yes Mr Power?'

'Will you marry me?'

# chapter four

Charlotte bent down beneath the umbrella her uniformed chauffeur was holding out for her and skipped down the few steps from the hotel to the open door of her waiting limo. Well, skipped in a manner of speaking, hobbled was more appropriate after the workout she had been enjoying all night, and the best part of this morning. Footballers – so full of energy, so desperate to demonstrate their skills! Wonderful lays, she noted. Nothing she had ever experienced had beaten sex with a footballer – especially foreign ones.

Settling back into her leather seat she pulled a mirror out of her handbag and checked her make-up once again – perfect, of course. Her skin glowed rosily from the recent exercise. She really ought to try sex just before a photo shoot, she thought to herself, and idly wondered when her next date in the studio would be. She'd have to co-ordinate it around the club's training schedule, or even during training – she remembered that time in the locker room. Locker rooms or hotel suites: that was Charlotte's rule for fantastic sex, the one fuelled by heat, sweat and danger, the other by champagne, decadence and luxury. What more could a girl want?

Her driver, the third the agency had sent to her this month, was now in his seat and had flicked on the intercom. 'Where to, ma'am?'

'London, Driver, please. Directly.'

'Very good, madam.'

'Ms Want!' she snapped back. If he said madam with that ridiculous grin on his face one more time she would have to sack him too. A pity, as this one seemed to be the only one who could negotiate exactly the right route, the one that involved a hold up only as long as a red light between her penthouse in Manchester and any meetings she might have in London.

Her agent had suggested it might soon be time for her to move to London, but Charlotte preferred the fame she enjoyed in Manchester. Away from where all the other, more famous, celebrities lived, Charlotte could lay claim to the city's title of most glamorous female resident, and all the party invitations and exposure that such a title afforded. There was not one single supermarket that had opened in the last year without Charlotte's blessing – after all she only had *Coronation Street* stars to vie with. In London, however, only mediocre celebrity awaited. Being the biggest fish in a smaller pond suited her far better than near obscurity in the capital. All that, of course, Charlotte hoped, would soon change.

'Sorry, Ms Want,' the driver corrected himself, and rearranged his mouth into its usual neutral expression.

Charlotte popped the mirror back into her bag and was about to snap it shut when the sparkle on her wrist caught her eye. Bringing it up to her face she twisted the silver bangle Silvio had given her in the glow of the limousine light. In the middle were three brilliant-cut diamonds carefully worked into the silver. 'Gorgeous!' she said out loud, turning it round in front of her. 'No,' she corrected herself as she examined the size of the stones properly, 'heavenly.' She let the jewels twinkle for a few moments longer before she rested her hand back in her lap.

Now that her physical needs were satisfied her mind was back on her work, and her most pressing concern was still what, in South Molton Street's name, she was going to wear to the Versace do. The stress of the impending occasion was beginning to bear down on her and Charlotte could feel the previous night's stock of relaxation already filtering away. She would need a massage, or a facial at the very least, by the time she got to London. God, if she was nervous now, then what was she going to be like on the night? Naked, at this rate, she thought to herself, *still with no bloody dress.*

There was no point in asking her agent Doug to help, he didn't know the first thing about fashion. And her PA was useless. Charlotte had noted with disgust yesterday that her suit had come from Principles. Principles! Not somewhere Charlotte would ever be caught buying anything. Her mother would doubtless want her to wear something way too chaste for the occasion just because Prince Charles was going to be there, so that ruled her out for advice as well. This party was going to be an A-grade flashbulb opportunity, and one she *had* to capitalize on, and there was no one to help her. If she was ever going to be big-league famous, then this was the party to launch her. Did no one understand this? she thought petulantly. Look what a dress had done for Liz Hurley – started her entire career. Yes, there was no doubt about it, the right look would land her photograph in the newspapers. Alongside Donatella's, Madonna's, Catherine's, Liz's . . .

And that was the trouble: every other celebrity in the land was going to be there; competition was going to be tough. She had already rung Versace and had been somewhat miffed to be told that, 'All ze dresses ave gone for zat night, Mz Want.' Charlotte suspected this was because she wasn't quite famous enough yet – only the A list were allowed to wear Versace to a Versace do. There was nothing for it – she would have to ring the one person who *would* understand. She picked up her phone and dialled Uncle Vic's mobile phone number. He'd told her that if she ever needed anything then she was just to call – and if she ever needed anything, it was now.

'Victor? It's Charlotte.'

'Ah, Charlotte my lovely, how are you?' Victor pushed the voluptuous Delia from his lap where she was conducting her audition.

'Vic, I've got a problem,' she simpered.

'What's that, my darling?'

'I haven't got anything to wear. It's this thing with Donatella Versace and Prince Charles next week, and I want to wear a really special dress, you know what I mean? A kind of career-making dress. But Versace hasn't got anything left for that night, and I don't know what to do.' Charlotte allowed her voice to crack a little with this last. Well, she was, after all, genuinely upset about the situation.

Charlotte's amateur dramatics aside, Victor's ears had pricked up immediately, his celebrity antenna on full alert. This was an important party for Charlotte and one she couldn't go to without making a statement. Charlotte was absolutely right: he knew just what to do. Or rather Adrian Fagge would. He promised to call her right back, after he had consulted his stylist.

Fagge was most emphatic, 'Jones, darling, she's gotta go to Julien Jones. Versace's so over now, anyway. Julien does the sexy stuff now.'

Fortunately, Fagge's particular recommendation already owed him a favour, luckily for Charlotte.

Power rang her back immediately.

'It just so happens I've just photographed this Jones character at home with his grandma, for *Hiya!*, so I'll give him a call and let him know you're coming. His studio's in Notting Hill. What time can you be there?'

Charlotte smiled to herself, she'd known she could rely on her Uncle Victor to sort her out. 'An hour and a half. Thank you so much, Vic,' she purred ecstatically down the phone, never one to miss an opportunity to capitalize on all the skills a woman possessed.

'My pleasure, Princess,' came the satisfied reply.

Two hours later Charlotte was standing in the middle of Jones's showroom in little more than a leotard. Except this leotard was pink, shiny, studded in glitter, and came down on one side of her hips in a demi-skirt, whilst just skirting her hips on the other. Luckily, Julien ('That's Julien with an "e" please, it sounds more exotic'), had also designed a matching pair of pink sparkly knickers. The dress, if that is what it could be called, was certainly going to get the flash-bulbs popping, and Charlotte knew it.

'Oh, Julien, it's fantastic! Thank you so much – you are *such* a honey! Such a *talented* honey!'

And Julien was. If there was one thing a gay Welsh boy from the valleys had had to learn how to do, it was to ingratiate himself with the girls. He had needed to: the boys had never liked him much.

'Now practise your pose, dearie. Lift your arms up, stick your tits out and PERCH that arse!'

Charlotte did as she was told and saw the effect was good. The 'dress' was hers for the night, said Julien, free of charge. How, after all, could he turn Power down when he had just written him a cheque for £10,000 for his inspirational story about life with his granny?

The first thing Charlotte did when she was back in her limo was call Power to thank him.

'You just won't believe it! If I don't make the papers in that dress, then I never will!'

'Fantastic!' agreed Power leafing quickly through his diary. 'Now, when did you say this party was?'

'Tuesday next week.'

'And *Hiya!* comes out on Friday. Right, Charlotte, I want you in next week's *Hiya!* If you're going to make the papers on Wednesday then you gotta be in the magazine on Friday to capitalize. This time though, it's gonna be different.'

'How's that then?'

'Lemme talk to Doug, but let's book you in for Monday. Monday all right for the shoot?'

'Yes, Monday's fine.'

'Talk to you later my beauty.'

Victor Power had a little shiver of excitement running through him. He knew exactly what sort of dresses Jones designed, and he knew her dress was likely to expose enough breast and buttock cheek to potentially make the front pages. *Hiya!* had to capitalize on this too, and there was only one place left to go: Charlotte's love life. He had cooked this plan up with Charlotte's agent a while back, but it looked like they needed to move quicker than expected. He hadn't been quite sure if he would be able to pull off the Versace invitation. Donatella had yet to take his money, but Elton had assured him he had put in a good word. Clearly, Elton had done his stuff.

'Douglas? It's Victor Power.'

'Victor, how you doing?'

'Very well indeed, thank you. I'm calling about the Want girl. I think it's time to move forward to the next stage. Can you get her to sort out a shoot with Ravelli on Monday night?'

Doug Bowser, a large, muscular, balding man of fifty, knew that 'no' was not the answer Power was looking for. Unlike Power, however, Doug harboured ambitions only for an easy life. He had worked hard and done well, and was hoping that in his old band mate's daughter he had the deal that would keep him and his wife (an ex-glamour model with breasts the size of Basildon), in pina coladas and suntan lotion for the rest of their lives. Their overseas subscription form for *Marbella Life* had now been running for over three years, and Mrs Doug had made it quite clear, on as many occasions as she could, that it was time for them to retire to the sun. So Doug was all too pleased to be moving to phase two of Charlotte's career: her celebrity boyfriend.

Keeping Charlotte in Manchester had proved fruitful. Her penchant for footballers had led to the most agreeable liaison between her and the demon Brazilian striker Silvio Ravelli, whose performance for United was definitely on the rise, and there was every reason to believe her association with him would have similar results. Deadly Doug dialled Charlotte's number.

'Charlotte, my darlin', how are ya?'

'Douglas, hello. How are you?'

'Proud of you, girl. Now, we need to talk about this next shoot for *Hiya!*'

'Oh yes?'

'Vic wants something different.'

'What's that?'

'He wants you at home with your lover.'

'My lover? Which one?'

'Which ever you want, my darling. Who's the latest?'

'Well, there's a couple –'

'What about this Silvio Ravelli?'

'How do you know about that?' snapped Charlotte quickly.

'Oh, rumours get around, sweetheart,' said Doug in an off-hand sort of a way, quite forgetting to mention that he had set the whole sting up with a private members' club beforehand. Only Charlotte and Silvio thought they'd met by accident. The whole team had been there that night, and Doug hadn't really minded which one she'd gone for, just as long as it was a striker. Ravelli was perfect – a real pin up.

'Well, we haven't been seeing each other long you know.'

'It's hardly betrothal stuff, Charlotte. It's just you two at home, you know, relaxing on the bed, cuddling up on the sofa, making pasta together, that sort of thing.'

'I can't make pasta.'

'No, but your boyfriend can.'

'He's from Brazil, Doug, not Italy.'

'Well, whatever. Take-away if you like. It's what Uncle Vic wants.'

'Oh. Is it?'

'It certainly is.'

Charlotte well knew that what Uncle Vic wanted Uncle Vic got. It was precisely because of his promotion that she was sitting in her limo right now. Charlotte might not always appear overly intellectual, but she certainly knew which side her bread was buttered. But she wasn't too sure about this. It was perhaps a little premature, or perhaps, even worse, something she didn't want to get in to at all. She liked men, but she liked playing with them, and just like when she was a little girl with her toys, she got bored with them very quickly. Most of Charlotte's relationships up until now had had the depth and durability of a two-week suntan, and it never took her long to find a new one to replace the last. Charlotte didn't have girlfriends because she was too busy having boyfriends. Having a *boyfriend* though – that was different. That was commitment, that was long term, that was – dare Charlotte think it? – emotional. It also, however, appeared to be work. And work, of course, came first.

'All right then, I'll ask him.'

'Good girl.'

'But Doug when do I get to really *do* something? You know make another record, or do some acting or something?'

'Soon, sweetheart. In fact, just as soon as we've done this shoot.'

'I don't want to be known for nothing you know. I've got talent, I want to use it.'

'I know that, Charlotte, but don't forget this is Victor's campaign too, and he knows a lot about this stuff, and he knows a lot of people in the industry, so I think we would be better off doing things his way for the moment, don't you?'

'Okay,' said Charlotte. 'But I'm going to need to earn some money soon.'

'Yes,' said Doug confidently, chewing on the stub of his cigar and thinking of his 2 per cent. 'Don't you worry, we will.'

# chapter five

Cas sat on the tube, juggling eyeshadow, lipstick and mascara on her lap while simultaneously trying not to let her newspaper slide to the floor, or her bag get nicked from under her feet. She was late again, and had had to leave the house without doing her make-up. She wasn't a particularly make-up friendly girl but as Tamara Yearbank – PBfH – wouldn't let anybody through the front door of her office without perfectly pencilled lips, Cas had little choice. 'No one works for my magazine with a bare face, it gives the wrong impression!' To whom, Cas was not awfully sure. It was a small issue and one that Cas had been prepared to give ground on: Cas was learning that if Tamara felt she was in control and that everything was originally her idea, then eventually Cas was able to get her way on some things.

Cas was also lectured daily by PBfH about her dress sense. Apparently, she would benefit considerably at work from being more chic with her wardrobe. But Cas was not the type of woman to follow fashion closely, even though her first journalism job may have been at *Vogue*, after winning their annual young writer contest. As far as Cas could see, most of the designers *Vogue* championed did not take womanly curves into account, and anything that looked sassy on a model only ended up poking out in all the wrong places on Cas. It also didn't help that Cas was the sort of woman who left her clothes on the floor at night, rather than hang them up, whose shoes were always found jammed under the sofa, and whose knicker stock was always at a permanently low level as all her nice stuff needed handwashing. A natural Voguette she wasn't.

As soon as she had established her name, Cas had left *Vogue* and gone freelance, appearing in magazines only as a by-line, which removed the need for fashion sense. Several features editors had picked up her name and she was soon getting the kind of commissions she wanted: she had covered the G7 capitalism riots, had spent two months working undercover at Huntingdon Life Sciences, the animal testing laboratory, had trailed Tony Blair on the last election campaign and had even been sent to Sierra Leone to investigate the diamond industry. It was off the back of this investigation that Susie Farlane had contacted her about a permanent position on the paper.

Cas shook out her newspaper and turned her attention to the more interesting events of the day. Unfortunately, they seemed to centre around the latest developments in the Madonna/Guy Ritchie marriage. Cas yawned and turned the page. Down the side of page two were the 'nibs' – the one-paragraph stories news editors deemed worthy only of mentioning. Cas always checked them out as they quite often yielded good ideas for features and today was no exception. A little boy whose arm and leg had been blown off by an IRA bomb had just left hospital with a new prosthetic limb (Cas made a mental note to contact his mother for an interview); the nightclub Cream had been granted a licence for a summer rave for 50,000 people (the new Woodstock? Counter culture goes mainstream?), and the body of a young Croatian girl had been pulled out of the Grand Union Canal. No one had been able to identify her and officials could only assume she was an illegal immigrant, and judging by her clothes had probably been working as a prostitute. Cas wondered about this last story – this was not the first case of its kind she had read about recently, and there was a theory on the news desk that there was an increasingly burgeoning sex trade among illegal Eastern European immigrants. Cas sucked in her breath as she reached the end of the story – the girl was estimated to be only fourteen years old. Where had this girl come from? How had she ended up in the canal? Now that would be a story. She tore out the cutting and put it into her bag.

'The child sex trade? You want to do a story on prostitution? Are you out of your tiny mind?' PBfH was shaking with mean, over-exaggerated laughter. 'Do you really think our readers want to read about that on a Sunday morning? Are you mad, Caris?'

Cas stood in Tamara's office and wondered which one of them it was who was mad. By now, she had no idea.

'Clearly, you've completely misunderstood the whole concept of this magazine if you are seriously trying to propose this as a feature. Where have you been since you arrived in this job? What do you think we do in here? Real life, for God's sake?'

Tamara Yearbank had a way of talking to her staff that made them feel they were the most stupid people in the entire world. At five-foot nothing, to say that she suffered from a Napoleon complex would be like suggesting a dwarf was vertically challenged. She used her height disadvantage as an entitlement to say everything at the level of a scream, and to stamp around in heels that announced her presence long before she actually arrived. Only when she met a celebrity or a VIP did the volume level drop, and she allowed her actually rather pretty face to relax from its normal screwed-up shrewishness. With her highlighted, glossy mane, perfect skin and fine features announcing her aristocratic pedigree and her circle of influential friends stretching from the House of Dior to the White House, Tamara Yearbank was a glossy magazine publisher's wet dream. Cas knew she secretly coveted the editorship of *Harpers & Queen*, but Cas also knew she had recently applied for the job and been turned down. This was another reason why she behaved so bitterly, and why Cas, who had absolutely no time for the deeply frivolous, appeared to be the butt of her anger. She was not the first though – three deputies in as many years had preceded her.

God forbid there should be anyone on the magazine who might pose even the tiniest threat to Tamara's own position. Little did she realize that no one could afford to get rid of her even if they wanted to – she earned far too much and her redundancy money would be astronomical. Farlane's answer had been to employ Cas.

Cas had never before experienced bullying like this, and wondered if in fact Tamara was quite all there. After all, Cas made Tamara's job easier for her. But logic, it seemed, didn't enter into this world of female competition and envy. On the only occasion when Cas had challenged one of her particularly vicious rants about the quality of Cas's work, Tamara had burst into tears and crawled under her desk where she had stayed for the rest of the day.

'Anyway, I've decided what next month's cover feature is going to be – the rise and rise of *Hiya!* magazine.' Her voice sounded like she had a gobstopper stuck halfway down her throat.

'*Hiya!* magazine?' repeated Cas.

'Yes, that's what I said, Caris. Have you seen the circulation figures published this week?' As far as Cas could work out the circulation figures of Tamara's rivals and future employers was all that she did read. 'It's had a year on year increase of over a hundred and fifty per cent. It's also the reason why we can't get any bloody celebrity interviews for ourselves any more. It's a phenomenon, and I think we should cover it.'

'Actually, I think that's a great idea,' said Cas slowly. 'You know who it's owned by, don't you?'

'No. Who?'

'Well, I'm pretty sure although I'll have to check, but I think it's Victor Power of Power Publishing – also proprietor of *Hot and Horny* and the rather lovely *Wet and Willing*.'

'He's a pornographer?' shrieked Tamara.

'Exactly. I think the *Guardian* tried to investigate him last year but for some reason nothing ever got published. There might be more stuff on record now – I bet he's got loads of dodgy stuff going on. We should get someone good on to it.'

'Hmm, well I was thinking more celebrities than pornography –'

'No, Tamara, I think you've hit on a great story,' cut in Cas before PBfH could shoot down her own idea. 'No one's done it yet either. I'll see if he will talk to us. Meanwhile we can get someone checking out his business interests. What an excellent idea!'

Tamara smirked. This was what deputies were for – ego massaging.

'Right, well you do that. I've got a lunch and I need to have my hair done beforehand so will you take conference at twelve? I'll be back by five to check the cover. Tell design I want at least three different versions to chose from. I'll drop in on Susie on my way out and tell her about the *Hiya!* idea. She'll love that.'

If there was one thing Tamara enjoyed it was sucking up to the editor. Oh, and having lunch. Tamara, who had talked to Cas for far longer than she had wanted to, made the end of their conversation clear by getting up, pushing past her towards the door, opening it and pointing outside.

'Okay,' said Cas resignedly, although she had plenty more to talk to Tamara about – like what on earth they were going to put in the magazine this week. 'You realize we haven't got an interview for next week's issue, don't you?'

'Well, that's not good enough, Caris, you better get one by the end of the day.' Tamara's voice was beginning to show her irritation and had gone up a tone from annoying squeak to frustrated yelp. Any moment now, thought Cas, the gobstopper is going to career out of her throat.

'Right,' said Cas, and practically fell through the door as Tamara slammed it shut behind her. Still, not an altogether disastrous meeting: she had escaped without being too badly mauled and she had actually managed to get a halfway interesting commission for the magazine in Victor Power. Cas went straight to the cuttings library to find out more.

When she returned to her desk with the cuttings file, there was an email waiting in her inbox from Tamara.

Scrap *Hiya!* idea. Have run it past Susie and it seems there's a problem. Think of something else instead and NOT PROSTITUTION!

Cas was amazed, just a quick glance through Power's file had revealed him to be everything Cas suspected and more. His tawdry collection of magazines plumbed depths that not even the most assiduous collector of pornography could imagine (he had once launched a magazine entitled

*Shaven Havens*), and the idea that this same man was secur-
ing exclusives with *Blue Peter* presenters was laughable. Cas's
heart had actually been racing – Tamara had unwittingly
stumbled on a fantastic story. She rang her immediately on
her mobile.

'Tamara? It's Cas.'

'What do you want? I can't talk to you now.'

'Listen I just wanted to tell you this *Hiya!* story is great.
I don't understand why you want to pull it. I've just been
doing some research in the library –'

'It's not me, it's the bloody editor – ask her.'

'What? Susie?'

'Yes. For some reason there's a problem, so you'll have
to come up with a better idea. I've got to go now.' And with
that she hung up.

Cas was mystified. Tamara clearly hadn't sold the idea to
Susie properly. It was exactly the sort of thing Susie normally jumped at, and Cas was not going to let it pass. She
went downstairs to go and see why.

Susie sat beside her desk and heard Cas out. She was
frowning, but Cas continued anyway, telling her everything
she had found out that morning. She had made a few calls
as well, in particular to a contact on the news desk at the
*Guardian*, Sam, with whom she had been to journalism college. Sam nursed a hopeless crush for Cas and had been
more than happy to look up the paper's entire investigation.
On that evidence alone there was enough to suggest there
was far more dirt on Power than had been so far recorded.
The *Guardian* had apparently been forced to pull their

investigation because of legal reasons, but they had located a substantial source of income to Power Publishing that had so far been unexplained.

'It's a top story, Susie, this guy is now best friends with half of Hollywood. He's trying to do deals with the Harry Potter cast while publishing pictures of topless – and bottomless models!'

Susie smiled wearily at Cas. 'You better shut the door,' she said eventually, sighing. Cas got up and shut the door. Something was wrong.

'What I am going to tell you now is in complete confidence, okay? I don't want anyone else getting wind of this, because, apart from anything else, I don't know if it's true. But Lord Appalling upstairs is trying to sell the paper.'

This was not good news. The rumours, it appeared, were all true.

'I saw the piece in *The Times* yesterday morning,' said Cas mournfully. 'I was hoping it wasn't true.'

'It is true.'

Susie Farlane did not enjoy the best of relationships with Lord Paul. He had employed her four years ago to breathe some life back into his paper, but he had not quite appreciated how maverick Susie Farlane actually was. After a fanfare arrival, relations between the two of them had cooled considerably – especially when circulation failed to go up. Lord Paul was now much more interested in ingratiating himself with the government than he was in the *Daily News*, but found his attempts to suck up to the prime minister were continually being thwarted by Farlane's front pages.

'I understand that it is Victor Power who is trying to buy it.'

'Power is going to buy the *Daily News*?' breathed Cas appalled.

'Possibly. If you do this story on *Hiya!* then old Appalling upstairs is just going to pull it and it'll be a waste of everyone's time and money. Now, as I said, Caris, that's between you, me and these four walls. If I hear it from anywhere else, then I'll know where it's come from. Just sit tight. Hopefully it won't happen and then we can run the story in full.'

Susie smiled at Cas, but not very convincingly. Cas walked back to her desk in horror.

No, she thought, they wouldn't let a pornographer run a national newspaper, would they? Besides, now she had started to look into the story, Cas was far too intrigued to leave it.

## chapter six

In the last month, Silvio Ravelli had found in Charlotte Want the only way to endure English life and enjoy English football. Just twenty-two years old, this was his second season for the foreign team, and this season was certainly proving to be much less of a disaster than the last. Every Saturday that Alex Ferguson marched the plucky little Brazilian out onto the pitch, there were more and more virtuoso hints of the flamboyant footwork, lightning flights down the centre of the field, perfectly poised headers and bullet-like free kicks that had made him the darling of his previous club. Silvio Ravelli was still a long way from being King of the Field of Dreams, but the accolade was now within his sights. And, as if to confirm his ascent up the ranks of premiership stars, Silvio's slight build which every week allowed him to dance his way past defenders (making him only just taller than Charlotte Want in her most vertiginous heels), coupled with his piercingly azure-blue eyes, dark shoulder-length locks and a body that rippled like a river whenever he moved, had won him this month's cen-trefold in *Cosmopolitan* magazine.

But Silvio's performance at the club had begun inauspi-ciously – indeed, his lifelong path to glory had been far from straightforward. Silvio had demonstrated his talent from an early age. The moment he had first stood up on his legs, his brothers had kicked a Coca Cola can across the room at him to try and knock him over, but he had simply parried it into the dustbin in the corner – with his left foot no less. With that, his entire family had realized that their lottery ticket out of the corrugated-iron shack in Rio's biggest favela was no longer an impossibility.

'Oh, my son, my son!' his mother Christina had cried and, gathering the stunned little Silvio into her arms, she had nearly drowned him in tears of hope and gratitude before disappearing off to the nearest shrine to lay down a hundred offerings to the Virgin Mary. Meanwhile, his brothers had whisked Silvio down to Copacabana beach where the talent spotters preyed. That day and every day for the next ten years they put Silvio through his paces on the city's golden sands until the great moment when he was finally plucked from the crowd and invited to join Fluminese juniors.

But problems soon became apparent. Fluminese, who always lost to their great team rivals Flamengo, suddenly started to come good. The reason? A rash of brilliant strik-ers brought up through their excellent training school, the most prominent of whom was a young man named Ronaldo. The result was that Silvio, a born striker, hardly ever got off the reserve bench. The position of star striker, which four years ago would most definitely have been his, now eluded him and with it the chance to be picked for the first team and win the salary and the sponsorship deals that would buy his mother the air-conditioned apartment he so wanted her to have.

As Silvio's teenage years passed by, so did his goal-scoring opportunities – until Alex Ferguson decided to take his team on tour to Brazil. On the day of the match against Fluminese, God smiled again on the Ravelli family (justly rewarding Christina for her recent six-hour prostration at the altar of Our Mother of the Holy Sacrament). Ronaldo was ill. A cold, said his girlfriend, although the manager sneered. Ronaldo's blonde, starlet girlfriend definitely inhibited his play, prompting a pre-match lecture to the rest of the team on the devious manipulations of Eve. Spitting on the ground in disgust, the manager called Silvio up to lead the team's strike force. Silvio did not squander his chance, leading his team to unexpected victory with two spectacular goals. That night the entire twenty-seven member strong Ravelli family descended upon the bars of Ipanema, where the city bought them drinks all night. Their son may not have brought them untold riches, but that day he bought them something much more important – pride.

The next day the call came: Alex Ferguson wanted Silvio for himself. With Silvio only months away from his twenty-first birthday the timing was perfect, and the lure of Manchester money was irresistible to the Fluminese manager. Silvio was told he could join at the beginning of the next English season. Before Silvio knew it, he had won a contract that paid him £10,000 a week plus a bonus of £1500 every time he scored a goal. His mother fainted.

Naturally, as soon as the news was announced, every company from chocolate-biscuit manufacturers to hair-gel suppliers were beating a path to the Ravellis' corrugated-iron door, and the riches that had eluded the family for so long came now in one great, big, fat moment. Within weeks the family were washing in a marble bathroom and everybody had a new pair of trainers. Their lives had changed in the space of ninety minutes.

So when Silvio arrived in England at the start of the season he was one happy boy. For about a week. Then suddenly he was homesick – very homesick. The golden sands of his city's beaches were a long way from the concrete precincts of this grey northern town, and the bitter, relentlessly wet weather began to close in on Silvio's psyche as the months progressed.

Silvio could also speak little English (school had never been very high up on his list of priorities as a favela-dwelling, football-obsessed Carioca), and he found it difficult and frustrating to learn. Furthermore, due to Brazilian red tape and FIFA complications, it took four months after he first arrived for the contracts to clear and the red shirt to finally dress his back. When he could at last be picked, the stars of the squad had established themselves already, fighting for a place now was even harder than it had been at Fluminese.

It seemed Silvio's career was condemned to the reserve

bench. His team mates were civil to him, but no one understood him or where he had come from. He wandered the city centre in the afternoons when he wasn't training and watched the pasty faces of the Englishmen screwed up against the winter rain. He found nothing of beauty to look at at all – least of all the women. For a boy who had grown up on the decorative beaches of Rio where the women wear nothing but dental-floss bikinis, and never wasted a chance to shake their bundas at the passing boys, Manchester girls, wrapped up in their huge parkas and combat trousers, failed to have a similar effect. For a red-blooded Latin male, this was devastating. Silvio felt very, very alone.

The club psychiatrist was at a loss to know what to do with him: as his enthusiasm vanished so his play began to suffer. Ferguson watched with dismay as his hot Latin star withered before his eyes. Finally, he knew all he could do to save him was to play him, and hope he could lift his game to what it once was. But if Silvio messed up on his debut, Ferguson also knew the fans would never forgive him, and he wasn't sure if Silvio would be able to come back from that. He had seen foreign players sacrificed on the harsh stage of the fans' judgement too many times before. It was all or nothing, but he gave Silvio his chance: he was picked to play at home against Arsenal, the great enemies from the south. Minutes before play started, Silvio kissed his crucifix, offered prayers to Our Lady of the Sacrament and bounded onto the pitch. Fifteen minutes later he was taken off on a stretcher. A foul tackle had brought him down in the penalty box after a spectacular solo run down the field, and he crashed to the ground in agony, writhing from the pain shooting through his left knee. The only consolation came when his team scored off the penalty and held the score to win the match, but Silvio had pulled a ligament in his knee and was now declared unfit to play for the rest of the season.

The next six months were spent in hospital and then in physiotherapy, with Silvio's mother constantly by his side. Ferguson owed it to Silvio to at least get him match fit again, before he could offer him the option of putting him out of his misery and sending him home where he could be a football star in his own right. Over the summer, with a few rays of English sunshine to coax him back to health, Silvio worked hard on his fitness. His mother constantly played him the samba and had Brazilian glamour magazines flown in which she posted over all his walls. His small Manchester apartment became a little Rio, but still Silvio mourned for his home town.

Eventually, the club physiotherapist pronounced him ready to play again. Ferguson called Silvio into his office, thanked him for the play that had won him a place in the heart of every fan for the rest of his career, even if it had resulted in months of recuperation from a horrific injury, and told him that if he wanted to go home, he could.

To his surprise, Silvio couldn't have been more insistent that he wanted to stay. He loved Manchester, he said. It was his new home, he couldn't think of returning to Brazil, even the weather wasn't a problem, the people were so nice.

He didn't need his mother here any more. Please, please, please, he begged, let him stay.

Ferguson was at a loss to understand the sudden change, but then he wasn't to know Silvio had just spent the night with Charlotte Want. For, as of ten o' clock last night, Silvio Ravelli had at last been initiated into the United squad, taken out to a private members' club to celebrate, and had fallen in love.

That had been a month ago, and as the plucky little Brazilian's passion had grown, so had his skills on the pitch. The more Charlotte agreed to see him, the more zest he had to run the extra yards. Ferguson could hardly believe his eyes. The more Charlotte giggled at his jokes, the more accurately Silvio passed the ball. The more she did what he asked, the more successful were his tackles. The kinkier she would be in bed, the more flexible he could be in the box. The more he made her shriek delightedly with pleasure, the more he found the back of the net. The last month had been a story of rapture and success: Ravelli hadn't known joy like it in his life, and Charlotte even found herself missing Silvio when she wasn't with him.

But Charlotte's work always came first. Something Silvio tried very hard to understand, but which was not part of his culture. In Brazil, sex always came first. Of course, he was very careful to make sure his manager was not aware of what was going on: that would not do. His Fluminese coach had drilled it into him; Ronaldo himself had taught him that much. One missed trick and it could be fatal to his career.

'Exactly!' said Charlotte. 'It's exactly the same for me! So you must understand that you absolutely have to, have to do this for me! Please Silvio – it's for my career!' Charlotte was stretched out over an enormous hotel bed in a La Perla black negligee. The sheets, the pillows, the chairs, were all over the room.

'But Mr Ferguson, he will KEEEELL me. I'm sorry, but no, I cannot.'

'Well then, I don't think I can see you any more.'

'NOOOooo!!!!' howled the Brazilian, in genuine pain. 'You must not say that!'

'But it's part of my career to have a boyfriend. I need someone to turn up to parties with, and I have a deal with this magazine and I have to do a shoot with a boyfriend. If it's not going to be you, then it's going to have to be some-one else, Silvio. It's as simple as that.'

'Noooo!!!!' Silvio had his head under the pillow, and was beating the mattress on either side with his fists.

Charlotte sat back against the bedstead, and inspected her latest manicure and the diamond studded bangle.

'I have to call him tomorrow, Silvio. If it's a no then that leaves me just the weekend to get a new boyfriend. I need to know if you're going to do this for me or not.'

Silvio stopped, in horror. 'You mean you'd do it, just like that? You'd just go out and get a new boyfriend?'

'Well, why not? I've done it plenty of times before. You know I'd much rather it was you, Silvio, but if you're going to be difficult about it then I'll just have to go elsewhere. Besides, it's only a small magazine, nobody reads it,' Charlotte lied.

'How small? Would Mr Ferguson read it?'

'Now that I very much doubt, Silvio.' Charlotte was pretty sure that wasn't a lie.

'And when would it be?'

'Monday, like I said, Silvio, in my flat in Manchester. We can do it after training if you like.'

'Ohhhhh . . .'

'Go on,' said Charlotte, turning to him with one of her smiles and slipping her hand down his shorts. 'Just think of how much fun we can have afterwards, when the photographer's gone!'

A beatific smile was beginning to spread across Silvio's face as her hand worked its magic under his shorts. 'And then on Tuesday we can go to this party together, and I could arrange for a car to take you back up to Manchester after the party, and no one would know anything the next day before the game.'

'Oh, you English girl!' exclaimed Silvio, rapidly ascending into a state of uncontrollable bliss. Not listening to anything his girlfriend was saying, simply concentrating on what she was doing, he acquiesced, 'You know you win!'

The next day, Saturday, Silvio scored two goals for United, and Sunday's papers proclaimed him the new hero of the north.

## chapter seven

Toby opened the door in his dressing gown. He saw absolutely no reason to get up before midday now he 'worked from home' and anyway Cas was out in the evenings so much nowadays that he left most of his work till night time. If he wasn't going to the pub. It suited him much better – leisurely lie-ins, a lengthy coffee session and no early morning scramble to work, just a stroll next door into the studio. So he had only just managed to shower and make himself a cup of coffee when the door bell rang at half past twelve. Consequently when he opened it, with his dark hair still glistening wet, his brown skin freshly scrubbed and his face languidly beautiful in the morning sunlight, the woman who stood at the door couldn't help but gasp despite herself. Which was nothing compared to what Toby did when he saw her.

Balanced on his doorstep was what Toby could only later describe as a 'visual freak', and his immediate instinct was to check up and down the street to see if there wasn't a camera crew following her. The street was empty, so he turned back to the woman and tried to take in the quite extraordinary sight of the lobster perched on her head. While she paused to stare at Toby's handsome, half-naked figure, he found it very difficult to look her in the eye without pointing out that she was under the not insubstantial claws of a crustacean. He presumed, however, that she knew, so he decided not to remark upon it, and instead mustered all his energy into keeping a straight face and asking, 'Hello. Can I help you?'

The apparition on the doorstep took a while to reply, studying as she was, 'that boy's damn good looks' as she was later to refer to them. This pause in proceedings also allowed Toby to take in the woman's carefully made-up face and neat black kimono, both of which suggested she was probably making a statement rather than that she was an escapee from the local mad house. Toby decided to give the lobster the benefit of the doubt for a moment longer. Giving him a lingering (and fairly lascivious) smirk, the woman finally replied in a strong New York accent, 'You sure can. I'm looking for Toby Hartley-Brewer.'

'Ah,' replied Toby, checking once again for the camera crew. 'That is me.'

'Great. Thought I'd catch you at home now. Mind if I come in?' And with that she walked straight through the door, past Toby and up the stairs before he could even ask her her business.

Toby followed her up as quickly as he could, but for such a small woman she moved pretty fast. As he rounded the banisters into the living room he found himself once again dumbfounded by the sight of the crustacean, and before he could ask what she wanted or go any further in their introduction he found it finally necessary to address the issue balanced on the top of her head.

'Your, um, hat. It's ah, quite . . . arresting.'

'Treacy, of course. His haute couture work, obviously, but the diamante-encrusted bit – that was my idea. It's particularly good for getting you noticed, which is of course, very important. Now Toby – mind if I call you Toby? – I'm here about your art.'

'My art?' replied Toby, half shocked, half pleased. What on earth did anyone want to do with his art?

'Yeah, sure. But as it is so damn early, I wondered if you couldn't fix me a cup of coffee first.'

'Why not?' muttered Toby, finally managing to drag his eyes away from the glinting – or was it winking? – shellfish.

While he located coffee, filter and mugs in the kitchen, he had a chance to observe the rest of the creature in his living room, as she busied herself with a cigarette holder and a bizarre-coloured cigar.

'Mind if I smoke?' she asked as she lit up without expecting an answer. She was, underneath the hat, small and thin: her wrist bones protruded, as did her cheekbones and her shoulder blades. She had short, jet-black, close-cropped hair cut in a jagged fringe across her forehead, and her face, for all its make-up, revealed the lines and bags of a forty something woman who had at one stage, and quite possibly still did, party very hard. The rest of her body was swathed in black silk and gathered at the waist with a pink jewelled cummerbund – to match the lobster, Toby assumed. Her make-up looked like it had taken hours of precision application, with her eyelids painted in stripes of pillar-box red, her face powdered albino white and her lips a neon pink. Toby had seen this sort of look in the pages of alternative fashion magazines, but he had no idea people actually looked like this in the street. Her right shoulder was exposed, tank-top style, despite the cold morning, to reveal an ornate butterfly tattoo on her upper arm. As Toby tried surreptitiously to take her in, the woman stalked round his sitting room surveying his and Cas's mess.

'Excuse me for asking,' said Toby politely as he searched for clean mugs, 'but may I know your name?'

'I,' said the woman, spinning on her heel with deliberate drama, 'am Cosima Beane.'

Cosima Beane? Toby had heard that name before. Cosima Beane . . . his brain scrambled for the recollection, he was sure he had heard someone talking about her in Harold Sweet's Art and Form class at the Slade the other day. She was supposedly the hot new dealer in the Brit art circus – she had just opened a gallery in Bruton Street and was upsetting all the traditionalists with her wildcard selection of 'artists'. 'Controversy is my calling card,' she had announced provocatively to the press. Apparently she had been displaying six-foot blue phalluses in her window the week she launched. Westminster council had taken offence and demanded she change the display, thereby granting her a glut of most welcome publicity. She was from New York originally, but had decided the art scene was more original over here, and had therefore decided to move across the Atlantic. She was someone Toby really should know more about, but didn't.

Unable to contain his curiosity, and having an inkling she would be flattered to know her reputation preceded her, he asked, 'Is that Cosima Beane as in, "The New Mistress of Shock"?' The question was posed with only the tiniest hint of irony, after all, he wasn't quite sure what she wanted yet. 'I saw an article on your gallery in the paper last week, I think. You're the New York art dealer, right?'

'I am.' She grinned. 'Thank you, honey, for the introduction. But allow me to correct you: I *am* from New York, yes, but I'm more than a dealer. I'm a *creator*, a *spinner*, an *inventor*. Which is the reason I am standing in your living room.'

Cosima Beane pronounced some words very emphatically, just to check the listener had heard and inwardly digested them.

'Right,' said Toby, and pushed his hand through his hair awkwardly. He then noticed he wasn't wearing anything and that Cosima was admiring his chest. He pulled his dressing gown around him and said, 'Mind if I go and put on some clothes?'

'Oh, you're fine as you are,' Cosima replied, clearly enjoying the view. Caravaggio-esque, she thought, mentally smacking her lips.

The importance of who this woman was and how she could change his life was beginning to dawn on Toby.

Suddenly, he felt quite nervous. At that point the coffee machine stopped gurgling and announced it was ready.

'Um . . . coffee. Coming up. How do you like it?'

'Long, black and strong.'

Of course you do, he thought, turning back to the kitchen. He panicked about the state of his studio: what could he possibly show her? His most important piece was at college, he was still working on it, he only had prototypes here to show her. At least, he presumed she was here to see his work. But how did she know about him? It must be through his tutor Harold Sweet at the Slade. He didn't have any work on display anywhere. Whatever, Toby knew this was a make-or-break moment. A dealer – a Bruton Street dealer – in his flat. Was this the point from which everything began to go right at last? He wished he could phone Cas right away and tell her who was visiting – imagining her relief and pride before his own.

'How did you know where I lived?' he began, noticing the lobster was now eyeballing him. It wasn't alive was it? Then realizing he had just asked a stupid question he tried again, 'I mean how did you know about me? Sorry,' he said, terrified he might sound as if he thought he was worth knowing about, 'I mean what do you know about me? Or rather, let me start again, why are you here?'

Toby kicked himself for sounding like an idiot. Like Hugh Grant. Damn! She had caught him off guard and then thrown him off guard still further by looking the way she did.

Cosima was grinning widely, and as she opened her

mouth to talk, she hammed up the drama of her presence by accompanying each sentence with a sweep across the floor of his flat as if she was in some terrible amateur dramatic production. With one hand on her hip, and the other wielding her smouldering cigarillo holder, she flung her arms about in a manner that attempted the coquettish, an intention underlined by the all too suggestive look in her eye. She sounded like – and looked like – a predatory old hag from a 1930s Broadway musical.

'Well, honey, I was talking with Harold Sweet last night, and he told me *all* about you. He said you were a *highly* talented sculptor and that you were *definitely* worth a look. As you know I have just opened in Bruton Street and am looking for new blood, and I have to say your story has intrigued me.

'I think, you know, that we could just have something here. I mean, all that *fantastic* class controversy, the inevitable parental confusion, the humiliation of the great British Empire's ruling elite, the racial complications, the genetic *absurdity* of it, the irony of that marvellous British characteristic: the stiff upper lip! And at the bottom of it all, we have *you* – the great common denominator, the symbol of social rejection.' Cosima paused and turned back to Toby. 'I have to admit, I'm hooked!'

Toby didn't have a clue what she was talking about. 'But you haven't seen my work –'

'Doesn't matter! It's the story that counts.'

'What story?'

'*Your* story! The colour of your skin! The history!'

Cosima said everything as if it was all one big exclamation. Everything she said, apparently, was too exciting for her to cope with. 'Have you any *idea* how appealing that is going to be to a country as race conscious and fucked up as my own? I think, young man, I definitely think, that you and I could make something of this.'

Toby couldn't be sure, she was American after all, but with a great sinking feeling, he thought she might be referring to 'Great-grandmama's Indiscretion', as his family liked to call it. Christ knew how she had come across that sort of information about him. It wasn't something he broadcast.

'Are you talking about the fact that I have Indian blood in me?' he asked slowly, his voice noticebly lower. Some people, especially the more bohemian, did sometimes have bizarre reactions to Indians. When he and Cas had been on holiday recently, a Spanish hippie had come straight up to him, asked if he was Indian, kissed his hand and then proceeded to ask if he knew someone called Sai Bubba.

'Naturally! Now look, I've got plans. First let's change your name to Tobias – much more artistic, much more aristocratic, that'll help underline your blue-blood embarrassment. Jay Jopling was telling me the other day that his brother knew you at Eton, which I gather is where Prince William went to school. Oh it's too perfect! Did you know him? Anyway, he says everyone used to call you Darkie. Was it traumatic, darling? Was it? You can tell me!'

Toby's pulse was beginning to race as emotion welled up inside him. He clenched his fists and tried to keep his voice calm.

'Excuse me, but would you please tell me what the hell the colour of my skin has got to do with anything?' he asked through gritted teeth. 'And I'm afraid I didn't go to Eton.'

'You didn't? Oh that's a shame. Let's say you did anyway. And as for the colour of your skin, what *hasn't* it got to do with?'

Cosima didn't appear to have noticed Toby's irritation, but then, thought Toby, she wouldn't – her brashness clearly went beyond her sense of dress.

'Darling, in the world of art you need more than talent, you need a story, and yours is such a fabulous modern diatribe on the links of our past to our present, an allegory for the hidden secrets that will out, the humiliations of another generation, the complexities of our racial hang-ups – don't tell me you cannot see the appeal?'

Toby was staggered. This woman, whom he had never met before in his life, had marched into his flat, started pronouncing about his provenance and dared assume a whole raft of insulting conclusions about him. He didn't know what to say. But then what do you say to a woman who wears a lobster on her head? Cosima used his temporary loss of speech to continue, in a slightly more gentle manner.

'Think about it, honey. That woman with the names sewn into her tent? It's only because she's so fucked up on booze and drugs that we're interested. Van Gogh? He was a nobody until he cut off his ear. Picasso? His rabidness for women is as celebrated as his art. It's no good just having talent. Talent, dare I say it, barely comes into it nowadays. Why, I've sold every one of those blue penises I had in my front window last week, even though they looked as if a child could have made them with papier mâché and a bucket of paint. Why? Because the man who made them had his penis severed from his body by his two lesbian lovers. It was all over the press. The penises are a statement, a statement of our times. That's what modern art is all about.'

Toby, who had recovered his tongue, but was beginning to be anxious about other parts of his anatomy, asked incredulously, 'And what was the statement your blue penises so boldly chose to make?'

'Castration of course! The castration of modern man by the rise of modern woman!'

This last was accompanied by another melodramatic sweep towards Toby's manhood. Which was one melodramatic sweep too many.

'Right. Well, thank you very much for coming to explain that to me, but I really don't think I'm what you want. Thanks for the thought, but now I am going to ask you to leave.'

'Oh? Why?' Cosima's crest, quite literally, fell, and her lobster seemed to topple from its perch.

'Because,' replied Toby through gritted teeth, 'you walk into my house uninvited, insult me and my family, display no interest in my work, and then tell me it's worthless if it wasn't for the fact my great-grandmother slept with one of her servants!' Which, as far as Toby was concerned, was quite enough reason to turn the only dealer who had ever displayed any interest in him out of his home.

Cosima examined him carefully and decided he was probably quite upset. Damn! She didn't quite have this communication thing over here sussed out just yet. Very sensitive these Brits.

'Well, you think about it,' said Cosima as Toby continued to stonewall her. 'I could turn your pieces of twisted iron –' and here she nodded at the piece that stood in the corner of the living room, the *Two Lovers* he had given Cas last year – 'into cultural landmarks of the twenty-first century. And I could make you a very rich man in the process. Here is my card,' she said leaving it on the kitchen table, 'and you call me when you've had a think about my words.'

And with that, just as abruptly as she had arrived, she was gone, leaving Toby, still in his dressing gown, seething with fury, coffee cup still steaming in his hand. If it hadn't been for the card, he'd have thought the whole thing had been a horrible dream.

# chapter eight

It was not late in the day, but already it was dark. Seven o' clock was a reasonable time to be leaving the office for Cas, but, she mused to herself, now it was autumn, she could soon look forward to leaving home in the morning in the dark, and leaving the office after daylight had well and truly disappeared. Pretty miserable living, she thought. Ahead lay winter, with its cold, its rain, its darkness and its interminability.

She was on her way to meet her old *Guardian* colleague, Sam, but what was usually a pleasant fifteen minute walk over the river was, in the rain, turning into a breathless, sodden dash, as she skipped over puddles and ran between shop fronts to avoid the downpour. But for all the dreariness of the weather, Cas was excited about what she was doing: increasingly it looked like she and Sam had a story on their hands. Susie Farlane telling her not to proceed with the Power story on business grounds had been like a red rag to a bull as far as Cas had been concerned – apart from anything else if this guy was seriously going to try and take over the *News* then someone had to stop him. Most importantly of all, though, this was exciting for Cas because this was the real world: this wasn't easy feed to satisfy the imagined salacious appetite of the public, this was proper journalism: a search for the truth. The latest report on Catherine Zeta-Jones's plastic surgery, a speculative piece about this Christmas's must-have party dresses – Cas could take or leave those sort of stories.

This – the shaming of a dirty tycoon – was the sort of reason why Cas had gone into journalism. Sure, she may have watched *All the President's Men* too many times as a teenager, and she did understand that you couldn't bring down corrupt and powerful men every day, but to do it just once – now that would be career-making stuff. And if there was more on this Power character than met the eye, then his position as a media magnate would be seriously compromised. As a passing car sped through a puddle and soaked her from the thigh down, Cas didn't even swear – she was too busy imagining herself and Sam as modern-day Woodwards and Bernsteins, the journalists who had brought down President Nixon.

Toby didn't quite see it the same way, however. He had called her an hour ago to remind her about the reception at the Slade they were meant to be going to tonight – an exhibition of one of his friend's work. It was important to him, he had said. London dealers and agents were going to be there and he would like her to be there for moral support. Cas had tried to explain the importance of her own meeting with Sam, but Toby hadn't seemed particularly interested. Apparently she had promised to go weeks ago, but couldn't he see that that was before she knew she had this story? It wasn't as if any of his work was going to be on display (What work? thought Cas), and there would be plenty more opportunities to go to his friends' exhibitions in the future, she had told him. Anyway, she told herself, this meeting with Sam was a fair enough excuse. Her story on Power was part of her career and therefore their income. How was Toby going to sculpt if she didn't support him to start off with? And if she couldn't stop Power taking over her newspaper, would she still have a job? Not an overly melodramatic summary of the scenario, she told herself, then pushed Toby to the back of her mind.

Sam was small, wiry and intense. Whenever Cas saw him he was always wearing the same uniform – Ted Baker shirt, jeans and trainers, and frankly he could pass for anything from a football hooligan to a dotcom entrepreneur, which was just the way he liked it, particularly when he was undercover. Sam was her age, twenty-nine, but had worked shifts on the *Guardian* newsdesk since he'd left college, which meant he hadn't got as far up the career ladder or earned as much as Cas did. But Sam was a great journalist. Not for him the selling-out to a glossy magazine to write about lipstick, reflected Cas, he did his job for the love of it, not for the prestige or the money.

The pub was an old hack's meeting place. As she dashed through its doors, emerging soaked, panting and flushed, she saw a number of people she knew or had worked with in the past. The windows of the pub had steamed up and inside the yellow light warmed the throng, who were gathered noisily around their tables, shouting, laughing and drinking. She said hello to a few people she knew while casting an eye round for Sam. Eventually she found him, in a far corner, his nose buried in some periodical, a pint of Guinness in front of him. She shouted his name as she made her way across the room, and noted the pleasure and warmth in her voice. She hadn't seen Sam in a while, and she suddenly realized, as she saw him sitting there, that she had missed him. Sam looked up, and his frown broke into a smile.

'Good to see you, darling,' she said as she hugged his small frame.

'Good to see you too, babe – long time. Ugh, you're all wet, come and sit down.'

'Thanks,' said Cas, shaking off her coat. 'Dare I ask when the last time was?'

'The teenage pregnancy in Darlington – don't you remember we were both sent to cover it? And you got the mother, but you let me take some of your quotes.'

Cas did remember. It had been last year, before she had taken the job on the *News* and was still a freelance. An eleven-year-old girl had got herself pregnant on a pretty rough estate, and she and Sam had both been sent to cover the story and see if they could get someone to talk. But of course no one would, until Cas went out and bought the girl's mother £50 worth of nappies – for that they let her in the front door.

She laughed.

'Glad you recall I helped you out.'

They chatted for a while, catching up. Cas told Sam about Toby and his sculpting. Sam had never met him, but Cas said he should, he'd like him. Perhaps he wouldn't, she thought, but she said it anyway, because it was the natural thing to say.

'And you? Fallen in lurve yet?' she teased him, trying to move on.

'Me? No. That would prevent me being such a ladykiller,' he teased her back. 'Anyway, it's good for my career. I want a foreign post next, and that would not go down well with Mrs Right, who probably has a nice publishing job in the centre of town, a flat and a couple of cats that will not be moved.'

'How well you know women,' mocked Cas, 'and how unworthy they are of you!'

For as long as she had known him, Sam had never had a long-term, loving relationship. As she watched his face across the table and looked into his eyes, she noticed in him a loneliness that had not been there before. His face seemed more pinched, his features harder. But otherwise he was the same, and it was just as easy for them to pick up the banter that they had always shared – whether it was sitting at the back of a college lecture hall, or in a bush staking out Bob Geldof's house after he had won custody of his children.

'So, this Power character,' began Sam, returning from the bar with another pint for himself and another double vodka and tonic for Cas, 'how far do you want to go?'

'How far is there to go?'

'Who knows? But there's a big hole in his accounts, and he's getting the money from somewhere. It would be easy to assume that if he's in the sex industry he may be running some kind of racket, but that may not be true. On the other hand, if it is true, what are we going to find?'

'Well, we don't know anything until we start digging. Tell me, why did the *Guardian* close its investigation?'

'Good question. It was when *Hiya!* magazine first started doing well and he became a bit of a figure. You know, photographed out and about with celebrities and that. People started asking questions about who he was, and the fact that he was in porn meant he sounded promising or, at least, worthy of a bit of investigation. I talked to the guy who led the team earlier today, and I have to say he didn't sound very encouraging.' Sam's voice had dropped a tone, and unconsciously, both leant their heads closer together across the table.

'What do you mean? Encouraging of us?' asked Cas.

'No – don't worry, I didn't tell him we were doing anything, as we agreed, but he said he began to get weird phone calls.'

'Like what?'

'People from Power's organization would ring him up, supposedly just for a chat and stuff, but would slip in information about him that they shouldn't have known.'

'Like what?'

'Like where his kids went to school, what kind of car he drove, where his parents lived. Creepy stuff.'

'That's weird.'

'Totally. He still sounded quite freaked by it. Anyway, he didn't get anything on Power, even though he was asking all these questions, and eventually the *Guardian* lawyers told him nothing was publishable anyway, and he sounded quite relieved to have been able to drop it.'

'Okay. Well, we learn one thing from that: to be careful who we ask questions.'

'Right.' Sam paused. 'So you want to do this then?'

'Do what? Investigate Power? Of course! I think it's disgraceful that one of our oldest national papers should be sold to a pornographer and a man who runs celebrity magazines. What's the point in newspapers if they are just there for titillation and gossip? Apart from anything else, Sam, it's a matter of pride. I certainly don't want to work for a paper that is all too likely to introduce a page three and run two-part investigations into the state of the latest Hollywood marriage. Would you? So why shouldn't we investigate him?'

Sam looked at her incredulously. 'Er ... because he's your future employer?' he said sarcastically. 'Because it could be way beyond our capabilities? Because it might get nasty? Because it looks like he is about to become a big media player and it might not be politic –'

'Sod politic, Sam! What are we in this for? The money? The title? I don't know about you but I have spent too much time recently sitting on my arse choosing nice pictures of actresses to accompany nice, sycophantic interviews, whose only newsworthiness is who they are currently shagging. I can't remember the last time I did something to get to the truth, to expose something, to try and change things.'

'Well, I should get off that crappy magazine and back to a news floor then,' countered Sam mercilessly, looking her right in the eye. Cas was taken aback. She didn't speak for a few seconds, letting what Sam had just said sink in.

'Well, I think that's what I'm trying to do right now,' she said eventually.

'Fair enough,' said Sam evenly. 'But tell me: why should I help you?'

Cas opened her mouth to speak, but one look at Sam made her close it again. She knew what she had thought. She had thought that Sam would do anything she asked him, because he had always done what she said and she had always taken advantage of it. But the expression on his face was quite defiant, and he looked like he knew what she was thinking. Cas felt slightly ashamed.

'The thing is, Cas, I haven't got life as easy and as safe and as comfortable as you. I've been slogging it out on the front line now for eight years, with bugger-all wages, no girlfriend to come home to, no awards, no promotions. I do this kind of work every day and get paid for it. Why should I want to do more in my spare time just to help you feel better about your career? Not to mention the fact that this guy sounds like he's serious and I could be putting myself in danger.' Sam was getting quite worked up, and Cas was not quite sure why.

'Sam, I'm sorry. It's no big deal. I didn't mean to ask you

to sacrifice anything. Forget it – I only asked you because I thought you'd be into it. Hey, look, let me get you another drink,' she said, trying to calm him down.

'Sure,' he said, relaxing the intensity of his gaze, and looking for his cigarettes. 'Whisky chaser, please.'

Sam lit up a cigarette. As he watched Cas walk up to the bar he remembered the promise he had made himself – not to fancy her again, not to harbour any stupid hopes of being with her, not even to imagine them being together, but it had all just floated away. He couldn't help himself, when she was near, she consumed him; had consumed him for years. That was why he was here now, that was why, stupidly, he would probably end up agreeing to her daft plot to unmask her future boss. To be near her. Even though he knew she didn't fancy him. Even though she had just spent twenty minutes telling him about her new bloke.

'Look Sam, I've been thinking about it,' said Cas, returning from the bar. 'You're right; there is nothing in this for you if, as is likely, we find nothing. And you're right about my motives for doing this. But the reason I asked you is because you're a damn good journalist and I'd want you on my side if I was picking teams. And I have the faint hope, as I'm sure you do too, that one day I'll find a big story, and I'll uncover it, and everything I will have done in my career up till that point will have been worthwhile. Even if I did spend this morning marking chocolate pots out of ten for tastiness.'

Both of them laughed and everything that needed to be said passed unsaid but acknowledged.

'God, I hate you Caris Brown,' said Sam with feeling. 'But I'm looking forward to working with you again.' He grinned broadly across the table at her. She stared at him to check he wasn't joking.

'You are?'

'I am.'

Cas smiled her relief.

'So where do we start?'

On the tube on the way home, steam spiralled off Cas's damp overcoat, a drop of rainwater fell from her nose. She could feel the alcohol coursing through her, and winced at the blinding white light of the carriage. She had drunk more with Sam than she had intended, but she hoped Toby might still be out so she could have a bath on her own, think about their plan, and fall into bed alone. It was not that she didn't want to see Toby, it was just that her head was full of Sam and Power. She was thinking about tomorrow, about going down to Companies House and checking the public records, about scrutinizing Power's magazines to see what he was into, checking his staff lists to see if there was an aggrieved ex-member who would talk, seeing who he had done deals with, and which deals had gone wrong. There was a lot to do and she was looking forward to it.

At Old Street she alighted, finally, and ran up the escalator (this she counted as excellent exercise, so she didn't have to go to the gym), out of the station and off towards Hoxton. Home! Nearly there. But as she fumbled for the key in the bottom of her bag she could hear music blaring from upstairs. Toby was in.

'Hi, babe,' she said cheerily, as she tried not to stumble up the stairs.

'Hi,' he replied, in a fairly deadpan manner, she thought.

'Want a drink?' she asked as she headed straight for the cooking sherry – she wasn't sure why, she just found herself going in that direction.

'No thanks,' he replied, untempted by Tesco's finest. 'How was your evening?' he asked slowly.

'Good. Great, actually.' Cas grinned. 'Sam has agreed to help me investigate this guy. Which is brilliant, because I'm not sure I could do it on my own.'

Toby nodded. 'Which guy?'

'Victor Power, of course,' Cas replied, spilling most of the sherry on the work surface. 'I've got a hunch about him. Something doesn't quite add up about his business. He's got too much money for a magazine publisher.' She looked up at Toby but his face was blank. 'Victor Power?' she said again. His face was still blank. 'You know, the guy taking over the newspaper?'

'No, I don't know, Cas, because you've never told me.'

Cas looked aghast. 'Oh. Sorry. Well, he is, and he's into lots of dodgy porn and a whole lot more besides – and I'm hoping to find out what and break a front-page exclusive that will lead to further investigation, an arrest, lots of glory for me, and you and me together for ever.' By this last Cas had managed to weave her way across the living room to Toby, give him a huge kiss, and start to go downstairs for her bath. At the stairs she paused, knowing she had forgotten something.

'How was your evening?' she asked.

'Fine,' said Toby.

'Good,' replied Cas, and proceeded to negotiate the stairs. Toby looked down at his hand where he held Cosima Beane's card. She had tackled him again tonight, at the exhibition, and even though Cas hadn't come, he had intended to discuss it with her. But she hadn't even remembered. Toby was hurt.

Downstairs in her bath, with her sherry resolutely refusing to make it into her mouth but instead choosing the path of least resistance down her chin and onto her chest, Cas wished Toby could understand her enthusiasm for this story a bit more and be a little less pissed off with her for not making his friend's exhibition. She had never even met this friend of Toby's anyway – he was hardly going to be offended with her for not coming – and as for moral support, well, Toby hardly ever asked her opinion about his work. He and his art friends were so clubbable, if you weren't into art then it seemed your opinion didn't count. When she had tried to offer up her thoughts to him and his friends before, they had just looked at her as if she was stupid. So she had learned to accept that what she had to say wasn't valid because, as Toby would quite frustratingly remind her, she knew very little about it.

She wondered why Toby wasn't more interested in what she was doing. Newspapers were her life, while Toby didn't even read them. Sometimes he would buy a tabloid on a Sunday to find out the football reports, but that would be it. And he had never once done more than glance at her stupid magazine. She had given up bringing it home for him. Fundamentally, thought Cas, she agreed with Toby's approach, life wasn't about slogging your guts out at the expense of the people around you. She had learnt that much from her father. He had spent so much time at work that he had eventually run off with his secretary. Cas couldn't remember him being around at all when she was little. She was ten when he had left and she had hardly noticed the difference. So she had fallen in love with Toby because he was exactly the opposite to her father: he didn't care about salaries and achievement. For years now she had worked hard at her job, putting in long hours, gaining credibility, watching her salary rise. But for what? She had all the clothes her wardrobe could hold, had invitations to more parties than she could possibly attend and had more friends than she had hours to give them. Increasingly Cas felt she was chasing her own tail, and the harder she worked the less time she appeared to be, well, living. Her stress levels rose, so she took a holiday. She was depressed about something going wrong at work, so she got drunk with her girlfriends. She was happy about something going right at work so she bought a new frock. And? Where was all this leading? Each morning she would wake up and look in the mirror and notice another line that hadn't been there the week before. So she would apply expensive Clarins vitamin cream and head off for another twelve-hour stretch in an air-conditioned office under strip lighting. Then Cas met Toby.

Toby was not like anyone she had ever known before. He was the opposite to her and it had felt like a cool refreshing breeze blowing through her life. She had been amazed by his mellowness, in awe of his considered ease, completely taken aback by his level approach to life. He wasn't in a hurry, he wasn't always trying to achieve some-thing, he wasn't desperately trying to get somewhere: no, he was quite happy where he was, thank you. And what's more, he made things. Real, proper, beautiful things that he spent months labouring lovingly over: it was such a refreshing change from the predatory show offs who prowled media nightspots in search of one-night stands: the ad men, the CEOs, the city boys, the marketing managers, the sales-men. Toby, Cas thought, was inspirational, and it was this that Cas's love for him was built on, she told herself and him repeatedly, rather than any, frankly pitiful, neurotic neediness for someone to 'support' or 'look after' her. She liked him for who he was, she didn't need him for what he could do for her.

Well, wondered Toby angrily upstairs, what was he really in her life for? A quirky alternative that had once made her think outside her box? She certainly didn't think about him much any more. And as for him being in her life, well, she wouldn't even talk to him about it, let alone let him in. Was he just a novelty factor for her? Like he was for Cosima Beane?

The trouble was that Toby lived his life on such a different level, thought Cas, losing the soap in the bath water underneath her again. He didn't know anything about what it was like to go into an office every day, to be bullied by someone you hated and had no respect for, to do a job, frankly, that you had seriously decreasing respect for, to be pulled in all sorts of directions, so you felt like you had no time for yourself any more.

She thinks that because she pays the rent that's all she has to do for me. She doesn't have to take an interest – and obviously she doesn't want to. So all I do is lose my pride and be at her beck and call. She doesn't even seem to want me for that any more. All it seems we have together now is sex. That's no reason to be together in the long term.

What did she and Toby do together now? Cas thought hard about it. Was it just sex?

## chapter nine

'Ravelli. In my office now.'

Silvio Ravelli had spent the entire game on the bench watching. His team had won easily without him: two goals from last season's top striker at AC Milan and one from home-grown Manchester talent had knocked Bayern Munich right out of the European Cup. But Silvio, the star of Old Trafford, hadn't even so much as been brought on in the second half. It was punishment, he knew, for the display on the front page of every one of this morning's papers (not to mention protection from the ribbing of the fans), and now he was going to hear it from the boss directly.

Ferguson, who had been congratulating the team in the locker room after the match while Silvio cowered at the back, had finished his debriefing by spitting out Ravelli's name and the summons to his office in front of all the lads. The flush of success had disappeared in an instant, and as the manager turned his thoughts to his errant striker his skin had pinched itself tight across his face in anger, draining away all the joy of victory. Then he marched past Silvio upstairs to his wood-panelled chamber ignoring his rather meek, 'Yes, sir.'

The boys around him nudged Ravelli in sympathy as he changed into his suit, knowing that the dressing down that was coming would be a damn sight worse than the ribbing he had taken from them and the fans before the game. He was lucky he hadn't understood what was being chanted. No one had offered to translate.

It was all hardly surprising: the picture had not been good. Silvio's jaw had been on the floor, incredulity pasted across his face as he watched his girlfriend, barely dressed in a pink leotard, flirting and preening and posing for the paparazzi. He hadn't judged the dress as that outrageous – after all Brazilian girls wore a lot less – but the British press had, especially when she had thrown her hands in the air and her left nipple had popped out. The headlines across all the back pages were asking exactly the same question: what was United's star striker doing at a party in London the night before a European game?

Upstairs, Ferguson wanted to know the answer to exactly the same question. He sat behind his mahogany desk brewing up a storm. Ravelli stood in front of him, eyes on the floor, and waited. Ferguson got up, walked up to him, so close Silvio could smell his chewing-gum flavoured breath. Towering over Silvio's small frame, he walked behind him so his mouth was positioned directly behind his ear.

He was FURIOUS, he said, so loudly Silvio nearly fell on the floor, about the IRRESPONSIBILITY of Ravelli's behaviour. His voice shook Silvio to the bone and it was all the little Brazilian could do to keep from flinching. What the HELL did Ravelli think he was playing at? Did he not understand he was a football player not a BLOODY CELEBRITY? Did he really think that the shareholders of this club, the very ones who paid his wages, wanted to see him CAVORTING around town with some TART in a swimsuit the night before one of their most important matches of the season? One that was possibly, depending on the form of the players, likely to net the club a LOT of money? Did he not understand how football worked? Did he not understand what his job was? What he was paid that ridiculous wage for? Because if he wasn't prepared to show that much COMMITMENT then he could bugger off back to Rio where he came from. That suited Ferguson fine because there were PLENTY of other very talented strikers out there who *were* prepared to show him the commitment.

'I'm sorry sir, it's just that she is my girlfriend and she asked me —'

'I don't care if she's your bloody grandmother, boy, it was the day before a European game!'

Silvio wisely decided that this was not a two-way conversation. He waited for Ferguson to calm himself and sit back behind his desk.

The problem was easy to see, thought Ferguson, the stupid boy was in love. Nothing but trouble, these foreign players. Nothing but bloody trouble.

Eventually, after a long, painful silence, during which Ravelli could not tear his eyes away from the pattern of the carpet at his feet, Ferguson, whose experiences with Charlotte Want and his players were not limited to Ravelli alone, said quietly and meaningfully, in an almost fatherly tone.

'A bit of advice young man: that girl is bad news.'

Too right thought Silvio – the bad news was that Charlotte was not available at his beck and call, because she was far too damn busy with her 'career', as she called it. But when she was with him, then she wasn't bad news at all, Mr Ferguson, no way, she was heaven. He refrained however, from saying this out loud. The trouble was that most of Charlotte's work seemed to be in London, and Silvio, utterly infatuated, could not bear to be apart from her for more than a few hours without his heart breaking. Ferguson's feelings on the subject of his relationship, were, Silvio could see, going to make his life very difficult. Especially as Charlotte always wanted to go out, and when she went out, it seemed newspaper photographers always went with her (she phoned them beforehand to let them know). So this was going to make hiding his whereabouts from his boss an even bigger problem.

'Do I need to bring your mother back to look after you? Are you not old enough to know what your priorities should be?' continued Ferguson in a mocking tone. 'Would your mama's pig stew keep you indoors?' he asked sadistically. Christina Ravelli had become something of a personality around Old Trafford during her stay, not least because she insisted on delivering huge pots of feijoada, her rather exotic pig and bean stew, to every player's house once a week. Silvio was riled. No one insulted his mother, but one look at Ferguson's face and he decided he would do better not to challenge him about it.

'The most important thing you can do now, laddy, is your job,' Ferguson said furiously. 'You are paid to score goals, not to run around at parties in London the night before a game. Or even before training for that matter. I did not spend millions of pounds on you because you've got a cute face and a celebrity girlfriend. Do you understand me?'

'Yes, boss.'

'Now, if I catch you doing this again then I will terminate your contract on behavioural grounds. Oh yes, the clause is in there. And then you will have to explain that to your mother when you get off the plane with your tail between your legs. Explain that her son has lost his chance to be a world-class football player because he fancied a bit of skirt. Do I make myself clear?'

'Yes boss.'

'Now what have you got to say for yourself?'

'I'm sorry.'

'And?'

'I will not do it again.'

'Now get out.'

Silvio needed no encouragement, and was out of the door more quickly than one of his free kicks. Outside in the corridor he wiped the perspiration from his forehead. His heart was beating fast and a feeling of nausea fluttered about his stomach. This situation was not good. One thing he knew he really shouldn't do was get on the wrong side of his boss. He was going to have to speak to Charlotte about this – he certainly couldn't be seen at her side too often any more. Or at least he was going to have to pick his moments carefully, and she was going to have to understand that. He was the man after all, and she the woman and she was just going to have to do as he said. That's the way it was in his country, and if she wanted Latino love then she had to have the whole package.

Charlotte had never had Latin before, Silvio thought, playing through the conversation in his mind, and how he would explain things were going to be different from now on. Latin was different, Latin was passion, integrity, fire and might. Latin was true, true love. But along with the Neruda poems and roses (both of which he had indulged her with ad infinitum) she must understand that she had to do as she was told. He wasn't going to be like one of these English boys and lie down and take it. No he was not. Silvio breathed deeply and began to feel better once he had resolved this. And as for that magazine interview, well, she was just going to have to tell them that they couldn't run it for a bit. Not until things had calmed down. There was no way he could risk his boss seeing that.

His mobile phone began to ring. Charlotte had programmed it with the tune to her one hit single and, as he was still standing outside the manager's office, the ring cut through the air like an alarm. Sprinting down the corridor and whipping the phone out of his pocket he saw it was her calling. Despite everything, his heart leapt just at the very thought of her voice.

'Darleeng, hello!' he whispered, charging down the stairs and out of earshot of the manager's office.

'Silvio, baby!' she replied.

A wild pattering spread through Silvio's veins, just the sound of her saying his name was enough to fill him with the honey of desire, to dispel all his worries, to concentrate his mind on – her.

'Have you seen the papers, darling? We look fantastic – and I've made every front page. I'm so excited! Vic is over the moon, I'm a star Silvio, I'm a star!'

'Yes, darleeng, I know, but there is a bit of a problem –'

'Sweetie, we've got to celebrate, you know. This is one of the best days of my life and I want to spend it with you!'

'Yes, my darleeng, I know, but I cannot come –

'I know you can't, baby, that's why I'm right here!'

'What? You are in Manchester?' Silvio's spirits flew up to cloud level.

'Better than that baby . . . nearer than that.' Charlotte giggled naughtily down the phone.

'What? I don't understand, darleeng, you have to explain.' Even though Sivio had been speaking English for more than a year now he didn't always understand everything that was said, especially on the telephone, and was aware he quite often missed nuances. Charlotte giggled some more and all Silvio could hear was what he could only imagine was the sound of a cork popping.

'Guess what I'm wearing?' she continued. Now this he could understand. He leaned back against the wall, closed his eyes and tried to imagine, a smile spreading across his face.

'Your black sexy leather dress?' he began. He learnt the word leather after just one date with Charlotte. She wore it a lot.

'No. Less than that.' Silvio unzipped the sheath dress in his mind and saw Charlotte stepping out of it, her generously curved body clothed only in . . .

'Your bra and panties – those little ones we bought last weekend?'

'No.' Charlotte giggled again. 'Less than that.' Silvio smiled to himself and saw her unfasten her bra, step out of her panties.

'Ah, I don't know . . . tell me,' he pleaded, feeling himself hardening at the thought of her.

'Nothing! I am absolutely naked. Just holding a bottle of Dom Perignon in my hand . . . '

Now Silvio was uncomfortably hard, and he put his hand down his trousers to rearrange himself.

'And guess where I am?'

Silvio tried to speak but couldn't: he was thinking only of Charlotte's full, big breasts, her chocolate-brown nipples, the dark triangle of hair betweeen her smooth, silky legs, the look in her eyes . . .

'I am in the shower, behind the curtain, downstairs in your locker room . . . '

'What?' Silvio's eyes shot open and a bullet of fear

passed straight through his body. In his hand his cock shrank back in terror.

'Downstairs? You are naked downstairs? Here?' Silvio extracted his hand and began to run. He had to hide her, this was too much. If she got caught, now . . .

'Come and get me, baby, I'm waiting . . .' Charlotte laughed throatily.

'How did you get in? How did you know where to go?' Silvio said panicking, darting down the stairs and sprinting through the corridors faster than he could move down the left wing.

'I've been here before, baby,' said Charlotte, but this was one comment too much for Silvio and he decided not to register it. He fled along the corridors, thinking: Please, no one find her before I do, and telling her not to speak. At last the door of the locker room came into view and thankfully there didn't seem to be anybody about. He crashed through it, glanced around, could see nobody and headed directly for the showers.

He pulled back the curtain and there she was, his girl-friend, Charlotte Want, completely naked, in the showers of his football team's changing rooms.

Silvio could hardly believe it, but even so the sight of her was already beginning to work on him. Suddenly, what he saw was not the locker room, but her dirtiest grin; not the team showers, but her slim shoulders curving towards him; not any possibility of danger, but just her bare breasts swinging his way, her dark pubic triangle unmasked and promising a thousand riches within. Despite himself, Silvio could feel himself hardening again, the panic of being found here with her already lending a frisson to the occasion that did not seem likely to assist him in preventing it.

She said not a single word but, transfixing him with her gaze, brought the champagne bottle up to her lips and began to lick the rim, her breasts swinging free in front of her, her other hand drifting down to between her legs, her fingers gently playing with the warm folds of her pink flesh.

'Want some?' she asked huskily, crossing one leg over the other, holding the bottle out to him.

Transfixed, all Silvio could do was stare. And the more he stared, the more he drank in the image of the sexiest woman in his world, standing naked in the place where only minutes before all of his team mates had been rinsing off the afternoon's sweat, the more he thought, Yes, I do want some. As he grew harder and harder all thoughts of smuggling her straight out of here left him and desire became too much. Now she was here, looking like this, he thought, now she wants me, needs me . . .

Drunkenly, Silvio stepped forward and took the bottle from her hand. Holding her gaze he lifted the champagne to his lips, let it pour into his mouth and dribble down over his shirt. The bubbles fizzed in the back of his throat, the alcohol encouraging his desire.

As he drank, Charlotte reached out and grabbed his tie, pulling him closer to her until she could push her hands up over his chest, feel the hard athleticism of his body and its quivering strength, perfectly poised, waiting to unleash itself on her. She knew the effect she had on him. That, plus the danger of where they were, the likelihood of them being caught, was making her feel very horny herself. She began to unbutton his shirt while reaching down with her other hand. A smile of satisfaction spread across her face as she felt his swollen cock throbbing against the material of his trousers.

'Hi, darling,' she said huskily, casually. 'Pleased to see me?'

Silvio couldn't answer, instead he pushed himself up against her, feeling the curves of her body press against his, her bare flesh crushed against his suit, thinking: I am due upstairs in the bar now for the press call, where everyone else is, but instead I am standing in the shower with Charlotte and a hard on and she is wearing nothing.

The roaring of the blood in his ears drowned out everything else. She loosened his tie, undid his trousers and he kicked them off, and his shoes and socks, thinking, I want to be naked here with her too. But she is bad, he thought, a bad girl, and while one hand was wrapped around the champagne bottle, the other, which was fondling her breast, suddenly pinched hard at her nipple – punishing her for her daring, and enjoying it all the same. He saw the pain and the pleasure flicker across her face, and she took the bottle from him and drank again. As she did so, he put the tie over her head and round her neck.

'You are a bad, bad girl,' he whispered to her, his voice thick with desire, and he tightened the tie around her. It was his cock now that was doing the thinking, not his head, nor his thudding heart. Charlotte's eyes half closed as she felt the material of the tie tighten on her throat, and she surrendered herself to his control. It had taken some courage to get in here, but today she felt as if she could rule the world and nothing was too much for her. She was on the front page of every newspaper: today she had made it.

So now, she was glad to sit back, be manipulated, to let Silvio's frustrated anger and desire take hold of her, feel his strong hands pawing at the skin of her back, caressing her neck, knowing they could and would tighten around her, knowing he was going to punish her and that the pain was going to feel good.

'I will hurt you for this now,' he said, shrugging himself out of his jacket. Taking the bottle from her hand, he ripped off the foil from around the neck, gripped her chin between his thumb and forefinger and jerked her face up so she was looking into his eyes, which were glowing with intention. This girl has to be controlled, he thought, and I am the one who has to do it. Forcing her legs apart with his knees he pushed the cold glass of the bottle up between her thighs. Between her legs he could feel the heat and the stickiness of her. She was turned on by herself and what she had done – this only turned him on more. He pulled tighter on the tie so it drew tauter around her neck. With the weight of his body he pushed her back hard against the wall of the shower, crushing her, controlling her.

'You must not come here like this,' he breathed, enjoying his position of strength over her, feeling like a man, in control of the situation at last. 'You are mine and you must do as I say,' he said and he worked the bottle up inside her, enjoying the sound of her groan. He pulled on the tie so her head jerked to the side and she knew she was helpless to his strength.

Silvio began to move the bottle inside her, until she moaned out loud, and he pulled her back from the wall against him and began to bite at her neck. She grasped at him with her hands, but he was stronger than she was and she couldn't move in his embrace. She scratched her long nails down his back but that just made him hold her tighter, bite her neck harder, push the bottle further into her. She cried out in pain but did not ask him to stop.

Silvio pulled the bottle from her and threw her back against the shower wall again. He stepped out of the rest of his clothes and his curved penis was now bigger than Charlotte thought she had ever seen it – the bottle seemed small in comparison. Her face had gone dark now with desire, and Silvio pinched her nipples hard in each hand. He moved her towards the shower gauge and pushed the button that released a jet of water over them both, to drown the noise of her. Pushing her up against the wall, the water flooding down between them, soaking them and Silvio's clothes, he picked her up, a hand under each buttock, her legs astride him and pushed his cock through her wetness and deep inside her. His eyes closed and his body was enveloped in the thudding that rang out in his ears. Her warm, dark place was invaded, holding him, all of him. All over him washed the water and all Silvio could feel, flooding through every pore in his body, was the cosy, comfortable, reassuring feeling that he was, at last, home. Charlotte could no longer see or hear, all she could feel was the hard, hot throbbing of her lover's cock as he began to move rhythmically inside her, the water pouring over her body and the groans of her lover's desire in her ear. She was lost inside him, he inside her.

'Ravelli, is that you?'

The couple stopped moving abruptly. There was no mistaking the voice – it was Ferguson's. It was coming from the changing-room area round the corner. The two bodies were absolutely frozen. Silvio looked down at Charlotte. To his disbelief, he saw a wicked gleam spread across her face. She looked as if she was going to laugh. Silvio was paralysed with panic – even if he could have moved, to put his hand over her mouth to stifle her laughter would result in his dropping her, and would make the situation even worse. Suddenly Charlotte felt heavy in his arms, then he saw the champagne bottle was just visible behind the shower curtain, as were his clothes. If Ferguson came round the corner he would certainly see them.

'Yes, sir?' he answered, trying and failing to keep his voice steady.

'I forgot to say, I want you here at 6 a.m. tomorrow for three hundred one-arm press-ups in the middle of the pitch. I want to watch them on the CCTV when I get in.'

'Yes, sir!' replied Ravelli quickly, thinking, please don't come over. Charlotte began to squirm against him. One look at her face and he knew she was enjoying this. She began to giggle and, unable to free either hand, he pressed his lips on hers to stifle the sound. He couldn't deny the terror was a turn on for him as well.

'Good,' replied his manager, and they listened to the footsteps, just audible above the splashing of the shower, and the door of the locker room slam.

'Now where were we?' asked Charlotte.

# chapter ten

Cas didn't get home until after Toby had gone to bed that night. As agreed with Sam a few days before, she had been down to the Berkeley Club, one of London's posher lap-dancing venues, to interview a girl by the name of Bentley Rhythm. The club had sent her profiles of all its dancers, but it was Bentley whom Cas had been after: one of the Power stable's favourite models for many years. Cas had found her featured in at least three of his magazines this month, on one as the cover star. On Sam's tip off, Cas had rung her agent masquerading as a model booker for another pornographic magazine, and had been informed Bentley Rhythm had a three-year exclusivity contract with Power Publishing – just as Sam had said. She had also, it was rumoured, once had a brief affair with him. Information on Power's private life was proving hard to come by, but Sam had done some asking around in the industry and Bentley's name had come up more than once. So she had seemed as good a place to start as any and, as in any industry, the sex trade was full of gossip, so Cas hoped she might learn something.

Sam was to spend the evening talking to an aggrieved ex-employee. The editor of *Women On Top* for seven years, he had been sacked a year and a half ago, and Sam had discovered him through an attempted court action he had brought against Power for unfair dismissal. The action had failed, and there was no evidence of a pay-off so he also seemed a likely source to talk. Sam had eventually found him editing *Girls and Guns* monthly up in Liverpool, but fortuitously he was down in London on business this week. He had agreed to meet Sam after some persuasion, although it had to be anonymously, in a service station on the M25.

'Hmm, let's see who got the short straw here: the one going to the Berkeley Club for champagne cocktails with a lap dancer, or the one going to Welcome Break for a cup of weak tea with a dirty mac?' asked Sam.

'Unlucky, mate,' Cas had teased.

Cover for the interview with Bentley Rhythm was the Sunday magazine's back-page feature, a slot called 'A Space of My Own', in which somebody talked about a space that was particularly important to them, and Cas had managed to get Tamara to agree to feature a lap dancer and her dressing room. It helped that London had decided lap dancing was the latest, most fashionable way to spend an evening. This had inevitably been triggered by the celebrity membership of a few of the clubs, celebrities mainly of the laddish sort, who had in turn triggered a spate of vacuous

style features on 'Lap Dancing – It's the New Cool'.
Tamara, therefore, had been in favour of it.

Cas had thought there was little point in going home
beforehand, so she had worked late in the office and then
taken a cab over to Mayfair at about ten. On the way she
sent Toby a text message saying, 'Will be home late – c u
2moro', and then cringed. It had got to the stage where she
and Toby were actually happier avoiding each other.
Normally they spoke during the day, but during the last
week neither had really wanted to talk to each other and
there had been no mid-afternoon chats about nothing in
particular, no giggling over inanities, no mock arguments
over whose turn it was to get dinner. She hadn't phoned
him and the couple of times he had called she had been in
meetings. When she had called back he had been out.

The Berkeley Club was certainly in the middle of
London's prime money ground. What Cas expected to find
was table upon table of flash-cash foreigners and half-cut
city boys cheering along some unenthusiastic, bony models.
Her expectation couldn't have been further from the truth.
The club itself was like a million other nightclubs all over
the world – red velvet upholstery, dance floor, several raised
podiums, booths and tables, and a dark ceiling decorated
with glitter to look like the night sky. But it wasn't just men
sitting around the tables, there were women too, young
women, not particularly dressed up (in fact they looked as if
they had come from work), but they seemed to be enjoying
the spectacle as much as the men. She spotted a few famous
faces – an It girl, who was quite used to posing with no

clothes on for men's magazines (was she trying to pick up some tips from the pros?), a forty-something singer who looked like he had put on quite a lot of weight and a writer whose exploits into the world of hallucinogenic drugs had earned him several fat book deals. The rest of the audience could have been from any background, it looked like a multi-national crowd, young, fairly trendy, and the atmosphere was light, open and only slightly tipsy. The lap dancing was going on in the background, no one was ogling, and the girls were looking rather pleased with themselves.

When she arrived, she was greeted by the owner cum manager of the club, a fairly experienced-looking fifty-year-old with a rockabilly ponytail and a huge glittering pair of highly suitable Elvis sunglasses. Quite how he saw through them in the darkness of the club Cas had no idea, but then as he expertly guided her to her table, she suspected he had had a lifetime of practice. Introducing himself as Rocky, he metaphorically charmed the pants off Cas who, after several lethal pink drinks in tall glasses (she had no idea what was in them but noted you could only buy it by the magnum), began to think she might like to give lap dancing a bit of a go herself. Cas asked him about the female punters.

'Why do they come?'

Rocky smirked, drew breath, and said, 'In my thirty-five years of experience in the nightclub business, darling, I've observed more men and women under the influence of booze and sex than I care to remember. All I can tell you is no one appreciates the female body as much as a woman, even if she is much more critical. There is nothing a woman loves more than coming down here and seeing other women in control, showing off their bodies and earning stacks of cash.' He turned to Cas and grinned, revealing a gold eye tooth studded with a diamond. 'I'll tell you another thing, though: women are much less afraid to fancy their own, no matter how straight they are. You ever seen a bloke buying tickets for the Chippendales?'

Cas laughed and said no she hadn't, but then the Chippendales had never much appealed to her either. Rocky gave her a look, and she told him she had a boyfriend and was quite comfortable with her sexuality thank you very much.

'No, no, no don't get me wrong,' responded Rocky, putting a manicured hand on hers, 'I'm not accusing you of that. I just think most women swing both ways, though in the end they find blokes ultimately more satisfying.'

'Maybe,' replied Cas, thinking neutrally of Toby, and watched a small girl with a bright-red bob removing her purple vest top to reveal two tiny pointed nipples and an enviably flat stomach. She could see Rocky's point.

The strippers themselves were excellent dancers, as well as purveyors of everything you needed to know about making love to a steel pole. The girls were protected by a club rule which was displayed prominently on all tables:

Clients are asked not to touch the girls (penalty: expulsion), and at all times knees must be kept no more than twelve inches apart – dancers and clients.

Cas couldn't help laughing at the prudery of this last but she saw that it worked. Seedy, the Berkeley Club was not.

The dancers all looked completely different from each other and each seemed equally comfortable with their different shapes and sizes. There was definitely no body fascism going on.

'My doing,' said Rocky proudly. 'I hand pick them myself'.

Some were blonde, some dark, some redheaded, some large breasted, some small breasted, some hippy, some voluptuous, some skinny. One girl even proudly displayed her caesarean scar with a glitter tattoo. They came over to Cas's table and chatted to her, one pointed out her husband in the front row, who apparently loved coming down here with his mates and showing her off. All were different nationalities: Russians, Croatians, Colombians, Americans, Swedes and Czechs, but only one was English: Miss Bentley Rhythm. She was clearly the star of the joint, judging by the way the regulars cheered and whistled her when she walked onto the dance floor, but then Cas did have to admit she had the most knockout body. She was at least six foot four, and had closely cropped peroxide-white hair. Her body looked like a non-plastic Brigitte Nielson with large, gravity-defying breasts, wide pink nipples, two apple-shaped cheeks for her arse and legs that went all the way to the centre of the earth and back. Her skin gleamed with baby oil as she writhed to the sort of vaudeville French cabaret music you might have found at Club Toulouse in Pigalle seventy years ago. It took her a full ten minutes to remove her sparkling gold Stetson and chainmail silver bikini, bit by tiny bit, and by the end of the performance, which included more contortions than Madonna's yoga teacher could have managed, she had the full attention of every single person in the club. Table after table screamed for more, and she danced privately (for extra cash, Cas noticed), for a few before taking a final bow.

'Ah, the jewel in my crown!' Rocky grinned contentedly, and tipped his girl a wink before she went off stage.

Bentley winked back: she looked like she was loving it. So much for Cas's downtrodden lap-dancer story, then.

Backstage in her dressing room, Cas congratulated Bentley on her performance.

'Yeah, it was all right, wasn't it?' she replied nonchalantly in a thick Scouser accent.

'You certainly know how to turn them on,' remarked Cas weakly.

'What about you?' shot back Bentley aggressively. 'Did I turn *you* on?'

Cas thought about it, momentarily shy. 'You know, Bentley, I think you probably did.'

Bentley chuckled to herself. 'Bentley's not my name, you know. I'm actually called Terri, but that's considered a bit common here in Mayfair, and besides, my surname's Ramsbottom and we wouldn't want that getting out, would we?'

'Absolutely not,' agreed Cas. 'That wouldn't help your career at all.'

'Aw, this isn't my career, love, don't patronize me with that crap. I'm just earning some money and having a good time.' Bentley pulled a towelling dressing gown firmly round her and lit up a Benson's. Under the harsh white dressing room lights her sex appeal seemed all of a sudden to evaporate. The stage show was just an illusion: make-up, lighting, a costume and a few moves could transform a woman completely. But then women had known that since time began.

'Mind?' Bentley asked, taking a deep pull on her cigarette.

'No, of course not,' said Cas, 'it's your dressing room.'

'Ah yeah, "A Space of My Own" – that's what all this is about, innit? Rocky told me it was "invaluable publicity" and to make up some crap about how special my dressing room is.' She scowled at Cas. 'Which was probably a bad idea seeing as I'm not too fond of journalists myself.'

'Oh,' said Cas, somewhat deflated.

'But he said you was quite insistent it was me. Any reason?'

'Well,' began Cas carefully, 'you seemed to me to be pretty much the woman of the moment. Cover star of *Come Inside*, in plenty of other magazines, and the star of the show tonight.'

'Buy those magazines often do you?'

Cas had expected Bentley backstage to be as friendly as the other girls had been out front, but this clearly was not going to be the case.

'No,' continued Cas calmly, wondering what it was she

had done to trigger such hostility, 'but I like to do my research.'

Bentley grunted, then turned to the mirror and began to take off her make-up.

'I'm not just a lap dancer, you know. I do other stuff – dancing, acrobatics, entertaining. This is just me bread and butter. If I could choose I'd be on the cover of *Elle*, not bloody *Come Inside*, thank you very much.'

Bentley threw her soiled cotton pad violently into the bin, and, using her reflection in the mirror, gave Cas a hard stare. Cas wondered what it was that Bentley was thinking about her, and decided her best approach now was to be direct. Bentley seemed to like directness.

'Pardon me for asking, Bentley, but do you think I'm here to take the piss out of you?'

Bentley turned round sharply to face Cas and looked her in the eye. Cas returned her stare and raised her eyebrows.

'I dunno – are you?' Bentley replied levelly.

'No, but I was trying to figure out why you don't like me here.'

'I'll tell you why, because I'm suspicious that you've chosen me. There's plenty of bigger club stars than me. What newspaper you from?'

'The *Daily News*.'

'And who owns that?'

'Well, actually that's a bit of a moot point at the moment –' Cas broke off. Bentley didn't know she was coming to see her about Power, did she?

'You're not here all of a sudden because you're trying to find out something about your new proprietor are you?' Bentley was grinning at Cas now, happy to be one step ahead of the game. 'Here I am dancing away for three years, minding my own business, and then all of a sudden there's a knock on the door: "Oh! Bentley you're a star! Can I come and interview you?" Nothing to do with the fact that I model for his magazines is it? Nothing to do with the fact that he once tried to get in my knickers, is it?'

'Look Bentley I don't know where you got that idea from, I'm just a magazine journ –'

'Yeah, right, and I'm just a cabaret dancer. Our sort don't talk to your sort. What's in it for us?' Bentley took a long, lifesucking drag from her cigarette.

This was interesting, thought Cas. What did Bentley know about Power taking over the *News*? She seemed to know more than Cas did herself. Would she tell her for money? Could Cas afford to pay her, and would she be telling the truth? Both women eyed each other suspiciously, like boxers circling each other in a ring. Then Cas's mobile went off. She checked the caller and turned it off.

'Who you hanging up on?'

'Um . . .' Cas hesitated. 'Actually, my boyfriend.'

'Well, don't mind me.'

'No. It's just I don't want to talk to him right now.'

'Lover's quarrel?'

'Ah – no. Well, yes. But I'm talking to you, so I'll call him later.'

'Aw, put him out of his misery. He's probably wondering where you are. You better not tell him!' cackled Bentley through her haze of cigarette smoke. 'Why've you quarrelled, then?' she added, this time though, her voice had gone softer, losing its accusatory edge.

'Oh, silly shit,' said Cas with a sigh, and looked at her feet. Cas had not come here to talk about Toby, but she saw she wasn't going to get anywhere with Bentley any other way. Besides, she could feel the pink drinks coursing through her bloodstream, and they were loosening her tongue. 'I'm just finding it difficult supporting him – he's a sculptor, and hasn't sold anything yet, though that's not his fault. I want to support him, but I don't feel he supports me. It's just a stupid argument about cups of tea.' Cas looked away so Bentley could not see the tears that had suddenly started pricking at her eyes. She didn't understand why she was suddenly getting upset – was it Bentley's hostile tone? The pink drinks had been strong, she thought, but she realized it was more than that. She was much more upset about things going wrong with Toby than she had dared to admit to herself. She had been pushing it to the back of her mind for so long and now she couldn't keep it at bay for much longer. She swallowed and with an effort forced herself to regain control, trying to wipe away a telltale tear as it fell down her cheek.

But when she looked up she saw Bentley's face had changed too.

'Oh girl! Now why are you doing that?' Bentley's voice was different, it had lost its harshness and, instead of folded arms, she was leaning towards Cas, putting a hand on her knee.

'I don't know,' Cas breathed. This was the question she had avoided asking herself – now someone else was doing it for her. 'I work hard all day, I take care of the rent, and when I come in at night he's sat there in the middle of this mess like it never happened. I have no idea what he does all day, but it certainly isn't washing or tidying. And another thing,' it was spilling out of Cas now, 'is that ever since we've moved in together I hardly ever *see* him. It's like we've lost touch – he isn't interested in my life at all.'

Bentley's face was creased up in sympathy. 'You've gotta understand blokes aren't cut out for that sort of thing. Anyway, going out with twenty-first century girl is tough – she doesn't need supporting, she doesn't need looking after, she's independent and demanding, and at the end of the day there's nothing left the bloke can actually do for her. And if she feels like the bloke isn't measuring up, even if it's in the tiniest little way, then she's so used to making every-thing perfect that she can't understand why he can't be either. All there is left for him to do is mate with her. But frankly after she's done a couple of rounds with Jessica Rabbit, he can't even do that satisfactorily either any more.'

'Jessica Rabbit?'

'Ooh, girl, don't you know? Get yourself down to Ann Summers and ask for one. They've revolutionized the vibrator market.'

'Really?' Cas laughed.

'Really,' replied Bentley, completely seriously. 'The thing

is, darling, all that new-man stuff never really worked. I should know, I've been through it too.' Bentley sighed. 'Men might try and understand women now, where they didn't even try before, but they're no more successful at knowing what to give you. You still have to tell them. Problem is, girls have everything they want nowadays, and so they can't quite figure out what it is they might ask for.'

'Love? Affection?'

'You get that already don't you?'

'Yes, I suppose I do. Actually, I think I need a wife, but I don't want my boy to be it. Too demasculating.'

'Exactly. Then you wouldn't fancy him any more. Blokes – they might say otherwise, but they still all want to be king of the herd. I should know, I married one.'

'Oh, yeah, who's that?' asked Cas, sniffling a bit.

A beatific smile came across Bentley's face followed by a pained frown. She passed Cas a tissue. 'Well, if we're going to talk about him then you might as well call me Terri. His name's Johnnie, and he works on a farm. So he gets to do all that macho stuff, you know, like riding tractors and stuff. Oooh, you should see him, he wears these checked shirts and his muscles just burst out – he's fucking fanciable, I tell you.'

'And how does he feel about you doing this?'

'Well, he doesn't like it. It was fine when when I was working locally, but now I'm down here in London trying to make a career of it, he won't have any of it.'

Now it was the lap dancer's turn to look away.

'So when was the last time you saw him, Terri?'

'Oh, don't,' croaked Terri, tears running down her cheeks. 'Last Christmas. You see it's tough for farmers at the moment, there's no money in it. So that's why I'm here, making us some money. But he didn't want me earning the bread – couldn't stand it. Then he wrote me this letter saying he didn't want to be married to me any more, didn't want me working down here. Now he's filing for divorce.'

Cas passed her back the tissue and Bentley blew her nose.

'Look, love,' said Terri, 'don't make the same mistake as me. You've got to let your man feel in control. He is not programmed to be your lesser half. I should have known that about Johnnie, but now it's too late. Don't you do the same,' she said affectionately, wiping away the remainder of the tears, and tackling the great pools of black mascara that had collected under her eyes. 'In the meantime, make up some crap about my "space" or whatever it is you want to write about. Throw in my husband, it'll make me look good. Just don't say he's divorcing me, though. And don't say my real name!'

'I won't, Terri, honestly! Look, thank you so much for listening, and I'm so sorry to have wasted your time.'

'Wasted my time? There's nothing I ever want to do more than talk about my Johnnie. Except he's not mine any more,' she said glumly, and Cas wondered if they were going to have to cry again. But then suddenly Terri switched, a shutter came down over her face, and she was Bentley again. 'About that Victor Power. What there is to know you'll find out soon enough.'

Cas looked at Bentley carefully. 'Find out what?' she asked. There was something Bentley knew, she could see it.

'Look,' continued Bentley, 'there's lots of bad stuff that goes on in this industry. You go and walk through Soho, you go into those little doors promising "Girls, Girls, Girls". You tell me how old those girls are, you ask them their names and you tell me if they understand you. You ask them again in Macedonian, in Thai, in Albanian, in Brazilian and you see if they understand you then.'

Cas nodded slowly, holding Bentley's gaze. Bentley was staring at her, and the hardness behind her eyes was anger. Cas didn't want her to stop, she needed to hear, she had to draw it out of her. 'And those girls, how have they got here?'

'Exactly,' replied Bentley. 'Exactly. Because they don't none of them have passports. And they all of them owe someone money for the passage. A lot of money. Money they are now trying hard to pay back, working all day and all night, sucking off men who don't get it at home, taking it any which way from some frustrated hooligan, getting fifty pounds extra for this, twenty pounds extra for that. Sold into slavery for a passage in the back of a lorry, crammed in behind crates of tomatoes with hundreds of others, to be spirited out on a layby on the A47. Then they realize they've reached the promised land, and it's not exactly what they thought it would be.'

Cas was incredulous. 'You're saying Power knows about this?'

'No!' snapped Bentley. 'I'm just saying that that's where

the money comes from in this industry. I don't know anything about him, I just know my business. But if you want a story, that's where you should be looking, because that ain't right. Those girls have not chosen what they do – they've been tricked into it.'

Bentley paused and drew out another cigarette. Cas watched her intently.

'Bentley, do you know any of these girls? Can you find one who will talk to me?'

'Don't be silly. I'm not risking what I've got here for you to get some story. Find one yourself. As I said, the country's crawling with them.'

'But they won't trust me.'

'They will if you pay them.'

'Bentley, if you can help me, we might be able to stop this –'

'Don't be ridiculous. If you stop one guy, then there will just be another to take his place. That's the way it works. Now if you want to stick your neck out and poke your nose into this dirty little heap of sordid shit then do, but you better know what you're doing because when there's money at stake – big money – someone is not going to want you going around spoiling it. All right? Now, I've already said enough. I hope you've got what you wanted.'

And with this the Amazonian blonde turned away, crushed out her cigarette in an ashtray, and went back to taking her make-up off.

'And another thing: I wouldn't tell too many people what you're up to either.'

'Thanks,' said Cas. 'I appreciate this Bentley, or Terri.' Bentley shot her a look. 'Bentley,' Cas corrected herself. 'I'll give you a call and let you know when the piece is coming out. In the meantime, here's my card in case you need to get hold of me. And – thanks for all the advice.'

Bentley's face softened again and she smiled at Cas.

'You look out for yourself, no one else is going to do that for you.'

'Okay, I will.'

'Well, then,' said Bentley, lighting up another fag. 'See you around.'

Cas flagged down a cab and asked for Hoxton. The clock in the cab said it was past two – she was much later than she had intended. She tiptoed into the flat to find Toby asleep on the sofa with the television still on. He looked like he had been waiting up for her. Gently she shook him awake and he smiled at her, and she led him downstairs to the bedroom, where they kissed and crawled into bed together. But Cas was exhausted, so she turned over, ignoring his obvious interest in more, and pretended she had fallen asleep.

# chapter eleven

Charlotte Want settles back into her plush leather sofa, takes a sip of her freshly squeezed carrot juice and pulls her dainty, perfectly pedicured feet up underneath her. 'I love it here,' she says sighing happily, 'it's my sanctuary.'

We are sitting in the immaculately decorated living room of Charlotte's stylish Manchester penthouse apartment. Black and white photographs of Charlotte by several well-known photographers line the walls, paying homage to Charlotte's sensational looks, but otherwise the penthouse is a temple to minimalist chic. A sheepskin rug lines the trendy stripped beech-wood floor that Charlotte had specially fitted, as well as an extension to the already capacious walk-in wardrobe. Otherwise the apartment has been left almost as Charlotte bought it – specially designed by Philippe Starck to capture the mood of twenty-first century living. And what better model could he have than

Charlotte Want as one of the first people to buy into his new concept in urban living?

Fast becoming an icon of the age, Charlotte has captured the hearts and minds of a generation, with her knockout looks, go-getter attitude and her immaculate taste in men, clothes and music. As if to reinforce this there is a state of the art stereo, and some key contemporary CDs lie on the floor at her feet; several invitations to forthcoming glamorous events line her marble mantelpiece.

Charlotte is a blossoming talent. Today she is wearing one of her favourite Gucci dresses made from the softest black leather, just like her sofa. A silver diamond-studded bangle that she fingers all the time, graces her elegant wrist.

When I ask her about it, she flutters her eyelids in a way that shows off her captivating eyes to their best effect, and blushes endearingly.

'It is a gift from the most important person in my life,' she says.

At that moment, as if on cue, Manchester United's Silvio Ravelli pads across the living-room floor from the bedroom, dressed in a towelling dressing gown, his coal-black locks still wet from the shower. He settles down on the sofa beside her. The two are the picture of utter domestic bliss, an example to couples everywhere, flushed and radiant in each other's presence. What a power couple they are: one of Britain's most beautiful and promising young personalities has fallen in love with one of the most talented and handsome footballers in the world! And for the first time, Silvio and Charlotte have chosen to open their hearts about the way they feel exclusively to *Hiya!* magazine, your number one for showbiz scoops.

*Hiya!*: Firstly may I congratulate both of you on behalf of the magazine on the happiness you have so clearly found.

CHARLOTTE (*giggling*): We just knew we were right for each other, as soon as we met, didn't we, Silvio?

SILVIO (*serious*): Charlotte is a beautiful woman and I am a very lucky man.

*Hiya!*: So how did you two first meet?

CHARLOTTE: It was in a trendy bar in Manchester – Quills. We had both been invited for the opening night. I was quite tired and wasn't planning on being there for long, but as soon as I walked in the door of the VIP room, I knew there was something special about the night. I spotted Silvio across the room and I thought, 'Wow! He's handsome', and I went straight over to talk to him. He was with all his team mates and he was quite shy at first, but I soon broke the ice, didn't I, darling?

SILVIO: Yes.

*Hiya!* So how long have the two of you been together now?

CHARLOTTE: Oooh, I think about a month now, isn't it, Silvio?

SILVIO: Thirty-seven days, yes.

*Hiya!*: And so how do the two of you spend your time together?

CHARLOTTE: Well, unfortunately Silvio has to spend a lot of time training, which is quite boring. But when I can drag him away from football then we like to go shopping a lot. Silvio needs lots of new clothes now he is my boyfriend so we go together and I choose lovely suits for him.

*Hiya!*: Do you like shopping Silvio?

SILVIO: Er, yes, it's okay.

*Hiya!*: What do you buy?

SILVIO: I buy Charlotte beautiful jewellery. She loves beautiful jewellery.

CHARLOTTE: We also eat out in lots of fashionable restaurants together, but I am watching my weight because of my job so I can't eat very much.

*Hiya!*: And do you ever go to see Silvio play at Old Trafford, Charlotte?

CHARLOTTE: No, I haven't been yet. I'm not that interested in football, actually.

*Hiya!*: And Silvio, have you ever been on one of Charlotte's modelling shoots?

SILVIO: Sorry? I don't understand?

CHARLOTTE: Silvio doesn't always understand everything. He's Brazilian you know. This is the first shoot he's been on with me. But he knows all the words to my pop song. (*Silvio smiles meekly*) He is sweet! The day after we got together he went to buy a copy of my record. I told him I was a singer. He couldn't find it in any of the shops, then in the locker room the next day the boys gave him a copy. I had given it to one of them last summer when I was dating him, and he gave it to Silvio.

*Hiya!*: And do you have any future plans you can share with us either of you?

CHARLOTTE: Well, obviously my Wella campaign is going brilliantly. My hair is so clean and fresh all the time and the company are very pleased with all the sales I'm getting. They say I'm really worth it!

*Hiya!*: And what about you Silvio?

SILVIO: I'm hoping to score more goals for Manchester United and be very popular here in Manchester, which is a town I love.

*Hiya!*: Because there were some doubts when you first came over from Brazil whether you were going to stay?

SILVIO: It was a bit of a problem at first because I could not play and it was very, how you say . . . frustrating?

CHARLOTTE: That's right, darling. His English is really coming on you know, considering he has only been here a year and a half. I can't speak a word of Brazilian!

SILVIO: Yes you can! *Gostoso!*

CHARLOTTE: Oh yes! I am *gostoso* apparently. It means good enough to eat in Brazilian.

SILVIO: And I eat her a lot!

CHARLOTTE: Sssh, Silvio!

*Hiya!* (*after laughter has died down*): So what does the future hold for the two of you together?

CHARLOTTE: Well, we are just taking it day by day at the moment. We are very much in love, but we don't want to rush anything. We are very happy, aren't we Silvio?

SILVIO: Yes.

# chapter twelve

The next morning Cas woke abruptly to the sound of the radio, which was unusual as she normally woke up precisely thirty seconds before the alarm went off. *Today*'s victim was John Prescott, spouting a series of nonsensical and increasingly irritable grunts back at James Naughtie. Cas winced – a double wince of embarrassment for the politician and for the thudding that had announced itself in her head. She groaned, and found that her breath tasted of the pink drinks of the night before. Toby slipped quietly out of bed and returned with a cup of tea for her. Cas appreciated the gesture, but she could feel the atmosphere between them was still thick.

'You all right?' he asked, his voice guarded.

'No, not brilliant,' she croaked, taking the mug from him.

'How was last night?'

'Interesting.' Pause. 'I cried with a lap dancer.'

'Really?' Pause. 'Any reason?'

Cas met his gaze and saw he was frowning.

'Just drunk I think,' she muttered, not quite confessing the truth. Toby sighed in exasperation as he got back into bed, then turned his back to her. Cas sipped her tea and felt her life with him slipping out of reach. An awful silence shrouded the room. Not even John Humphrys' belligerent baiting of a cabinet minister could hide it. Cas looked at the clock.

'I'd better get going,' she said, and her words felt like exploding shells in the delicate no man's land between them.

She moved her body carefully so as not to disturb her pounding head. As she gingerly pulled herself up from the bed, Toby flipped over onto his back, and watched her retreat into the bathroom. He opened his mouth to say something, then shut it again. Instead, he stared at the ceiling.

She came back, dressed and slapped on her make-up with the radio on loud to hide the fact they weren't talking to each other. It didn't work. Then she spilt talcum powder all over herself, peppering the clothes she had just put on with immovable white dots. She drew breath.

'Start as I mean to go on,' she said to herself calmly, and began the dressing ritual again. She noticed her drawers were full of clean clothes.

'Thanks for doing the washing,' she said casually, as if it didn't mean anything significant at all. Anything to avoid confrontation – particularly this morning.

Then he said it: 'Cas – we need to talk.'

'Yeah,' she said, looking round for another pair of tights.

'Come and sit down,' he pleaded.

'I can't now, I've got to go to work . . .'

'Ah yes – work.' He couldn't keep the irritation from his voice. 'Any point at which you will not be working?'

'One of has to, Toby.' They glared at each other.

'I'm going to see if I can get my old bar job back.' Toby had been thinking about this yesterday but he had only just decided then and there that he would.

Cas frowned. 'Well, what's the point in that? You won't have any time to spend on sculpting and we'll be back to where we were six months ago.'

'Yes, but at least you won't treat me like this.'

'Like what?' she demanded, the delicate state of her head making her more defensive than she had meant to be. She wanted to be gone, for the situation to diffuse. 'I've got to go. We'll talk tonight, okay?'

Then, without looking at him, she moved over to his side of the bed, kissed him goodbye (on the forehead) and ran out of the flat.

Work did little to ease the pain in Cas's head. When she got in, she found Susie Farlane had called an editorial conference for the entire staff. Which could only mean one thing.

'Everyone, I have some important news for you. You've probably been reading stories in the press about Lord Paul's intention to sell the *Daily News*. Well, I have been kept in the dark as much as you have, until this morning when I was rung up by the publisher Victor Power wishing to take me out to lunch as, according to him, he is, from today, our new proprietor.' Susie sighed and registered the disbelief on the faces of all her staff. 'So, yes,' she continued, 'all those emails Lord Paul has been pumping round the company asking us not to believe the stories and categorically stating that the *News* was not up for sale, appear to have been complete lies.'

A quiet murmur went round the newsroom, everyone's fears now confirmed.

Farlane continued, struggling to keep the anger from her voice, 'Unbelievably, I have still not yet heard from Lord Paul, who apparently is too busy even to come down here and tell us whether we have been sold or not, so I can only gather that Power is indeed our new owner.'

Everyone on the paper twittered with mixed feelings.

'At least it's all over.'

'He can only be better than Appalling.'

'Does this mean lots of *Hiya!*-type coverage?'

'Can only be good for the showbiz page.'

'Disastrous for the newsdesk.'

'Listen,' continued Susie Farlane, 'I know nothing more than that at the moment but I'll let you know as soon as I have anything to confirm –'

At that moment Sky news, which most of the newsroom monitors were tuned into, beamed up a picture of Victor Power announcing his takeover of the *Daily News*. The newsreader confirmed the story. Susie Farlane had become quite flushed with rage. In front of the entire staff, she picked up the nearest phone and asked to be put through to Lord Paul, who this time it seemed had the decency to take the call.

'Richard? Susie here.' Farlane's face was creased with anger, and had that barely suppressed tone of controlled fury that actually made her voice go quieter. 'I find it incredibly discourteous that you have not even had the politeness to inform your own newspaper staff of their takeover before you inform the rest of the press, although granted it's symptomatic of your entire CRAP management style. As I and all my staff are standing here watching Power announcing his takeover on the bloody television, I think it's only fair that you come down here and tell us yourself!' Then she slammed the phone down.

Needless to say, Appalling failed to appear and Susie Farlane beat a miserable retreat back to her office. His management style had always left much to be desired, but Cas guessed he was actually too much of a coward to show his face. He had been duping his own staff for so long he could not now come clean about what he had done. He had always denied accusations that he had bought the paper for prestige, but as soon as it had failed to get him what he wanted he had sold it – to the most unscrupulous of owners, it seemed.

It was going to be hard for Susie Farlane to ignore Power's business. As one of the liberating feminists of the seventies, how on earth was she going to square working for the publisher of *Women on Top*? Farlane was a popular editor, she stuck her neck out for the things she believed in and was always running round among the staff inspiring and motivating them. Generally, people loved working for her. She got to know her staff well, inviting them to parties at her house, seeing them socially when she could, and had gained a fierce loyalty from them in return. If Farlane went, then probably most of the staff would go too, provided they could secure the right pay-off terms.

Half an hour later Lord Appalling managed a global email that was, like most of his circulars, three thousand words too long so that no one actually bothered to read it. He had treated his staff at the end like little more than monkeys in a cage, and he had shown the lack of respect in which he held the *Daily News*, a paper that had been printing for over one hundred years, by selling it to a porn merchant. Everyone from the tea lady to the news editor felt nothing but disgust for him. A ripple of fear was now running through the paper – everyone's jobs were suddenly in danger.

The only person who seemed in the slightest bit cheered by the news was, of course, Tamara, for whom the prospect of working for the proprietor of *Hiya!* magazine was thrilling. Cas suspected she was already composing a crawling letter welcoming Power to the paper and 'trusting he liked what they did with the Sunday magazine'. It made Cas feel even more sick than she did already, especially when for the first time since Cas had started work on the magazine, Tamara didn't go out to lunch, but waited patiently in the office for the moment when Power might arrive so she could introduce herself. Everyone else went to the pub, where the landlord felt so sorry for them that he gave them all drinks on the house.

At three o' clock Power arrived. He might as well have had trumpets outside and a red carpet thought Cas, as he rolled up in a stretch limousine to a fanfare global email from 'The new management'. With him, linked arm in arm, was an elderly woman with a blue rinse and a tweed suit. She wore a buttoned-up white lace shirt with a cameo brooch clasped to the collar. Behind him stood a muscular shaven-headed man who looked like the sort of minder who would get a convincing bit part in a British gangster film. Cas could quite comfortably picture him, with his shaven head and bulldog looks, slamming someone's head in a car door. He was, in fact, Mike Pitts, someone whispered to Cas, Power's right-hand man and 'Executive Editor' of Power Publishing.

Power arrived on the newsroom floor, smouldering Monte Cristo in hand (ignoring the no-smoking policy, much to the delight of all the smokers), with his face lit by a beam of newly whitened teeth. He introduced the elderly lady on his arm as his wife, and the minder as his 'Right-hand man, Pitts.' He might have fitted the bill, but she was hardly the sort of spouse one would expect from a pedlar of soft porn, but then, thought Cas, maybe that was the desired effect.

'*Hiya!* everyone!' he began, cracking up at his own joke. Seventy-two editorial staff stared in horror. 'This is one of the most fantastic days of my life! I've always dreamed of owning a newspaper, and now I do. I'm sure you will all work very hard for me, and I shall return the favour by pumping into the *News* the money this paper really needs.

One thing I do have a lot of is money, and that's what you'll all be getting.' Power paused and grinned at them. The assembled throng merely exchanged glances of incredulity. 'I think you've been doing a great job so far,' he continued, 'but clearly there are places where we can tighten up and that's where we'll be concentrating our efforts.'

And then he began, one by one, to shake every single member of staff by the hand, and introduce them to his new wife. Mrs Power, so recently elevated from her position as secretary to wife, seemed very mild-mannered indeed, perfectly demure and even pleasant, conveniently counteracting any ideas anyone might have had that he trailed a flock of bunny girls in his wake. The promise of more money obviously also did much to cheer everyone up, and the personal touch also helped – no one could remember if Lord Appalling had ever actually been on the newsroom floor. They thought probably not.

Cas was more dubious, however. If just some of what Bentley had intimated was true then the prospect of working for such a crook was not a happy one, and she could only assume Power's purchase of the paper was a self-glorification trip and an opportunity to get a foothold further up the ladder of power. It was hard enough now finding somewhere that actually took journalism seriously; a creeping attraction for the lives of celebrities was beginning to take over newspapers and the *Daily News* had deliberately sought to buck that trend. Its sale to Power, thought Cas, must signal the end of that era.

As she put the finishing touches to the magazine cover that night (Tamara had long since gone home – in fact the moment after Power had left the building), Cas weighed up her options: the day's news changed the complexion of what she was doing. Could she in all honesty carry on working for Power at the *News* while simultaneously investigating him with Sam at the *Guardian*? Could she afford not to? She thought about her position and she thought about her bank balance and in the end she decided to equivocate and not make a decision at all – for the moment. She desperately wanted to ring Toby and see what he thought. She dialled his number, but hung up before the call went through. She knew he wouldn't be interested, and besides, relations between them now precluded discussing anything that wasn't 'us'. Maybe she could talk to him later tonight. She used to talk to him about everything – how had it ended up that they held each other's lives in such contempt?

Sighing, she decided to call Sam instead. Sam, of course, wanted to know everything that had gone on that day as it had great gossip value, and Cas enjoyed giving him a blow by blow version of events. When she mentioned her quandary he told her to stop being so ridiculously moral and to stay put – she was much more helpful to any investigation if she stayed where she was, he pointed out. She might get closer to Power now they shared the same office building. Cas shuddered, remembering the hard grip of his hand round hers when she had shaken it earlier this afternoon and the menacing stare of the bulldog in his wake. Who knew where that hand had been, who knew what the bulldog got up to in his spare time?

'The good news is, Cas, that you've got your way. Now it has been announced he's bought your paper the news-desk here have put me on to Power anyway. They are planning a big profile on him and want me to do some digging.'

'That's good. By the way, how did you get on with your ex-employee?'

'Oh, can you believe it? He didn't show.'

'He didn't show? But he said he would.'

'I know. I waited an hour and a half. Drank enough shit coffee to irrigate the entire motorway. How was your lap dancer?'

'Actually very interesting. From what I can gather the big money in this industry is pouring in from the illegal immi-grant sex trade.'

'Whoah. That's serious shit, Cas. Is Power involved in this?'

'I don't know. That's what we've got to find out. We need to find one of these immigrants – see who she works for, who they work for and so on. Follow the money, I believe is the phrase.'

'Right. Sounds like a good plan. I'll phone some contacts tomorrow, and do some asking around tomorrow night. Don't suppose you fancy coming up to King's Cross with me, then?'

'Ooooh, you don't half know how to treat a girl, Sam!'

'Oh go on, it'll be miserable on my own.'

Cas hesitated. What about Toby? She glanced at her watch – to her horror she saw it was already nearly nine.

'I don't know Sam,' she said quickly. 'I'll do my best. I'll let you know tomorrow.'

She put down the phone, turned off her computer and ran out of the office. As she walked across the bridge she dug in her bag for her phone so she could call Toby and tell him she was on her way. Shit! She had left her phone on her desk. She broke into a run.

## chapter thirteen

Back in the flat, Toby watched the kitchen clock tick round to nine. He shook his head – Cas had said they would be talking tonight but where was she? She hadn't even called him to tell him she would be late. He picked up the phone and dialled her mobile number, but there was no answer. She really doesn't care, he thought, and put his head in his hands.

Perhaps she was trying to tell him something? The thought had occurred to him that she had lost interest in him. She seemed less keen on sex recently, turning away from him in bed and nowadays there wasn't a lot left of their relationship other than that. He paced up and down the kitchen wondering what to do. He felt trapped by her. She had insisted he give up his job to concentrate on his sculpting, but then she punished him for it. It didn't even seem like she was particularly interested in what he did anyway, she was too damn consumed by her own job.

He waited, as he had done all day, pacing the flat, trying to work out what would be best to say, trying to work out what she wanted to hear. But now it looked like she wasn't even going to do him the courtesy of turning up. He played a game with himself: if he hadn't heard from her by 9.30 then she wasn't interested. The clock ticked on. The half hour passed and there was still no sign of her. Not wanting to admit her disinterest he rang her again. Still no answer. Painfully, he pictured her somewhere – in a bar, at an opening, at dinner with some contact, hearing her phone ring, checking to see who was calling and then throwing it back in her bag. Sadly, he picked up his wallet and left the flat. He was going to the pub to ask for his job back.

By the time Cas got home, it was half past ten – obviously the tube had managed to impede her progress home on the night she most needed it to work. She burst through the front door calling Toby's name, but he wasn't there. Her heart sank. She sat down on the sofa and waited.

She was anxious now: she was late and felt guilty that he had probably waited for her and then given up. Now she would just have to wait for him to come home. She looked about the flat taking in the signs of his day to day living – a history of art book open on the table, a notepad with some sketches scribbled on it. She picked it up and looked at it – rough outlines of bodies twisted into unnatural shapes. She stared at them, admiring the curves, working out what he was trying to say. She was reminded again of his talent, and glanced across at the work he had given her in the corner of the room. For a moment she felt a rush of pride, swiftly followed by a rising lump in her throat. Oh! how she needed him to hold onto. She realized that for weeks she had really been wanting to spend proper time with him – to go for walks together, like they used to, or wander into the West End on a Sunday afternoon to catch an exhibition. They had done none of these things recently. Suddenly she felt the keenness of how little she knew about what was going on in his life, let alone what was going on inside his head. She tossed the notepad back on the table in anger and willed him to come home. She turned the television on to pass the time, but there was nothing on, and in irritation she switched it back off. She picked up a magazine, but it failed to hold her attention. She badly needed something to take away the pain of what was happening between her and Toby, to distract her from the gnawing anxiety about her job and their income. In a frenzy of misplaced emotion, she began to tidy the flat up.

She scooped up the papers from the table, threw the cushions back on the sofa and rounded up her discarded shoes. She wiped surfaces, tidied magazines and rearranged their CDs. She cleared up the kitchen, disinfected the surfaces and watered the plants. Then she noticed the floor was dirty too and heaved the vacuum cleaner out of the cupboard and began to hoover up the stairs and around the living-room floor, ignoring the tiredness in her head and the heaviness in her chest.

Lying face down on the floor underneath the kitchen

table was what looked like a business card. Must have fallen out of my bag, she thought, and reached under the table to pick it up. She turned it over to see whose it was. It said 'Cosima Beane' in large pink letters, and then 'Art dealer' underneath. A handwritten scrawl across it said 'Call me'. Cas screwed up her eyes, then read the card again. She wondered if she was hallucinating – such had been the events of the day it seemed like almost anything could happen now, but no: the card was still in her hand, and still said the same. Everything else in her life suddenly disappeared, as a shot of adrenaline-fuelled excitement pumped through her, and a series of hastily imagined possibilities jumped into her head.

How had Toby come across this? It was Toby's wasn't it? If it was, then this card could be the way out of trouble for them both. It could, in one fell swoop, release Cas from her job, get Toby the recognition he deserved, and that would make them both happy together again. 'Call me' said the scrawled handwriting in blue biro. As if we could afford not to, thought Cas.

At that moment she heard Toby's key in the lock. Her heart thumping loudly, buoyed up by the excitement of her discovery, she ran down the stairs calling his name. She threw herself on him as he came through the door.

'Babe!' she cried, 'I've just found this! Is it yours?'

Toby looked at the card Cas was now holding in front of him, and his heart sank.

'Yeah,' he said slowly. Then, when she looked at him like she wanted more, 'It's a long story.'

'Oh my God. Does she want to buy your stuff?' asked Cas, her words tumbling out over each other. 'You know who she is don't you? She's total hot shit!'

'Yes. Thanks Cas,' he replied tightly. 'I do know who she is, and she's not hot shit.' This was the last thing Toby needed, Cas jumping to conclusions. He cursed himself that he hadn't thrown the card away.

'What do you mean?' An edge had entered Cas's voice that Toby had anticipated and did not want to deal with. 'Of course she's hot – Charles Saatchi has just bought half her collection.'

Toby took a deep breath. 'I mean she's a rude, offensive fraud.'

'Toby what do you mean?' Cas was paralysed with incredulity. 'This woman could *make* you!'

'Like I said, it's a long story, Cas.'

Cas looked at Toby appalled, not daring to guess what this 'long story' might be. Cosima Beane was exactly who he needed, and Toby was calling her a fraud.

'Toby, I don't understand. Explain.'

Toby looked at her, her eyes sparkling with misunderstanding about the card, and thought, is that all she cares about?

'Look, Cas, why don't you just calm down, go upstairs and we'll talk about this properly?'

Toby's words were heavy, his voice low and sad. Cas didn't understand. All she knew was that she didn't like the sound of what was coming.

'Okay,' she said, trying hard to contain her desperation to

hear what had happened, and they both trooped upstairs and sat awkwardly next to each other on the sofa. Cas held Cosima's card in her hand.

'So?' she asked, failing to keep the urgency out of her voice, letting him know how badly she needed him to tell her something she wanted to hear.

Toby looked at the card in Cas's hand, and then looked at Cas.

'She came to the flat,' he said abruptly.

'She what?'

'She was here the other day, in her full glory, looking like a peacock on acid.'

'You're joking!' replied Cas, hardly able to believe what she was hearing. 'To see you?'

'No, not exactly,' continued Toby, who was thinking how much he had wanted to confide in Cas about the visit for ages, but now felt as if he was undergoing the third degree. 'She actually came to lecture me,' he said with disgust at the memory.

Cas had an awful feeling that this conversation was not going to end in the way she wanted. Why was Toby being so evasive?

'Lecture you on what? Does she want to sell your work, Toby? Tell me! This could be brilliant!'

Toby decided he had to put a stop to Cas's enthusiasm.

'No, it wasn't brilliant actually, Cas. She marched in uninvited, looking, frankly, like she had just escaped from a lunatic asylum, talked utter twaddle for about ten minutes, during which she managed to insult me and my family with some claptrap about hidden family secrets and my Indian blood, didn't so much as ask to see a single piece of work, and left.'

'And?'

'And what?'

'So is she going to try and sell any of your stuff?'

Cas wasn't listening to him. He looked at her. Was she hearing what he was saying?

'No. Actually I told her to leave,' he said, anger beginning to creep into his voice.

'You did what?' Cas was incredulous. This was too much. She threw her hands up in the air. 'Toby, this is the biggest break you've ever had. One of London's hottest dealers offered to make your name and – let me get this straight – you threw her out of the house?'

'She insulted me!' Toby was shouting now, hurt that Cas could not see it from his point of view, that she cared more about this woman than what he thought.

'So what?' Cas shouted back, unable to control the tension the day had built up inside her, which was now threatening to explode. 'Do you think we are in a position to be picky here?'

'Look, Cas,' he said through gritted teeth, 'she's not interested in what I make, she just wants to pimp me to the general public as some kind of freak, a walking aristocratic embarrassment because of the colour of my skin. So I told her where to put it.'

'Toby, you idiot!' Cas was not appeased.

'What do you mean, *idiot*?' Toby was incensed now too.

'Listen to me, Cas. Listen to me for once. She was a nightmare!'

'Yes,' replied Cas slowly as if talking to a small child, 'but she can make you a success. You can sell pieces and make money, so I don't have to pay the rent any more. You can buy your round in the pub and we can make some choices about the way we live rather than how we *have* to live. And I can have a choice about who I work for.'

'Enough, Cas,' said Toby, holding up his hand. 'I've heard the word rent too much recently. I've been back to the pub tonight to ask for my job back, and as soon as they have a vacancy I'm going to start work there again.'

'Why? You're a fool! You're telling me you would rather work as a barman for peanuts than have someone sell your work for thousands? After all the support I've given you for the last year, you finally have your break and you turn it down? I don't understand you!' Cas was shouting now, her emotions way out of control.

'Support? Oh yes, you've paid for me, Cas, but have you let me know about it.' Toby was seething with anger now. 'I'm grateful for it, sure,' he said, his fists clenching and unclenching by his side, 'but what I am not grateful for is the way you treat me now as if I'm a useless idiot and some sort of burden round your neck. I'm not your lover any more, I'm just your punchbag when you get in at the end of the day. Well, thanks, but I have enough self-esteem left not to sell myself to the first hypocritical witch who wants to make a mockery out of me.'

And with that he got up and walked down the stairs.

'Where are you going?' shouted Cas after him.

'Out,' he replied, slamming the door shut behind him.

Cas looked at the card in her hand and then threw it onto the table. Damn Toby! He had the key to their future in his hands and he chucked it away. Tears stung her eyes, and she thumped the cushions on the sofa in exasperation, before burying her face in them. Damn him!

Toby did not come back that night and Cas slept fitfully, too full of anguish to sleep properly. When she woke in the morning, she was almost grateful for him not being there – at least she could get up and face the day at work without another difficult scene.

In the office, the mood was one of trepidation. Power had apparently installed himself upstairs in an executive suite on the same floor as Lord Paul. But no one could quite believe it was going to be as good as he said it was. They were waiting for the Mr Hyde to appear from behind the Dr Jekyll. After all, it was generally agreed, the man who had made his money publishing pictures of forty-something housewives in their knickers could not be as straightforward as he claimed.

Someone went upstairs to see him and reported back that his wife was sitting at the desk outside his office taking his calls, which seemed a little strange, but she had apparently been perfectly civil, insisting she 'would go mad if she stayed at home'. Susie did not comment at morning conference, and remained tight-lipped throughout the day, which did little to relieve the air of tension.

Plans were announced late in the morning to move *Hiya!* magazine to the floor above the *News*, which excited Tamara no end – the chance she might be sharing the lift with one of *Hiya!*'s featured celebrities had her practically skipping down the corridors. Only Tamara, it seemed, thought Power an unqualified good thing. After all, he was on first-name terms with all the celebs, her idea of social bliss, and she saw in Power a passport to celebrity heaven. It appeared Cas had been right and that she had indeed written her letter to Power, because she announced amid all the morning resentment that she was off to lunch with Power himself. Cas noticed she was wearing a particularly low-cut top.

Tamara's promotion to favour could mean nothing but disaster for Cas, as Cas was the last person Tamara wanted to work with. She had a thousand friends with long blonde hair and three syllable names ending in the letter 'a', whom she could bring in instead, and Cas gloomily predicted that Tamara was already agreeing Cas's severance terms. With her chances of survival at nil, Cas's instinct was to call Toby but then she remembered with a rush of anger that she couldn't. How dare he walk out last night? she thought. How dare he abandon her now?

Instead she rang the bank to check what their financial situation was, and instantly regretted it. She would have very little time to find another job if she got fired from the *News*. Suddenly, she felt very alone, very vulnerable. This was not a feeling Cas was used to, she was used to being in control. She wanted Toby very badly indeed. She shut her eyes, trying to imagine that nothing had happened between them, that she had the security of knowing he would be at home that night when she got in, that she would hear the gentle, calming murmur of his voice, the touch of his fingers on the back of her neck, the strength of his arms as they enveloped her, the safe warm strength of his body next to hers.

She wanted to hear what he had to say as well, to hear what he thought she should do. She wanted to discuss everything with him. But she didn't know if he was even going to be at home. She couldn't stand it any longer and began to call his friends, one by one, crushingly having to ask them if they knew where he was. She eventually found him.

'Hello,' she said gently. 'How are you?'

'Not brilliant.'

'No, me neither.'

Neither said anything, waiting to see who was going to give in first. Neither did. Eventually Toby spoke.

'I've been thinking.' Cas didn't like the sound of this. 'You and I are too much in each other's faces at the moment. I need to think about things.'

Cas swallowed. Not now – not when she needed him more than ever. But she couldn't say it. All she could say, was, 'Okay'.

On the other end of the line Toby's heart sank. He hadn't wanted her to say that. He had wanted her to say, No, don't do that, come home. But she hadn't. So he was right, she *was* losing interest. Well then, he had to do what he had to do. Give her a chance to get away from him.

'I think we need a break. Or I do. To think about things.'

The lump in Cas's throat had swollen to the size of a tennis ball and she couldn't trust herself to speak. About her, in the office, people were pushing past her desk. She had her face buried in her keyboard.

'All right.'

And that was it.

She gently put the receiver back on its hook and looked up at her screen. Her eyes were flooded, and she dug her nails into the skin of her palm to stop the flow. Eventually the mist cleared, and she saw that new mail flicked up on her computer screen. It was from Sam.

> How are you fixed for tonight? Fancy a wander
> around N1?

Cas hit the reply button. Good old Sam, at least she wasn't going to have to sit at home alone.

> Marvellous, can't wait. Do you want to get some
> dinner beforehand?

As she pressed SEND another email pinged up on her screen. It was from no.one@hotmail.com. Inside was no message, just a web address: www.edengirls.com. Curious, Cas pressed the web-link address, and gradually, the screen filled with the pixilated image of a young girl. She had

Eastern European features, and looked just a child, certainly younger than sixteen years old. Underneath her were
the words, 'Buy me.' Excitement, tinged with horror, welled
up inside Cas. She felt her heartbeat quicken and tried to
scroll down through the site, but she saw you needed a
password to get any further. The email had to be from
Bentley, or someone Bentley knew. She sent an email back
to the hotmail address.

> no.one – tell me more. I need a password. Help
> me . . .

She waited. No reply. Then new mail, but it was from
Sam.

> Sounds good. I'll be in the Eagle from 8. See you
> there.

Excited, Cas immediately forwarded Sam her email from
the hotmail address.

> Check this out – just been sent it. Could this be
> Power? Can you track ownership of the site? Too
> risky for me to do it here. This could be the dirt we
> are looking for.

Cas felt genuinely excited. All thoughts of Toby were
discarded for another time, another place. This had to be a
breakthrough. Well done, Bentley! She knew there had to

be more to Power than he was claiming; after all, where had he got the money from to buy the *News*? Did he really have £100 million lying around in spare cash? If they could link the ownership of that net business to Power in any way, then they had him. He had to be smarter than that, but if that email had really come from Bentley (and who else could it come from?), and that really was his business, then the net was beginning to tighten.

Sam called her twenty minutes later, even he sounded excited.

'Well, I've checked the registration details of the site through its ISP. The company is called Rapture. I've cross-checked that with the Companies House website and it seems there are two directors registered, and their address is – wait for it – the Pacific Island of Nauru.'

'Nauru? Where the hell is that?'

'It's about eight miles off the equator, and the last time anyone looked, it housed several palm trees, one mud hut and two giant computers.'

'It's a tax haven then?'

'Exactly – and a notorious as one as well. It operates a strict law of secrecy and has the easiest application for a banking licence in the world. Half the Russian mafia are registered on that island. Once a company goes off-shore it can hide anything behind a couple of nominee directors. Chances are that whoever is behind Rapture is seriously dodgy if they have resorted to this scam. But then you can see that from the site.'

'So what can we do now?'

'Well, we have to see if there is another, more reputable company donating to Power Publishing that is using Rapture income. Which could take me a very long time indeed.'

## chapter fourteen

Some days later, Toby found himself staring into an inglenook fireplace. Beside him lay a piece of iron, a small piece, about a foot square, but one he had been wrestling with for the last fortnight. He was trying to twist it into the shape of a woman – a curvy, voluptuous, fertile, woman, but it wouldn't go. It kept turning inside out with the breasts pushed back to where the spine should be, the buttocks coming out of her stomach, the legs not the full thighs and slender calves he was trying to create but lumpy, distorted shapes of hideousness. It was like a nightmare, or one of Picasso's women on a very bad day, thought Toby wryly.

He had brought the shape into the bedroom his mother had made up for him in their cottage. He wanted just to stare at it, fix it with his glare for a while. He thought if he did this he might see a way of breaking the puzzle, turning it so it fell into place and transformed into the figure he had in his mind. But the metal confounded him, he could see no way through. He turned instead to the fire which glowed in the grate, teasing him with shapes among its flames which came and went, came and went, so nothing stayed the same. Every idea he managed to fix on disappeared as soon as he had a hold on it, each an ephemeral thing.

Outside, his mother was clattering in the kitchen. He was close to his mother, much closer than his elder brother Stephen, who was much more his father's son. Stephen was a few years older than Toby, nearing forty, with a wife and kids. He ran a farm near Highgrove where he bred organic pigs and tried to cash in on the publicity that surrounded the Prince of Wales's farm. He struggled, but he also enjoyed the Prince's patronage and the rich soil of that part of the country. Toby's father couldn't have been more delighted that Stephen and Harriet, his rather horse-faced but wealthy wife, had been invited to Highgrove three times now, and would trumpet the fact at local cocktail parties.

Toby's father, St John, had led a life of disappointment. Part of the landed gentry, he had inherited from his father the title of the Earl of Wensleydale and an estate nestled in the beautiful, oh so English, Yorkshire countryside. But he had also, Toby had been told, inherited his father's debts, debts from a lifetime of louche living, and had faced an uphill struggle to try to hang on to each family asset, and he had lost the fight spectacularly every time. First it had been the family silver, then the paintings, then the antique furniture, then the collection of vintage rally cars, and, finally, the huge draughty stone hall nestled in the middle of the

Yorkshire Dales. The family seat was now a two-bedroom cottage in Shropshire, with enough land for his wife to keep a cow and some chickens and tend a small kitchen garden. As far as Toby could see, his father had never done a day's work in his life, but had dealt with crisis after family crisis with increasingly large amounts of whisky. He had spent long hours in his study, when Toby was a boy, but he had never been quite sure what his father did there. He would watch the level in the whisky decanter go down in his father's tantalus, and daily Toby would be summoned to fetch the decanter and take it to the cellar for a refill.

These refills would encourage violent tempers, that cowed St John's poor wife Emily into a mild acceptance of everything he commanded, and the demand that she act on it instantly. Toby despised the way his father talked to his mother, but, at Emily's pleading, had learned eventually to bite his tongue. His childhood had been spent in silent rebellion from his father, who would look at him and the colour of his skin as if it were an insult. When people came to visit, Toby would be sent out to play with Bob the gamekeeper, and encouraged not to come home until after dark. Emily would fill his pockets with apples and sandwiches, and Toby would skip off joyfully to Bob's hut, and they would spend the day prowling the estate, laying traps for foxes, shooting rabbits and building tree houses. This, of course, suited the young Toby fine. Stephen would fume at having to get dressed up in tight itchy tweed suits and stand around being polite while Toby got to tear around the countryside.

Toby had been sent away to boarding school when he was eight, but had been recalled at twelve because there was no money left to pay the fees. After that, Toby attended the local comprehensive where he took the preliminary battering from his schoolmates about his large house and posh family, but once he had challenged a few of them to a fight in the playground and won, they stopped.

Toby was strong, lithe and beautifully muscular. He had been born that way and his life outdoors had honed his body. He was bright too, and gained three A levels which took him to Edinburgh University, where he read art history. It had been a struggle funding himself through it – he had worked as a barman all through the holidays for almost four years, and his debts had been immense by the time he graduated. Emily had helped out wherever she could, although Toby never knew where she found the money. She always made him promise not to tell his father – just like when she occasionally treated him to a pair of football boots, or a new school blazer, or the Christmas presents she secretly gave him when his father had passed out in front of the Queen's speech. Toby could only assume she scrimped and saved the money from her housekeeping allowance.

It was at about this time that Toby decided he preferred making art to learning about it. His father had always discouraged arts subjects at school. Toby's A levels had been in physics, chemistry and art history, the former two due to his father's thundering insistence, the latter to his own choice. Up in Edinburgh his father could not reach him, and he began to take evening classes in sculpture. As everything he touched was transformed by his elegant, long-fingered hands, he received more and more encouragement from his tutors, eventually winning a scholarship to the Slade after he finished his degree course. His father tried to stop him going, but Toby was a man now, and didn't have to listen to his alcohol-addled father any more.

As for St John, he had become so twisted and bitter by his life of disappointment and failure and the bullying of his wife and younger son, that nothing he said made sense any more, either to himself or to those near him. Emily would just wrap a blanket around him as he muttered in the rocking chair by the fire. For the first time, she could dictate her own life: she could tend her garden, her hens and her cow. She was happier than she had ever been, thought Toby, as he watched her, free to live her own life, her monster of a husband quietened by approaching dementia. There was something soft and ashamed on Emily's face, always had been, but this new lease of life had granted her, along with the recent proximity of her son, a new light in her eyes again, and the beauty she had once enjoyed as a young woman was returning.

'Toby,' she said, quietly putting her head round the door. 'There's some lunch for you if you want it.'

Toby turned to her, glad to break from the confusion of the fire and the iron. Emily smiled at him reassuringly, but saw the pain in his eyes.

She had met Cas a couple of times – twice when St John had allowed her to go to London and Toby had sent her the train fare (which she had returned), and once when Toby had brought Cas up to the cottage. His father had been so vile and offensive, however, that the weekend had turned into a disaster and Toby had vowed never to expose Cas to his father again.

Emily, on the other hand, had liked Cas a lot – she was warm-hearted, interesting, interested – Emily actually found herself having conversations with Cas, not something she was used to. She could also tell that Cas loved Toby deeply, something it was important for a mother to see in her son's lover, as she could also see that the feeling was more than returned. She had crossed her fingers for them both and hoped it would turn out right.

And then a few days ago Toby had turned up on her doorstep looking miserable. He wouldn't talk about it to her, he was too choked, so she just did what she knew mothers could do best: looked after him, cooked him food he wouldn't eat, and waited. Eventually Toby had admitted that he and Cas were spending a few days apart. He said she had something big on at work and he only seemed to be getting in her way. Emily couldn't offer advice – after all who was she to give advice? She had had one of the unhappiest marriages in Christendom, she thought, and one of the most tragic.

Toby shuffled into the kitchen and sat down at the table in front of a bowlful of soup. He had no desire to eat at the moment, but he tried because he knew it made his mother happy. St John was left in his rocking chair in the sitting room for mealtimes, it made them much more peaceful.

'Have you spoken to her today?' began his mother gently, desperately wanting to draw something out of her son. She could not bear to watch him like this.

Toby looked up, put down his spoon and sighed.

'No. I don't know what to say.'

'What does she want you to say?'

Toby paused. 'I don't know if there is anything I can say. I don't know if she wants me any more. I think I'm a burden to her. All she wants me to say is that everything is all right.'

'And you can't say this?'

'Well everything is not all right, it's in shreds. And I don't think what she is doing – chasing around at this newspaper trying to prove something to people who are not worthy of her, is good for her or all right. She's just this ball of stress and washed-out energy that snaps at everything. And I don't think I want to sell my soul.'

'What do you mean?'

Toby looked at his mother. He couldn't explain this bit. It was something the family had agreed, silently, not to talk about, and something Toby had no desire to go into again, as it had caused him enough shame and embarrassment for most of his life. But it looked like it still wasn't going away.

'She wants me to sell my work through a dealer who is pretty unscrupulous and who I'm afraid I don't respect,' he replied, with only a small part of the truth.

'Will this dealer sell your pieces?'

'Probably.'

'Is that so much to ask?' asked Emily gently, speaking from a lifetime of increasing poverty.

Toby stared at his mother, then looked away. He couldn't tell her the whole story, it would hurt her too much.

Emily continued. 'Toby, you and she had a good chance of being happy together. From what I saw that girl was in love with you. That is something I strongly advise you not to throw away. Life is about compromise you know, and occasionally we have to do things that we do not like to make things better in the long run. Maybe this is that time for you.' Emily got up from the kitchen table and walked over to busy herself at the Aga so Toby could not see the tears on her face.

Toby thought about what Emily had said. Maybe he was trying to have his own way too much. Cosima could sell him on this dreadful story, but the notoriety would soon pass and he could be his own person in his own right, with his own talent and his pieces worth buying because they were good, rather than because they were made by someone who was from the landed gentry but was clearly half 'Paki'. The more he thought about it, the more he realized he was steeling himself to do it. Perhaps it wasn't such a big deal after all. The colour of his skin had only worked against him up to this point, maybe it was time it worked *for* him. He found his wallet and drew out Cosima's card, fingering it as if it were the devil's gold. Maybe his mother was right.

## chapter fifteen

The Cosmopolitan Hotel had become something of a by-word for the cutting edge of London's contemporary social scene. Since opening in the late nineties, it had established itself as the de rigeur London residence for ageing rock bands, crisis-prone Hollywood stars trying to regain their sense of cool, wannabe pop tarts desperate to make it, newly celebrated starlets on a stopover and, with this kind of clientele, a steady trickle of super-rich male executives trying to impress good looking women into bed with them.

Its adjoining bar, open only to the visitors of the hotel and a carefully picked band of urban movers and shakers, had barely been out of the headlines. Where the Groucho provided intellectual chic, Soho House fashionable chic (or so both liked to think), the Cosmo bar added itself to London's lengthening list of private members' clubs as the place where you went simply to behave unashamedly. Where, in the Groucho, you would be expected to deliver a diatribe on Karl Marx as you hoovered up your cocaine (indeed the toilet cubicles all came complete with works of philosophy), and where in Soho House you would have to drop someone's name in film or television whoseyacht-youhadjustbeenstayingon to get so much as a second glance, in the Cosmo Bar you could just lift up your top and shout 'Look at me!' – which suited the vacuous fashion and pop worlds perfectly.

Plenty of celebrities now, as a matter of course, ended raucous nights on the town with a visit to the late-licensed Cosmo, ensuring their exit was to the heralding flash of the tabloid photographer. Every well known face from Robbie Williams to Leonardo DiCaprio had been photographed appearing from its portals quite considerably the worse for wear – a fact that only served to enhance the hotel's reputation as the epicentre for London's gilded nightlife.

But that was not all. It also, in the form of its restaurant Bonu, had created the city's premier eaterie. The food was to Japanese cuisine what Albert Escoffier had been to French cuisine – it stretched it, polished it, glamorized it and made it the best it could possibly be. If the Cosmo had style, then its restaurant proved it had substance. The one, tiny drawback was its prices: at £65 for a starter, perfection didn't come cheap. But for those who wanted to buy a ticket into the world of glamour, Bonu was the perfect invitation.

And so it was that Bonu had become Victor Power's favourite meeting place. It was impressive even to the most jaded Hollywood star, it remained unremittingly stylish

('The Ivy is so yesterday. Who wants to sit around in that room with all that naff coloured glass?' – Adrian Fagge), and it was expensive – My name is Power and I make money. By off-loading the best part of £5,000 there a month, Power ensured that he was where the celebrities were and that the celebrities knew where he was.

Inside the restaurant everything was white – the floor, the ceilings, the walls, the furniture, so you felt like you were in some kind of futuristic dreamscape, or were coming round from an anaesthetic and couldn't quite figure out if this were the afterlife or a hospital ward. The only colour was provided by the waiters, who looked like they had stepped out of a Calvin Klein advert (and probably had), and the restaurant goers. White had been a wise decision on the designer's part – the kind of international jet set who booked into Bonu deserved undivided attention in their own right: giant leggy models with skirts that only just grazed the curve of their buttocks sat next to Prada-ed architects in shiny moddish suits; over-dressed fashion queens flirted with T-shirt and Brylcreemed male models who were too busy looking at their reflections in the surfaces to notice. Every table told a story of wealth, mischief and intrigue and, indeed, the restaurant had even featured in one of the previous year's most high-profile court cases when a Grand Slam tennis champion's love child had been conceived in the Bonu broom cupboard. It seemed some people could not quite take their sake.

The food itself was exquisite, delicate, dainty and delicious: little glass cradles of chopped sashimi nestled in great bowls of ice decorated with pansy petals; huge great green banana leaves bearing the delicate twisted morsel of a glistening Pacific prawn; hollowed-out frozen bamboo stalks loaded with vintage sake. The Japanese head chef was famous for his skills with the ceramic knife. The secret of great sushi and sashimi, he claimed, lay not only in its freshness but also in the way it was cut. He now travelled the world and in time-honoured fashion had become a celebrity in his own right. A personal appearance at your dinner party could set you back by well over £20,000, and that was before he had even severed a fish head.

Victor Power always enjoyed taking five minutes to survey the scene in the restaurant. He would make sure he was early for any lunch or dinner date in order to give himself plenty of time for rubber-necking. His magazine aspired to the very society that Bonu attracted. *Hiya!* gave every hairdresser frequenter and dentist's waiting-room patient a bird's eye view of the lives and stories that were being played out at each of Bonu's tables. Many had accused the magazine of creating an unrealistic impression of the world of glamour, but as far as Power was concerned, the evidence of its reality could be felt all around you at Bonu.

Tonight, noted Power, was no exception. The reservations book was a veritable style-file of the rich and famous: Julia Roberts was being dined by her film company in one corner; the Wong couple, Hong Kong and now London's most vivacious party throwers were in another; a boy band were sulking near the centre (when would their manager get the hamburger thing?); Marco Pierre White was holding court at another table; and Vanessa Feltz and her dreadlocked fitness instructor were making eyes at each other at another.

To Power's delight, most of those present had succumbed to the lure of his big fat cheques, occasioning everyone, out of politeness, to at least acknowledge his presence as he strode majestically through the room to a table in the centre ('It's sooo worth paying an extra £250 for the right table.' – Adrian Fagge). Although tonight, the nodded heads and polite good evenings were accompanied by raised eyebrows and twitching lips, for on Power's arm this evening was his new bride, Winifred Wattle. As most of the restaurant goers were used to seeing him walk in with someone under the age of twenty with a pair of breasts large enough to topple her over should she neglect to lean back adequately, this certainly counted as gossip.

Mrs Power, who on no account ever let anyone call her Winifred, even her new husband (to his relief), found the scene rather amusing. She had become quite accustomed, in her husband and employer's company, to seeing things she had never witnessed before, and this was no exception. But being a stalwart sort of a gal, she liked to take new experiences in her stride, and would remark on them always in the same way, 'Very nice,' or, if particularly impressed, a brusque, 'Quite lovely'. Her mother had taught her over the years never to gawp at anything, and that emotion was only one step away from hysteria and therefore the preserve of the undignified. Straight back, chin up and mind your Ps and Qs. Never be impressed by anything, her mother had lectured, as the sorts of things that seek to impress you are never impressive in their own right. (It had taken the young Winifred a couple of days to unravel this one.) It was easier for Winifred's mother, however, because she generally found little to her taste anyway, so being impressed was never much of a problem. But Winifred had learned her mother's lesson well, and nothing could have prepared her better for the world she had just entered. Despite being installed in her own personal wing of Power's Surrey mansion, with her own jacuzzi, sauna and gym, Mrs Power remained exactly the same person who had inhabited her Hounslow semi. Her tastes stayed utterly modest, but her curiosity grew and grew. Her sheltered life meant she had seen little beyond school, teacher training college and her mother's retirement home, so the wealth and variety of other people fascinated her (making her, as Power had so astutely recognized when he first employed her, *Hiya!*'s dream reader).

Marriage to Victor Power facilitated her exercise of this curiosity, but not once did she allow herself to consider herself part of such lives. Oh no, she considered herself far too old and set in her ways for that. She was also wise enough to recognize her marriage as nothing more than it was intended to be: a veil of respectability to facilitate Power's social ascent. The apex of which, he had promised her on their wedding day, would surely be a visit to Number

Ten. Oh yes, he had gloated, the prime minister himself would no doubt soon find time in his schedule to welcome them into his 'nu' establishment. (Mrs Power could not help noticing her husband's growing annoyance that such an invitation had not yet appeared. He may have married her to keep up appearances, but Mrs Power could also see that the entrée into ruling society her husband had been expecting had not, as yet, quite materialized, *Daily News* notwithstanding.)

Power's marriage had only grated with one member of his staff, and that was Adrian Fagge. Much to his disgust, Mrs Power had refused to accept his advice on how to dress as a lady worthy of her new position. Mrs Power had always regarded Fagge as a faux, a word her mother used to describe someone she had taken a dreadful turn against, and his was the one presence she could not abide. When he suggested a shopping trip to Jil Sander to replace her wardrobe from the Edinburgh Woollen Mill, she shuddered. When he suggested a quick trip to Daniel Galvin to sort out the blue rinse, Mrs P merely flicked off the request like a stray hair on her overcoat. Indeed, when he so much as uttered a word, Mrs Power would completely ignore him as if he did not even exist. He was the only element of her new husband's life to which she took exception and, as far as her husband was concerned, if that was going to be the extent of her unrest then he was a lucky man. The jacuzzi full of beauties he enjoyed several times a week might have occasioned more fuss, but no, Mrs Power understood exactly the parameters of their relationship. And it suited her fine: just as long as she didn't have to pay any attention to the dreadful Mr Fagge.

Charlotte Want, on the other hand, was quite a different creature. She had indeed benefited from the advice of Adrian Fagge – 'Never be seen in public without perfect hair and make-up. Never swear in public, it's very common.' Unlike Power, she liked to arrive impressively late for every appointment, as Fagge had told her, only the vulgar turned up on time. Dressed in a plastic, pink Barbie dress with a caveman-esque bone choker, she led the Gucci-suited Silvio by the hand through the maze of Bonu tables towards that of Victor Power's. The couple were being put up in the hotel courtesy of Victor Power: he had invited them to dinner as he had some news to announce, he had said, and he also wanted them to join with him in celebrating his takeover of the paper. Unfortunately phone calls to more famous contacts had been met with a polite 'No', but Victor was learning that with Charlotte whatever he wanted, he got. Besides, since the couple had 'come out' in *Hiya!* they had become quite the talk of the town. Charlotte's celeb rating had been radically elevated and Ravelli had hardly been off the back pages – not least because of Ferguson's very public dressing down of his star following the interview. Silvio now somewhat regretted appearing all over *Hiya!* magazine; not only was his boss now well aware of the nature of his relationship with Charlotte Want, but so were the fans, and some of the chanting at Old Trafford had become quite obscene.

As the couple entered, all the women in the room did a simultaneous double take and several cracked their necks in the process. Silvio outshone any male model in the place a thousand times over, his turquoise eyes glittering with joy at being so close to his loved one, his lithe body displaying the easy confidence of one who has only recently enjoyed orgasm. His olive skin and shiny black hair glowed with love and admiration for the woman who was walking before him, and while most women could not suppress a twinge of envy, they also inwardly cried, 'Aaah . . .' at the sight of such innocent young love. (Well they had all read the interview last week.)

Charlotte, who was always receptive to the way people were reacting to her, did not let the effect of Silvio's presence at her side slip by unnoticed. Power, it seemed, was absolutely right: there was strength in celebrity numbers, and Silvio had a following that was global to her national one. Farmers in Uttar Pradesh wore Silvio Ravelli's name on the backs of their football shirts. Charlotte reckoned she was lucky if the shoppers in Chester Arcade could remember her surname. But Silvio was changing all that, and already it was having an effect. Just before she had left Manchester for London, Doug had called her with the news she had been waiting for: Virgin wanted to release a single with her. Virgin Records! Nothing could have delighted her more and she had shrieked in delight (Doug could testify to that – his right ear was still ringing). Her agent had tried to calm her down, telling her it was only one single, not an album deal, it was just to see how it was received, but this was enough for Charlotte. All she needed was one chance to show them (it wasn't her fault that last time the stupid songwriter had walked out). They were going to put her with their best songwriters, producers and choreographers, and even spend some money on the video as well. At last her talent would out, she told Doug and her mother and Silvio and anyone else she could think of. The offer had apparently come on the day the *Hiya!* interview with Silvio had hit the stands. Suddenly, Charlotte felt right with Silvio: he was hers, and together they would grow in stature and fame.

Up until now, however, Charlotte had done a good job of repressing any feelings she may have had for Silvio. A little affection was fair enough, but there was no way any emotional obstacles were going to come between her and her steely ambition for global fame. This had always been Charlotte's approach with men: she had assumed from the history of her own parents that men were essentially useless, though vaguely necessary as bread providers. It was women, however, who really made things happen. Her father had wanted to be a pop star: he ended up as a computer salesman. Her mother had been a groupie: she had ended up as the rich lady who lunched in Cheshire. But Silvio, it seemed, was already one step ahead in that game: apparently, he was rather good at football (something which had not really registered with her before). If this brought him fame, which in turn reflected on her, then she should, she thought, probably develop the relationship. As she teetered her way between the tables, all eyes on her, she turned round and threw him a devastating smile. Silvio melted for all to see.

After they had sat themselves down at Power's table Charlotte clasped Silvio's hand possessively on her lap (she was pretty sure everyone was still watching). Silvio's eyes had not left her from the moment they had walked in the door. Power (and Mrs Power) observed the young couple approvingly and Victor gave his young protegée the benefit of a proud grin. She'd done well so far, had Charlotte Want, and with his backing if she wanted to go further, then she most certainly could. Snaking his arm around her back, Power peered into her cleavage approvingly, and squeezed her arm as he pulled her towards him.

'You look like a princess tonight, my darlin'!'

This, however, did not go down particularly well with the Latin Silvio Ravelli, who looked on appalled as this rather grubby older man pawed his girlfriend. His disapproval flashed in his eyes, but Power affected not to notice, Charlotte was his, and the only reason why Ravelli had her was because he had fixed it that way.

'Mr Ravelli – what a pleasure to meet you at last!' began Power, in his most oily voice. Silvio decided instantly that he did not like this man, and that he was a threat to his relationship with Charlotte. He stared at the glistening, grinning tycoon before him, until Power was forced to drop his arm from Charlotte's back, and failed to respond to Power's greeting.

Power shifted uncomfortably in his seat, but decided he

would continue to be gracious. 'How was your game today?' he tried again, knowing very well Silvio had scored his team's winning goal.

Silvio shuddered. He turned to Charlotte to register his disapproval of this man, but found her staring at him icily. She willed him to be polite. She had spent a long time before dinner explaining exactly how important a benefactor Victor Power was to her. Silvio, who was by now becoming increasingly sensitive to Charlotte's moods, saw what she wanted, and on behalf of his angel and in response to the tightening squeeze she was now employing on his hand, collected himself and replied with reserved politeness.

'Thank you, it was going very well,' Silvio spoke quietly, the brief nod of his head encouraging little more conversation.

Mrs Power watched the exchange with interest.

'He shot a goal,' added Charlotte helpfully, 'but he also got a yellow card, didn't you, Silvio?'

Again Silvio nodded, keeping his eyes on the tablecloth in front of him and his head down. It was only when Power turned to chat to Charlotte that he looked up again, to stare at Power's face, coolly studying his movements. He definitely didn't like the way Power looked so approvingly at Charlotte, he didn't like the way he called her 'my girl' – she wasn't his girl, she was Silvio's – and he didn't like the way Charlotte was being so flirtatious back. The more Charlotte giggled at Power's jokes, the more she allowed her hand to flutter on his arm – and once Silvio thought he saw it rest on his knee! – the more jealousy began to creep into Silvio's heart.

In order to spare his guests the embarrassment of deciphering the menu, it was Power's custom to place his table in the hands of the chef, who would invariably serve them with his own combination of courses of tiny delicacies. Silvio, who would go to Sao Paulo frequently for matches, loved Japanese cuisine. With the largest Japanese population outside Tokyo, Sao Paulo had a thriving Japanese quarter where Fluminese would always insist on staying, and his introduction to Japanese food had been of the very highest quality. Normally then, he would have delighted in his meal, but tonight all he could do was shuffle the morsels around his plate. Power put this down to a lack of sophistication, and offered to bring him here as many times as it took to customize him to 'the high life' as he so crashingly named it.

'Something you'll have to get used to now you and Charlotte are . . .' and a wink of his eye and a crude leer of his lip was quite enough to make Silvio turn away in utter disgust. He said nothing in response, but finding himself in a distinctly uncomfortable situation began to swig his sake in tennis-star-like fashion.

Meanwhile, Charlotte twittered on about her Virgin deal, her hopes for the recording studio, the designs she had in mind for her stage outfits, the continuing saga of her search for a London flat. 'I must talk to Adrian about this. I mean Notting Hill is a bit passé these days isn't it? But then Clerkenwell is so grey, Kensington so middle-aged, and St

John's Wood so boring. Maybe I should just go for Mayfair. What do you think Mrs Power?'

'I think that would be very nice,' she replied politely, not really seeing what the difference was, but enjoying watching Silvio's morose attempts to refill his glass.

'The trouble is, it's hardly edgy is it?' chattered on Charlotte as Power smiled benignly at her. 'I do so want to be edgy. It's the only way to get any credibility in the pop world nowadays with all these manufactured boy bands about.' Charlotte sighed and Power said he quite agreed with her.

'I had a chat with the editor of *Smash Hits* the other day and he said it was absolutely imperative I got myself a stylist. What do you think, Victor?'

Power gritted his teeth. Give these girls an inch and they take a mile. Did she have any idea how much it was costing him to keep her chauffeur and PA on the payroll already?

'I think you have quite excellent taste already, Charlotte,' he said firmly. 'But if you need advice you know you can always call Adrian. After all it was his idea to put you in Julien Jones, you know.'

'Oooh!' screeched Charlotte excitedly at the memory. 'And that definitely worked, didn't it!'

'It certainly seemed to,' breathed Mrs Power.

Silvio glanced up at her curiously, wincing at the memory of Ferguson's fury the following day.

'So how is everything going at the paper?' asked Charlotte, forgetting to talk about herself for once.

'Ah, coming along nicely thank you very much,' said

Victor tightly, shifting a little in his seat. 'Although the scrutiny from the rest of the press is not exactly helpful.'

'What's that about then?' asked Charlotte. Silvio pricked up his ears again. But Power didn't seem to want to talk about it. The truth was that the instant recognition and entrée to the governing elite that Power had assumed would come with his purchase of the paper had not exactly materialized. Irritatingly, politicians were refusing his lunch invitations and the rest of the press were having a field day with his 'moral unsuitability'. But Power was not someone to give up without a fight and already he was preparing his next step – an enormous party, the like of which London had never seen before, at which there would be the cream of society. If he could not tempt the movers and shakers of Westminster to sit up and take notice of him, then his circle of celebrity influence certainly would. With the kind of party he was now planning, no one would be turning down their invitation.

So, as a huge plastic grin threatened to split open his face, he replied bullishly, 'Nothing to worry about. Plans are now in place, shall we say.' Then, as if announcing the arrival of the queen, Power drew back, spread his arms wide and, pausing for dramatic effect, announced, 'I am going to have a party.'

'Party? You're having a party Victor?'

'Certainly am, Princess.'

Silvio winced at this term of endearment.

'Ooooh!' squealed Charlotte in delight. 'That will be amazing!'

'But it's not just going to be a party. Oh no. This is going to be an Event. Everyone is going to be there, and no expense will be spared. It will be held to celebrate three years of *Hiya!* magazine, and anyone who has ever appeared in it will be invited, or indeed,' Power muttered to himself in a lower voice, 'ever intends to appear in it again.' Woe betide those who failed to turn up: already Fagge was putting the word around town that this was going to be a must attend event. Power continued, 'Mrs Power here is going to help arrange it and Fagge will of course be responsible for organizing everything.'

'It'll be quite lovely,' agreed Mrs Power loyally.

'It will, of course, be excellent publicity for the paper too, which I shall also be cross-promoting on the night, so I want plenty of celebrities to turn up. I trust I can count on you both to be there?'

'Of course you can!'

'Silvio?'

Silvio stared at Power. 'I will be with Charlotte,' he muttered, and glowered into his sake cup.

'As for the paper, well, once I have managed to downsize the ridiculous amount of staff, and we can cheer up the content with a lot more showbiz, fashion and gossip, I am confident the *Daily News* will be a huge success, don't you think so, Mrs Power?'

'Oh yes, absolutely,' she replied nodding vigorously. 'I have suggested there should be a bigger section on hair tips. I think women readers like to read about that.'

'Very good idea,' agreed Charlotte.

'Actually, I wanted to ask the two of you if you would visit the paper when you are next in London,' said Power. 'That would give it some good publicity and I think it would be helpful for both of you and your press coverage. Charlotte, you could talk to the showbiz editor and Silvio, perhaps you could chat to the sports desk. I also thought it would be a nice idea if the two of you contributed a column once a week. It would give you invaluable publicity and a good opportunity for you to plug your music career, Charlotte.'

Silvio glanced at Charlotte. She wasn't going to agree to this was she?

'Victor, I think that is a brilliant idea!' she said clapping her hands together.

Silvio was overtaken with horror. Just because he was going out with Charlotte didn't mean he had to help this man out too, did it?

'Excellent!' said Power, looking very pleased with himself. 'You see how my little cross-media fertilization is going to work here?' he said turning to Mrs Power, who nodded in a rather bemused fashion. 'Everyone's a winner!'

Silvio emptied the rest of the sake bottle around his cup.

Dinner over, Charlotte decided it was time for her and Silvio to make their entrance into the bar. The bar was not Mrs Power's scene at all, and Power himself had business to attend to, something to do with his assets, he mumbled and, looking at his watch, the grin that had been plastered across his face all night, momentarily fell. As they got up to leave the table Silvio stumbled and accidentally fell into

Power. Power took hold of his arm to steady him, but Silvio jumped at his touch, and shook him off like a bad smell.

'Silvio!' cried Charlotte.

'Little unsteady there, are we?' asked Power patronizingly. Silvio's attitude had not gone unnoticed.

The Powers went on ahead, leaving Charlotte alone in the lobby of the hotel with Silvio.

'What was all that about?' she demanded.

'I'm sorry.' Silvio shrugged, not wanting an argument and noticing that Charlotte did not look as though she was too happy. 'I just don't like that man,' he mumbled. 'I don't like the way he speaks to you. Like he owns you.'

'Well, he's my boss so you just have to like him, Silvio!'

Although Charlotte, in her new resolution to fall in love with Silvio, couldn't help thinking there was something rather endearing about his jealousy.

Silvio himself – or was it the sake? – suddenly found desire rapidly replacing disgust. Winding his arm territorially around her waist he pulled her into him, tracing the line of her bottom with his other hand.

'My darling, you are very attractive when you are shouting,' he slurred into her ear.

At that moment Charlotte spotted a famous Italian fashion designer coming down the stairs from the restaurant behind Silvio, and not wishing to create anything other than a scene of perfect domestic happiness allowed Silvio to embrace her. As she pulled away from him she saw the designer smiling at the erotic affection of the couple. She nodded to him and made a mental note to ring him the next day for some clothes.

'So where is this famous broom cupboard?' asked Silvio, to whom the idea that drink might drive away any possibility of performance had not occurred. But Charlotte was not going to be caught in flagrante in what was tantamount to her workplace, especially when there was important networking to be done in the bar.

'Another time, darling,' she said firmly and, grasping him by the hand, marched him over to the Cosmo bar.

Now, the problem with buying a drink at the Cosmo bar was that invariably it was three people deep. The place was utterly jammed anyway, and practically the only thing you could buy were very expensive cocktails served in tiny Martini glasses. By the time you had fought your way to the front of the bar, been relieved of thirty quid for a couple of drinks, and then attempted to fight your way back again, there was nothing left in your glass anyway, most of its contents having been jostled to the floor. Silvio found this extremely frustrating, and with what could only be described as a single-minded attempt to obliterate the memory of the entire evening, he remained at the bar, downing the contents of several Martini glasses one after the other off its polished silver surface.

Meanwhile, Charlotte's attention had been caught by a well-known record producer who quite fancied her, which left Silvio free to be chatted up by a Brazilian model in a revealingly tight slashed top, who said 'she admired his moves'. The model introduced herself as

Floriana. Through the haze of alcohol Silvio dimly recollected that he had heard her name before, she had created something of a scandal when she had given birth to the love child of an ageing rock star, putting an end to his long-standing marriage and propelling herself on to the front page of every newspaper and magazine around the world (for a fee). Little more than a calendar girl back then, she had not once missed an opportunity to parade said love child, who bore an unmistakable resemblance to his father, in front of the cameras and was now something of a global superstar. Still, if there was one thing to recommend her – and the rock star had seen this too – it was the size of her unfeasibly large breasts, and consequently Silvio could not help admiring *her* moves either, particularly when she wiggled them provocatively in his direction. After several minutes of conversation, Silvio noticed that her slashed top had worked its way (or been worked?) down her torso so the slash now revealed one of her nipples. Said slash made it very convenient for sticking your hand in, noted Silvio after his sixth cocktail. The model, for her part, was absolutely delighted to have such a famous footballer pawing at her bits and pieces. Still, she was smart enough to keep one eye on the footballer's girlfriend. Charlotte was sitting with her back to them and so the model considered herself free to encourage Silvio's clumsy advances as much as she could. But groping in the bar was very quickly not enough for her, and Floriana invited the unsuspecting Silvio downstairs 'for a little livener'.

Silvio had no idea what she meant but rather hoped, now that he was so blind drunk that his less intelligent fleshy appendage could do the thinking for him, that it involved a broom cupboard. All thoughts of Charlotte had now disappeared from his head, dispelled firstly by fury and secondly by alcohol. Besides, he was a Latino, and therefore he was allowed several women at once.

Floriana led him by the hand downstairs towards the toilets, and once they were round the corner and out of sight, he pinioned her against the wall and forced his tongue inside her mouth. Grabbing at her breasts and buttocks, he tried to lift her up, but she pushed him away.

'No – not here!'

'Yes, here!'

He tried again, not fully able to focus on what was in front of him, except a large, protruding nipple. Just as he was about to slip off her top to reveal more breast, he felt a piercing sensation in his backside as something small and needle-like entered his behind.

'Owwww!' he yowled and whipped round.

There was Charlotte wielding a swizzle stick and looking like thunder. Floriana charged swiftly into the ladies' and locked herself in a cubicle.

'What do you think you're doing, Silvio?' demanded Charlotte.

'Darleeng!' began Silvio.

'Don't you darleeng me, you drunkard! Now straighten yourself up, we're leaving and there are hundreds of photographers outside.'

'But aren't we staying in the hotel?' asked Silvio, confused.

'Yes, but we need our picture taken first or there's no point in us even being here,' snapped Charlotte. Silvio appreciated he was not in a position to argue.

'Now, take my arm and remember to smile when we go through the doors. We'll talk about this later.'

She swept back his hair and straightened his shirt collar before pulling the top of her dress down to reveal some more of her cleavage. Charlotte never wore a coat – she would much rather freeze and show off all her assets. Silvio allowed himself to be led back upstairs, across the bar to the door, but, unfortunately, just as Charlotte opened it, the full impact of his evening's drinking chose that moment to make itself felt and, as he lunged out of the door, he managed to projectile-vomit the sake- and martini-stewed contents of his Bonu meal all over the steps, and some of it over Charlotte's shoes, too. Just as the flashbulbs went Pop!

# chapter sixteen

Cas's eyes flicked open and she looked at the clock. 4.36 a.m. She shut them again tightly, hoping, praying that in that half life between sleep and wakefulness something would be different. But the fantasy eluded her. She stretched her legs out, searching for the warmth of Toby's body that wasn't there. She turned over, still not wanting to believe his absence, but the bed was empty, just cold space and acres of sheet where he should be. Tears welled up in her eyes, a lump swelled in her throat, her heart creaked. At this time, when she was not at work, when she was not distracted, when she was not hurrying from one appointment to the next, when she only had herself to look into, she was forced to ask – what was her life without Toby?

For the weeks since he had left she hadn't been able to sleep properly, couldn't be bothered to eat. She was torn between anger at Toby abandoning her at such a moment and the the constant feeling gnawing away at her that this could be her fault. She knew she had been caught up in herself, in her work. She knew Toby had been feeling redundant, but all the time she had thought he would understand. After all, much of the reason she was in this situation now was because of him: she had taken this job, rented this flat and (now vacant) studio expressly for him.

But she was beginning to think that something irreparable had been done. They had hardly spoken since he had left, both it seemed were angry with each other and the conversations they had had, had been cursory and dull. Like a plant she had neglected to water, she wondered if she would be able to revive the sagging leaves of what the two of them had once had.

And then she would be forced to wonder if perhaps she and Toby *were* too different, maybe they *couldn't* make things work. Maybe Toby was right to leave. His style of life – laid back and easy – his different set of priorities, might never suit her, and if they stayed together then maybe they would clash all their lives.

This thought, which had been playing round in Cas's head for days now, did little to ease her pain. She loved Toby more than ever, his absence just pointed this up, and forced her to reflect on their relationship. She had to admit she shared with him an intimacy and an understanding she had never reached with anyone else. But was this enough to make the relationship work? Was she still going to lose him all the same?

She grasped the pillow where his head should have been and pulled it into her in place of him, sobbing with great dry convulsions. There were lots of different kinds of crying and she had been through them all since he had gone: self-pity crying, anger crying, tired crying, pain crying. But this, this was the worst. This dawn light, tear-streaked hopelessness was a mind-disabling wretchedness, and with every day that passed it just got worse.

What was he doing at his parents' home? He said he was working on a piece, waiting for her to decide if she was ready, but she didn't understand what he meant by that and he wouldn't explain. All she knew was that without him she carried around an unbearable ache, one that underlined everything she did, everything she said. But what was she meant to do? Call him and tell him she was sorry she worked too hard? She was doing it for him. Pride had made her stop short of admitting that she missed him.

She could distract herself sometimes, at work, or with Sam, with whom she seemed to be spending most of her time now. Occasionally for sweet moments, she would not remember at all. But every morning she would wake, in this witching hour, and the loneliness would be brought home to her: the prospect of a life ahead without the joy Toby had brought her. She wanted him back, so badly, but she didn't know how to go about it. There was just nothing now where once there had been the two of them together.

Cas thought about the day ahead. It stretched out so interminably, so unpleasurably, so tediously, until the evening, when she would meet Sam. Then she could fill her head again with Victor Power and discuss new leads and talk about scenarios and forget. What she was doing with Sam was the only thing keeping her going at the moment, the only way she could make any sense out of her life, and so she had thrown herself into it completely.

As for her day to day work, the reality of office life with PBfH was worse than ever. The atmosphere on the paper was so awful now, a strain of uncertainty, dread and fear resting on everybody's shoulders. Already redundancies were being announced. Would they have a job tomorrow? What kind of person were they now working for? And all around everyone was making plans to leave, talking about giving up what they had, moving on. It was a dreadful place to be every day. If she didn't have the Power investigation, which had now become something of a crusade she noted to herself, then what would be the point in anything? The one uplifting element of her life had been Toby, but now he had gone. He was her future, and now that had disappeared under a veil of uncertainty.

In despair, Cas turned over and over, hugging the pillow closer and closer, squeezing it into her, but sleep and its sweet peace did not come. Five, then six, then finally the time came when she had to start again, put on her face and pretend she was functioning. She dressed and left the flat. On the way to the station she picked her mobile out of her bag, wanting so much to call Toby, to hear his voice, but she couldn't – not while she was crying. She was the strong one, she couldn't admit she wasn't coping without him, either to him or to herself. So she dropped the phone back in her bag, wiped her tears away on her sleeve and bought a newspaper, desperate for other thoughts to fill her mind and push out this misery.

The other passengers on the tube stared at her, one concerned woman in a blue suit asked her if everything was OK. Yes, fine. Obviously. Biting her lip, she forced the words on the page into her head to push everything else out. At her stop she got off and walked out of the station. The grey office block that was her daily house of torture loomed large over the river. She walked into its shadow and then in through its maw.

Within the building, Power's Mr Hyde had made his appearance. Any initial hope that Power cared more about the paper than his predecessor had been crushed by a series of senseless changes. Changes that anyone who worked at a paper could see displayed a singular lack of understanding of the needs of journalism. Five days after he took over, Hyde had cancelled delivery of all other newspapers and restricted access to the internet. Too costly, apparently. So anyone who wanted to find out what the news was, or what their competitors were actually up to, had to go to the local newsagent. The news editor had lost her temper, and stormed into Farlane's office shouting, 'Does this man have any fucking idea how to run a newspaper?' As the news editor was normally a quiet, reserved woman who would flinch at the machismo of her colleagues and whose capacity for calm under stress was enormous, this outburst came as a shock. Even she had cracked. Fortunately, once Farlane had vociferously persuaded Power of the essential need for news in a newspaper, he agreed to reinstate the papers. His next great act of misunderstanding was to put a stop on the telephone lines for all international calls. This left the foreign editor in something of a fix as she had three international correspondents and seventeen stringers waiting for her direction – and she wasn't able to speak to a single one of them. Foreign stories, it appeared, were no longer on the agenda for the *Daily News*.

Following this cost-cutting exercise came a freeze on courier bikes, taxis, and – of all the meannesses – photocopying paper. So much for Dr Jekyll's promise of more money.

Next came the issue of content. Power, it seemed, was not particularly interested in current affairs, unless celebrities were having them. His first move was to insist the editor of *Hiya!* sit in on the newspaper's morning conference, supposedly to contribute any stories he might have, but the ruse was obvious: it was so he could report what was going on back to Power. Every day at five o' clock, Farlane would receive an email from Power asking her what the splash would be on the front page the next day, and she would tell him. Every day Power would suggest something different. On one particularly memorable occasion, when the foot and mouth crisis was bringing rural Britain to its knees, the Selby train crash had claimed ten lives, and the blizzards sweeping the north of England had left hundreds of thousands of homes without electricity, these had all been rejected as front-page stories – Power wanted the tale of teenage pop star Billie's stalker as the splash. Farlane had humoured him, as she herself was (if somewhat hysterically), beginning to see the funny side. The next day the *Daily News* was the laughing stock of Fleet Street.

Cas, meanwhile, had one project she could bury herself in, and the changes at the paper, in Cas's eyes, affronts to the very nature of journalism, just made her more determined than ever. A week after his take over, the *Guardian* ran a profile on Power, written by Sam, minutely detailing all his most graphic porn publications and the few biographical facts on him they had manged to glean.

Power's personal wealth, the paper reported, was now deemed to be in the region of several million pounds, and he lived ostentatiously in a large house in Surrey, sparing himself few luxuries. He owned a private jet that flew him around the country at need, ran a fleet of cars from limousines to urban jeeps, and whenever he was seen about town, in the finest restaurants, he was dressed expensively in tailored suits from the hottest name on Savile Row.

The inner sanctum of his staff is tight, the paper continued, those closest to him have worked with him for years and their loyalty is absolute. His relationships with women had been fleeting, until recently when he had married his secretary of many years, Winifred Wattle. Little was known about her either, only that she was a number of years older than her husband. She, like Power, had no surviving family and few friends.

This was about as much as the paper had been able to legally report, but Sam and Cas both knew there were still questions about how Power had originally come by his fortune that the paper was not able to go into – was it from magazines alone? They were both suspicious and had spent much of the last few weeks trying to unravel Power's tangled accounts, whose twists and turns were unpredictable and complex. They were beginning to detect large amounts of money channelled through Power Publishing that appeared to have no explicable source, and which appeared to be creamed off the system through a series of 'expenses' before they could be accounted in the company's annual profits. The amounts were substantial: up to £20 million in the last two years, but they had been well hidden. So well hidden that it seemed the Inland Revenue had yet to pick them up, or at least to question them as legitimate expenses.

Based on his findings, Sam and Cas had also begun to uncover an elaborate system of self-funding within Power Publishing. Only by funnelling profits from one part of the company to the next was Power able to sustain an illusion of wealth. Moreover, the purchase of the *Daily News* looked like it had been a heavy burden on the health of the firm, using up most of the company's collateral. Unless the *Daily News* went into massive profit soon, the two surmised that Power was going to have a problem.

The financial holes, however, were nothing like as damaging to Power publicly as the coverage other papers devoted to the anatomically graphic content of Power's media interests. There was little British papers enjoyed more than defaming their rivals, and to have stumbled on such a rich source of scurrilous material about one of their own was a joy to them all. Pages and pages of Power's pornographic material were re-printed in all the nationals (perhaps a little lasciviously), and the coverage was acutely embarrassing for Power, particularly as all his celebrity best friends were now left in little doubt as to where their cheques came from.

Power himself was incandescent with anger. Barely able to control himself while he had been reading the *Guardian* report, with what he perceived as its hypocritical moral tone, he had roared with fury and screwed the paper up into a ball and chucked it across his office. Mrs Power had flinched in her seat and kept a very low profile. Power had then summoned the news editor and directed her to find something on as many of Fleet Street's other editors as she could.

'Get me some dirt on these hypocritical bastards and get it now! I want it splashed across the front page of the newspaper tomorrow!'

The news editor was not quite sure how she was going to do this, but she dutifully pulled four of her eleven reporters off the daily news agenda and instructed them to dig around the personal lives of Fleet Street's finest. When they failed to come up with anything, Power was forced to disappear off in his limousine to his anger therapist. On the way back, calmer, he mused that all this scurrilous backbiting in the pages of the nationals was building him a worse reputation, not the better one he had hoped for when he bought the *News*. Well, if he couldn't be a serious figure, then he would be what they wanted him to be – an entertainer. He countered his defamation by announcing the party in the pages of his own paper, the showbusiness editor was instructed to run a story about it every day, and now it seemed little filled their proprietor's head other than the expanding guest list for his grand feast of celebrity.

Following his obsession with such trivia, and the daily revelations in other papers of the more graphic aspects of his other publications, the high-profile columnists of the paper slowly began to quit. The foreign editor announced she was off to Ceefax, and the science editor to the BBC. When Farlane went to discuss the science editor's replacement with her proprietor, rumour had it she had been told Power did not want him replaced at all: there were, apparently, plenty of science stories on the internet which could be used instead. Why didn't she just 'use a work experience to dig them up?'.

On top of this, word had got out that Farlane had been asked to make a hundred redundancies across the paper. Power, it seemed, thought the newspaper could be run by a team of just forty people. Farlane had since stopped talking to him, and would now only communicate by email. 'It's the only way I can control my blood pressure.' He, of course, was trying to force her resignation, but she refused to go before she had fought a rearguard action for her staff's jobs or redundancy packages. All information came by gossip alone, and each new day brought fresh rumours: nothing was certain, and everyone now worked as if the sword of Damocles was hanging over their heads.

The only person who had actually benefited from Power's takeover was Tamara Yearbank. She and her new proprietor were now the best of friends. Power had promised her that he was going to up-page her magazine and turn the entire thing fully glossy, with her in charge. He also promised her a constant supply of celebrity scoops and interviews secured by *Hiya!* magazine and passed to her free of charge. PBfH, much to her staff's irritation, was cock-a-hoop, and set about spiking every single feature idea Cas had in production. Any suggestion Cas made was met with, 'Victor won't like that,' and then snide comments hinting at Cas's imminent demise, usually along the lines of how much better any of her friends would be at Cas's job than Cas herself.

Cas could only deal with this by concentrating on exposing what she now felt sure was the rottenness at the core of the Power empire. Once Tamara had left the office for the evening she would trawl the internet and the library for further evidence of Power's lewd business interests. The other papers' revelations about Power may have damaged his reputation, but this was not enough to remove him as proprietor of the *News*. Soft porn was a cause for debate, but it certainly wasn't criminal. If there *was* something more, Cas resolved she was going to find it. Then Power would be removed and her job, and she, would be safe.

As Cas arrived at work, make-up hastily applied in the ladies' to hide her red eyes and the bags that graced the bottom of them, Chris the designer came racing up to her.

'You'll never guess what's happened now!'

'What? I hope you're excited for a good reason. I don't need any more bad ones.' Chris, a talented boy of twenty-one, had little to lose at the *News* and was thoroughly enjoying the catastrophes following Power's takeover.

'Apparently he's selling off his porn sites!' Chris beamed. 'And the magazines too! That means he's cracked – the pressure's got to him, he's not prepared to stand up for what he is!'

Cas was intrigued by this news. According to her investigation of Power Publishing, the only profitable bits of the company were the porn-oriented titles. If he was selling them then where was he going to get his money from?

'Where did you hear this, Chris?' Cas asked, knowing that if the information was true it could have a disastrous effect on the cost-cutting plans at the *News*.

'It's in the *FT*, on the business pages. The city editor spotted it.'

It was true. The reason for the sale could only be speculated about, but the *Financial Times* suggested that because of the intense scrutiny over his other publishing interests, Power had decided the only way he was going to be able to continue to hold his head up in public was if he disassociated himself from pornography entirely. But it also suggested that Power Publishing was not as confident and as well-off as it liked to convey – the decision to sell was motivated by a desperate need to raise funds. The question now had to be asked: could he actually afford to keep the *News*?

'Actually it's not good news, Chris. It's terrible news. Hang on, because your redundancy cheque is coming round the corner. If he flogs off his porn titles and the

*News* doesn't make money quick, there'll be no money left in his pot to pay anybody.'

'Caris! Get into my office. Now!' shrieked Tamara from behind her door.

Unbelievably, she was in before Cas and was actually working.

'Yes, Tamara?'

'Could you do something useful rather than spreading idle gossip, please?'

Tamara was standing behind her desk, purposefully shouting loudly enough so the rest of the staff could hear. 'I also want to take this opportunity to tell you that I'm fed up with your negative approach to the new ownership. You've got to accept the situation; change this magazine with me or frankly you need to find another job!'

'Right,' said Cas, not sure how to respond.

'Next week Charlotte Want and Silvio Ravelli are coming into the office. They will both be writing a column for the magazine and I want you to edit it.'

'What?'

'You heard me. Charlotte will be sharing her beauty and fashion tips, Silvio will be writing about health and fitness. Oh, and we want lots of detail on all the parties they go to together as well.'

'But Silvio Ravelli can barely speak English – how's he going to write it?'

'Of course he can speak English.'

'He can't, he's Brazilian. I heard him being interviewed on television and he can hardly string a sentence together!'

Tamara's face flushed beetroot-red with rage. Her lips pursed and seething with fury she replied, 'Well, in that case you're going to have to write it for him. I've arranged for you to meet them both this afternoon at Charlotte's agent's offices. Two p.m. sharp. You will do the columns every week. Now – get out!!!' she yelled, slamming the door behind the fast-retreating Cas and leaving the walls of her cage juddering.

'Oops. Think I overstepped the mark there,' said Cas quietly and sat down at her desk and put her head in her hands. Writing a society column for Charlotte Want and making up 'ealth tips' from a footballer – what was her job turning into?

On her desk her answer machine message light was blinking and she turned it on. There was a message from Toby, asking her to call him right away. If anything was calculated to throw her further off balance then this was it. With trepidation she dialled the number of his parents' house. Every time she spoke to him now it seemed to worsen the situation.

'Toby? It's me.'

'Cas.'

Long pause.

'How are you?'

'Okay. You?'

Cas bit her lip. 'Okay. I think.' Longer pause. 'I mean things are a bit hairy at the paper.' Why didn't she say what she meant – without you.

Toby swallowed. 'Cas, I've been thinking about what

you have been saying. If you really want me to do this Cosima Beane thing then I'll do it.' There, he had said it – he had given her what she wanted. He did not feel any better.

Cas tried to take this in. Was this really what she wanted? 'But you mustn't do this for my sake, Toby. Do it for yourself.'

'No, I'd be doing it for you. I love you and if this is what you want, then I'll do it.'

'No, it's not what I want. It's what I want you to want!' Cas replied with infallible logic.

'What?' replied Toby, bemused.

'Do it because you want to, because you want to make a success of things.'

'Cas, I'm telling you that I will do the thing you said you really wanted, so don't try and make me take responsibility for it as well. I can make a success of things another way. Left to myself I would not choose my family's sordid secret as the basis on which to launch my career, but if you think I should, then I've just told you – I will.'

'Is it really that cut and dried Toby?' asked Cas, losing her cool, feeling the emotion welling behind every word.

'Oh, look, forget it, Cas. I wanted to talk it over and you're shouting again.'

'I'm not shouting,' replied Cas, shouting. 'I'm just worked up – I've got a lot going on here.'

'Okay. Well, ring me when you've got time.'

And they hung up.

\*

Toby ran his hands through his hair in exasperation, and turned to leave the room only to find his mother standing in the doorway. She seemed frozen. He looked at her closer and saw that she was stricken. The cottage was tiny, there was no way his mother hadn't heard. He remembered what he had said and he felt his heart bump against his chest.

'Sordid family secret?' breathed Emily.

'Oh look, Mum, it's all a disaster. Let's just forget it,' he said as he tried to push past her, but she wouldn't move.

'No, Toby. What is this about?' Emily's voice was calm, determined.

Toby looked at her. Maybe he should tell her, maybe the weight of it all pressing down on him was going to get too much. Maybe this family should have it out after all.

'It's about the colour of my skin,' he said accusingly, looking her, at last, in the eye.

The force of her son's gaze took Emily by surprise and she gasped and looked away.

Toby continued, 'The art dealer I was telling you about thinks I'm some kind of anomaly because I come from an aristocratic family and I've got Indian blood in me. She thinks this is a selling point. Don't ask me why.'

Emily swallowed and took a deep breath. 'Toby there is something I have to tell you, something you should know.' Toby didn't like the sound of this. Steeling herself, Emily took a step closer to her son. Laying a hand on his arm, she said at last, 'I am your mother, but St John is not your father.'

## chapter seventeen

Charlotte Want was impatiently tapping her pink satin Jimmy Choos against the leg of the leather armchair. Outside, the warm autumn sun was streaming through the windows of Doug Bowser's agency, but inside the atmosphere was so frosty it might have been winter. This, fumed Charlotte, was far from the ideal situation. She pushed her large Dior sunglasses further up her nose, thrust her chin in the air and, clenching her teeth and sucking in her cheeks even further, tried to imagine herself a thousand miles from this room.

Opposite her, a miserable heap of tracksuit bottoms and sweatshirts held the slumped body of Silvio Ravelli, who had sunk so far down his chair into his baggy training clothes that he had almost succeeded in the illusion he was trying to sustain of not being there at all. Between the pair, rather uncomfortably sat Doug Bowser, whose capabilities as a RELATE counsellor had never been called on before in his line of work, and were certainly to be found lacking now. The large man shifted in his chair, and longed for the end of the day when he could leave all this mess behind him, settle behind the wheel of his second-hand Mercedes (personalized number plate: DEA D1Y), and drive up the M11 to the arms of his missus, or at least to the rather more welcoming arms of his black comfy TV chair. But for now he had his most difficult client, Charlotte Want, to deal with. Inwardly, he cursed the day he had met Gloria the groupie – if it wasn't for her and her incessant yammering at him, then he would not be here now. The frozen silence in the room prevailed. Only the click, click, clicking of Charlotte's heels on the chair leg cut through the heavy air, and the occasional mournful sigh from the Brazilian.

After Silvio Ravelli had made something of a fool of himself outside the Cosmo bar, not to mention the mess he had made of her favourite pair of Manolos, Charlotte could hardly countenance the sight of him any more. Disgusted and humiliated she had unceremoniously dumped him there and then – though, obviously, only once they were out of sight of the cameras. Despite the ungodly hour of the morning, and the promises she had made to herself about the benefits of sharing her fame, she had thrown him out of her hotel room in a blazing fury (one in which Silvio received several body blows from her vomit-strewn shoes), and had forced him to spend the rest of the night in an alcohol-sodden heap on the floor outside her door. When he had eventually come round from his alcoholic stupor, Silvio had sheepishly slunk back up to Manchester in one of the Cosmopolitan's thoughtfully provided limousines and spent the rest of the weekend in hiding from the clamouring press and the ribbing phone calls from his team mates. The picture of the pair leaving the bar in such an undignified manner had, of course, made it on to the front page of every tabloid newspaper that morning.

The following afternoon however, Charlotte had received a disquieting phone call from Doug congratulating her and Silvio once again on making the front pages, and passing on a request from 'Uncle Vic' for 'a full and frank' interview for the next issue of *Hiya!* about how both of them were dealing with Silvio's alcoholism. Nothing Charlotte could say would change Doug's – or rather Uncle Vic's – mind.

'You're too much of an item, my darlin'. You're hot, hot, hot, as they say,' Doug said persuasively. 'It's got to be said, darlin', and I'm only saying this to you as a professional, mind, but with that Ravelli kid by your side you are double the celebrity you would be on your own. Treble, even, dare I say it. People love him, you see darlin'. He puts more balls in the back of the net than all the other premiership strikers put together, and that makes him big news!' Doug drew breath in the silence that followed, not sure how this last bit of information had gone down. 'He's good for your career, my girl,' he said soothingly.

Even in her rage Charlotte could see the truth in what her agent was saying. She had never made the front pages before, but since she had been going out with Silvio the paparazzi wouldn't leave her alone. There were two or three camped permanently outside her front door right now, much to her delight, even if the only questions they ever asked her were about Silvio.

Annoying as this was, Charlotte was smart enough to realize there was still a large pool of fame by association to be tapped by continuing her relationship with Silvio. After two days of sulking, much cajoling from Doug and her mother, and finally a rather distressing phone call from Doug in which he had explained that both Wella and Virgin were a little nervous about her image – they absolutely wanted her as one half of a celebrity couple, rather than as a single girl about town – she had eventually relented and rung Silvio to allow him to apologize.

His response, however, had not been quite what she was expecting, for the scales had finally fallen from Silvio's eyes. Somewhat put out by the manner in which he had been dumped, not to mention the excruciating pain of having to endure two hours of watching her encourage 'her slimy boss' to dribble all over her and several skin-puncturing blows from the vomit-covered shoes, Silvio, wounded inside and out, had decided that Charlotte Want was not quite the girl he had thought she was. And even when Charlotte had turned up on his doorstep dressed persuasively in a leather coat and little else, he had managed to resist – which was quite something for the sexually charged Brazilian. Charlotte, unused to being spurned and not in the least bit happy about it, had therefore resorted to the last line of defence. She had informed him via his answer phone that unless he went out with her again she would give a 'full and frank' interview to *Hiya!*, the *Daily News*, the BBC – and indeed anyone else who wanted to listen – about how he had smuggled her into the locker room of the Manchester United football ground and made love to her while his boss stood on the other side of the shower curtain.

Already in enough trouble with Ferguson as it was, Silvio could do nothing else but agree to her demands and the two spent an excruciating morning posing for the *Hiya!* photographer while the interviewer made up their responses to questions like: 'Has Charlotte been very supportive to you through this difficult time?' and 'Do you think Silvio's drink problems have tarnished your image at all Charlotte?'

Banned from any more public appearances, Silvio had spent the last three weeks arriving at Old Trafford at six in the morning for four hundred one-arm press-ups before training. Eventually, his boss had let him back on to the team, just as Silvio received another phone call from Charlotte Want demanding he start writing a health column in the *Daily News*. He wailed in protest, but Charlotte had one over him now and told him he had to continue to appear by her side for another six months before she would let him go. No one turned her away from their doorstep when all she was wearing was just a leather coat.

So, thought Charlotte, as she tapped Doug's armchair with her nails and heels, here they were again. Opposite her the stricken Silvio sat with his head in his hands avoiding any kind of exchange whatsoever, and between them sat Doug, whose only contribution to the whole proceedings was the occasional suggestion that it was perhaps in the best interests of all concerned if the two would just kiss and make up. Charlotte had told him to shut up.

Into this jolly atmosphere walked Cas.

'Hi. I'm Caris Brown, from the *Daily News*,' she said charmingly as Doug's secretary showed her into the room. Doug, leaping from his seat and delighted to have someone else in the room to break the tension, introduced her first to Charlotte and then to Silvio.

'You're late,' snapped Charlotte, withdrawing her limp hand from Cas's the moment they touched. Charlotte was never particularly well disposed to other women, and especially not after she had noted Silvio look Cas up and down with undisguised admiration.

'Ees no problem,' cut in Silvio, clearly delighted to be presented with such a fine specimen of English beauty. But this was not what Charlotte wanted to hear at all, and unable to contain her jealousy and fury, she jumped up, spun on her heel, gave Silvio a look of mock hurt, then flounced out of the office, slamming the door behind her. Both Doug and Silvio stared after her in shock.

'Was it something I said?' asked Cas, in surprise.

Silvio grinned, and Doug, recovering himself, ran out to try and retrieve Charlotte.

'Es not you, es me.' Silvio laughed and gestured to Charlotte's empty seat, inviting Cas to sit down.

'Oh dear,' replied Cas. 'No one seems to be able to hold down a relationship these days!'

'You too?' asked Silvio, already imagining the possibilities with this rather fetching journalist, whose figure-hugging dress showed off the sort of body of which even Ipanema beach would be proud.

'That's another story,' said Cas brusquely, but she liked the soft look in Silvio's eyes and decided she was probably going to get along with him. 'Now, this column of yours,' she began.

'Psshhh . . .' Silvio waved his hand in dismissal. 'Write what you like. I have nosing to say. Zis is somesing that Power man want. I don't care.'

Cas looked at Silvio carefully. 'Victor Power?' she asked.

'Yes, he want zis. Not me. My boss – Mr Ferguson – he will be very angry about zis, but zere is nosing I can do. So, write what you want.'

'So why are you doing it?' asked Cas, incredulous that Power's tentacles could reach so far.

Silvio smiled. 'Anozer story, as you say.'

But Cas was not going to let this opportunity slip away. 'Do you know Mr Power?'

'Yes,' said Silvio, with open disgust.

Now Cas was really intrigued. 'Why don't you like him?'

Silvio shrugged his shoulders and looked out of the window. 'I just – I just don't like him,' he said eventually, and Cas wasn't sure if it was the language or something else stopping him from saying any more.

The truth was, Power had wounded Silvio's ego, a dangerous thing to do to a Latin man.

Whatever it was Silvio had against Power, Cas wanted to encourage him and she decided to risk taking him into her confidence.

'Listen, Silvio, if there is something you know, you must tell me. I work for Power now too, but like you, not out of choice. I think there is something dodgy about him, and if I could just find out what, then –' Cas broke off: Silvio was looking at her strangely, but his face was open and honest. 'Look, perhaps I shouldn't say any more, but . . .'

'No, no, go on please. You are right, he ees a bad man, I can feel it,' said Silvio.

So Cas told him that she didn't know if he was bad, but that she had her fears for the *News*, that she was trying to find out as much as she could about him. Silvio sat bolt upright in rapt attention, his piercing blue eyes not once leaving her face, transfixed by her voice, her lips, her eyes, her manner – everything. It was almost as if he didn't want her to stop talking, and Cas, not immune to Silvio's physical charms, said perhaps a little more than she should have.

'But listen, Silvio,' she pleaded. 'I could be in real danger here, so I beg you to keep this information about what I am doing to yourself. Please – you mustn't even tell your girl-friend. Promise me, please, or I could be in real trouble!' Cas waited nervously for a response. But Silvio did not move. The contrast between this well-meaning girl, the softness of her voice, her quiet determination, and the beautiful way her eyes begged him to keep her secret, and the monster he was trying to rid himself of could not have been more pronounced. Once again it seemed, like a thunderbolt right to the centre of his being, Silvio had been smitten by an English girl.

'Silvio?' Cas tried again. No response. Cas wondered if something was wrong with him – he looked ill. 'Mr Ravelli?'

Slowly, Silvio began to shake his head in wonder. 'You – you are so beautiful!' he whispered, in a voice struck with awe. It was the kind of comment that only a foreigner with language problems could get away with. Cas was taken aback, blushed and looked away, but she was not altogether insulted.

'Well, thank you,' she muttered, feeling herself blush even more. There was no denying that Silvio was pretty damn gorgeous himself, she thought. She smiled and looked back at him, but he was still slowly shaking his head. She wondered if he had heard a word she had said. She cleared her throat, 'Um, I was saying that –'

'You have my word!' began Silvio in earnest, 'anysing, anysing, I will do it for you. Don't worry about Charlotte – we are finished, no more talking, nosing. Zis is just for the newspapers so she can be famous. It's all she want – she use me,' he said, with perhaps a little more hurt in his voice than was needed. 'But Power, you are right, zere is somesing about zat man, but I do not know anysing now. But maybe, for you I can find somesing. Give me, please, your phone number.'

Cas pulled a card out of her bag and handed it to him. As he took it, he let his fingers rest on hers for a second. Then he caught her hand and looked beatifically up at her face. He smiled, a heart-melting smile, and again Cas blushed. It was at this moment that Doug chose to re-enter the room. Hurriedly, Silvio dropped Cas's hand, and they both looked at the floor. If Doug noticed anything, then he chose not to remark upon it.

'Charlotte has asked me to tell you that she will telephone you with the information she would like to include in her column,' he told Cas. 'I'm afraid she is late for shooting the video for her new single and has had to leave now. So perhaps for this week, if I give you her diary and all the parties she has been to, you could write something for her?'

'Oh yeah, that's fine,' replied Cas, quite relieved she wasn't actually going to have to deal with Charlotte directly now. Anyway, this was the journalistic norm for party girls' columns, Cas had heard. 'I'll bash something out and fax it over to you for her approval.'

'Good. And do you have everything you need from Silvio?'

'Um, yes, I think so. We are going to write about . . . um . . . er . . .' Cas floundered around for a subject and looked at Silvio, but his face was still gazing at hers. 'Um . . . nutrition! Yes, this week it's nutrition.'

Silvio looked puzzled. 'She means food, Ravelli,' explained Doug, who had little time for the Latin Romeo.

'Oh!' Silvio nodded, then returned his gaze to Cas.

'So?' said Doug.

'Yes,' agreed Cas, who knew a hint to leave when she heard it, and handing her business card to Doug said, 'and please give this to Charlotte, she needs to call me every week by Wednesday to make the press deadline.'

'Well, you'll see her next week anyway as Silvio and

Charlotte will be visiting the *Daily News* offices for a photo opportunity.'

Silvio's head shot up, this was clearly not something he knew about. Doug glanced at him and nodded his head, 'That's right, Sunshine.'

As she left Deadly Doug's Agency, Cas felt quite giddy from the footballer's attention. But she was also no fool, and knew not to take it seriously. Still, she allowed herself to enjoy the flattery. Amusing too was the apparent state of the Want/Ravelli relationship – not exactly as it appeared in *Hiya!* magazine, then. As she strode along Shoreditch High Street, the warm autumn sun on her face, she allowed herself to enjoy the moment – the first in a while. The silence between her and Toby had been wearing her down. She had called him twice now and he had returned neither call.

As she headed towards the tube station, her mobile rang. It was Sam, saying he needed to see her urgently. As the 'interviews' had been somewhat short, she had time to fit in a quick drink before heading back to the office.

Sam was impatiently twisting his glass in his hand when Cas arrived in the pub. As soon as he saw her, his face broke into a smile and he jumped up from his seat to welcome her. Cas laughed at him, 'What is it Sam? I came as quickly as I could.'

'The newsdesk want me to carry on investigating Power,' said Sam.

'Um – great. I thought you already were?' replied Cas.

'Yes. But look, I've come up against a paper brick wall.

The affairs are so tangled and so far there is no tangible evidence linking Power with anything not above board. This morning the editor called me in for an update and I told him everything I knew including our suspicions – and I showed him edengirls. I've done some research into people-smuggling, and frankly the profits are mind-boggling. The going rate for the one-way trip from Eastern Europe is about five hundred and fifty pounds per person, and with forty people to a boat, or a lorry, that works out at about twenty-two thousand pounds a go. Then you add on to that the revenue you get from them once they arrive, either through forced prostitution, or slavery, or whatever – and believe you me, it goes on – and you are sitting on a very agreeable sum of money. Easily enough to explain away the millions that are floating through Power's account that we can't trace. I showed him all Power's figures and he agreed with me that there is enough circumstantial evidence to link Power with something dodgy like this site.'

'Yes? So?' urged Cas. Sam was excited, she could see it in his eyes, hear it in his voice.

'He's agreed to send me to Nauru.'

'Fantastic!' gasped Cas delightedly. 'That's brilliant Sam! So if he does have stuff running through that island, and he's left any trace, we'll nail him.'

'Exactly. It won't take much, a signature, a company name, even a hotel record of his having stayed there, or one of his employees. The editor thinks if I don't find anything there's still a story in it anyway. So I leave – with a photographer – on Monday.'

'Sam, this is the best news. I'm so pleased.'

Sam beamed and finally Cas felt she could stop feeling guilty for coercing him into helping her with this story in the first place. Sam had excitedly explained that no journalist had yet been to Nauru, and, at the very least, there was a good feature to be written on this unknown island and bent finance, whether he found a link with Power or not.

'Listen Cas, I've been thinking,' continued Sam, his voice quieter now, his head leaning closer towards her. 'This investigation is about to get serious. We need to do everything we can to get the stuff we need. Look, I know it's dangerous, but I wondered if there was any way you could have a sniff around Power's office? All we need is something to prove he has an interest in Rapture, or even just Nauru, and then we are almost ready to go to the police. You've got access to the building, it seems a shame not to do it.'

'Actually, I've been thinking the same,' replied Cas. 'Christ, if you can go to the Pacific, I can at least walk up the office stairs. I've been working late quite a lot recently and checking out the security. I know the guards well anyway, and they know me. They keep copies of the keys to the office doors, I'm sure I can think of an excuse to get Power's. Leave it to me – I'll give it a go if I can.'

Sam smiled at her. He could see she was nervous, but he knew she would do it.

Cas enjoyed Sam's company – it was better than being on her own, and certainly better than being in the office.

On impulse, thinking of her lonely flat, she invited him round for dinner that weekend.

'So we can talk about your trip,' she added hastily.

Sam could not have been more delighted. Cas didn't know if it was the right thing to do, but frankly she needed the company.

'Another drink?' asked Sam, eager for more of her.

'Sam, I've got to shoot. You are not going to believe this, but I've got to write up the social diary of Charlotte Want and Eating Healthily with Silvio Ravelli.'

'Your job kills me,' responded Sam, shaking his head.

## chapter eighteen

Victor Power settled back into the deep seat of his chauffeur-driven Bentley. He let out a long sigh, smoothed back his oiled hair with his hand and fixed his gaze out of the passenger window, cradling his chin in his palm. In front of him, in the lamp light reflecting off the falling rain and puddles, the crowded streets of south London unfolded, each shop window a bright picture of the life within. A Chicken Express, a late-opening hardware store, a pub, a Pricecheck, an off-licence, all of them box-like havens from the life on the street outside. By every cashpoint sat a beggar, some covered by a thin blanket against the cold of the evening, some clinging to the dogs that were their only companions and friends. Most who passed the beggars pretended they weren't there, none ever gave from the wad they collected at the hole in the wall. Their cupped hands remained empty, their scribbled signs 'Hungry and homeless' were ignored. On a street corner a gang of teenage boys, dressed in the regulation tracksuits and trainers of their favoured brands, loitered, looking mean, knowing nothing. A group of lads on their way to football chucked a ball about, two girls hurrying along under a brolly vainly attempted to keep their ironed hair dry. The wind picked up and whipped the rain; their brolly turned inside out.

The Bentley passed deeper into the boroughs, drawing admiring glances from the pedestrians on the streets. It passed under railway arches, smoothly rolled past the card-board-box dwellers, most living from one fix to the next, all resigned from hope a long, long time ago. Two older, bearded men were engaged in a fight, neither one wanting to let go of their cans of Tennants Extra, stumbling about drunkenly as they tried to land a blow. A woman, her hair matted and her clothes torn was screaming after them, the spittle arcing from her mouth.

Victor Power shut his eyes and tried not to remember. Folding his hands together he rubbed the heavy gold signet ring he wore on his little finger, he felt the smooth expensive material of his trousers, he let his hand drop on to the reassuring leather of the car seat. All still there.

He opened his eyes. The car had stopped at some traffic lights on a dark street. Beside him a woman bent down to the window to look in at his face. You could see she was still young, perhaps still in her teens, but she looked much older, the pasty whiteness of her face and the red rings around her eyes giving away her vicious game of drugs and prostitution. She wore nothing on her legs, which were clenched tight together in the cold and rain. Her feet were perched precariously in open-toed platformed high heels.

Her skirt was barely longer than a belt and an outsized dirty anorak was her only protection against the night. As she bent down, she let the anorak fall open to reveal her tired cleavage and rapped on his window pane with her chewed hand. She was saying something – he couldn't hear through the pane of the glass, but he knew what it was and he shook his head slowly, turning away to stare at the head rest of the driver's seat. The woman wandered off and the car pulled away. All over London, all over the country, he thought, a thousand women like this were making their living, serving a need. Some in better conditions than others. None as well off as his girls.

He picked up a paper from the seat beside him and glanced, bored, over the umpteenth 'business profile' on him. They had nothing new, none of them did, and he didn't understand the attraction. Why were they all so interested? They were gunning for him – viciously – and it angered him, not because it wasn't within their rights but because their motives were so dishonest. Every time they mentioned his name they called him a pornographer, not a business-man. What did it matter what the nature of his business was? Every time they mentioned his publications the names were preceded with the adjectives 'seedy', 'dirty', 'grubby' – just like they were themselves, he thought. Nothing had been more hypocritical than the salaciousness with which they had, in vast detail, reproduced the content of his pub-lications, letting their readers savour it while tut-tutting at it at the same time. It was amusing, he noted wryly to himself, that sales of his magazines had gone up, thanks to all the free publicity. What was the difference between the pictures in his magazines and the Page Three girls? What was the difference between *Hiya!*'s content and the life stories of the Hollywood stars who graced their supplement covers? Give a newspaper a good picture of Tom Cruise and his latest girlfriend, or even Charlotte Want and her footballer boyfriend, and it's straight on all the front pages, World War Three or not. Hypocrites, that's what they were – hypocrites. Well, he would show them. He would outsell them eventually, he at least was honest about what his readers wanted. He had a proven success record, and there was no reason why the *Daily News* should be any different.

The flurry of bad press must have been instrumental in his being ignored by the ruling establishment. He had been expecting seminars at Downing Street, consultations with cabinet ministers, meetings with decision-making committees – at the very least an invitation to a Buckingham Palace reception. But nothing. Worse, he was still blackballed from the clubs that extended membership to all the other newspaper proprietors. More than ever, Power found himself isolated outside the circle of movers and shakers that mattered. He shook his head and stifled a growl in his throat as the fury rose in him again. The impossible British establishment, would he never be accepted? What was so wrong with him? Well, he would show them, he resolved, the more they pushed him away the more he would fight. He would become such a powerful figure that in the end they would be reduced to coming to him. And it would begin with this party.

His phone rang. It was Pitts sounding nervous. More bad news. Someone had been asking questions about his accounts and the Inland Revenue wanted to know more. Who were these pesky journalists? As a result of all this invasive coverage he had had to offer large chunks of his empire up for sale, in an effort to claim the respectability all the others believed they spoke with. He had been made to understand that it was the paper or the pornography, one or the other. And this from an industry that had invented the Page Three girl.

But what irritated him most, what really made him angry was the personal detail. His own staff had clearly been briefing other papers on the way he behaved at work, on the things he said. How dare they? He paid their wages, didn't he? Who did they think they were working for? He was used to absolute loyalty. This informing was not acceptable and he wanted as many of them fired as quickly as was decent, so he could replace them with his own people. As for that ridiculous leftie feminist who was cling-ing onto her editorship, he had to get rid of her as soon as possible. She was only hanging around for a pay-off, he knew that, but he'd break her first, force her to resign before she was pushed. Didn't she know when she was not wanted?

At last, the limousine slid through the gates of his home, his beautiful, dream mansion, that had taken him almost three years to build. Every time he saw it he could not resist a smile at the grand Roman columns on either side of the front door, the statue of Eros fountain in the front drive, the gold twisted door knobs, the manicured lawns, the box hedges. As English and as upwardly mobile as it got. He smirked. Screw them all – he had what he wanted!

As he strode in through the front door and handed his coat to the butler, Winifred was making her way down the sweeping gold staircase.

'Mr Power! How are you? You are late. I've asked the cook to keep some supper back for you. I hope you are not too tired?'

He grinned at her. She was the perfect wife, so attentive and caring (perhaps more of a mother than a wife – how good was that?). Now there was loyalty for you.

'Just some business I had to attend to, my dear. I am tired, so I am going to bed, but do ask the cook to send me up some dinner. I'm afraid I'm going to be late again tomorrow night, I've got some people to visit in town.'

'Yes, I saw that in your appointments diary Mr Power – down at the Berkeley Strip Club. You *will* be late.'

'I know. I'm sorry. We haven't had dinner together in ages, but I shall see you in the morning. Shall we ride in to work together?'

'That would be lovely Mr Power. I was just going to catch the end of *Midsomer Murders* then turn in myself. I shall talk to the cook straight away.' And with that she bustled off down the corridor. Power flicked through his post – nothing interesting – and strolled into the library, where his stock of precious cigars was kept in the walk-in humidor. He picked out a Cohiba no.3, and sitting back in his armchair cut off the end, braced a match against its box, placed the brown stub in his mouth and puffed gently till it was lit. He let his mouth fill with the earthy flavoured smoke, shut his eyes, and blew it out in quivering smoke rings towards the fireplace. He opened his eyes, and watched the grey circles drift up in front of the full-length portrait of himself that hung over the mantelpiece.

Upstairs, John Nettles having once again saved a Cotswold village from another serial killer, Winifred Power flicked off the television and began to ready herself for bed. First she unfastened the cameo brooch her mother had given her from her collar, and carefully placed it in its box in her meagre jewellery chest. Then she began to unbutton her high-necked silk chemise, her fingers struggling slightly with the tightness of the buttonholes, pulling out the paper hankies she kept up her sleeve and dropping them in the wastepaper basket. She sat down on the floral quilted eiderdown of her overly large bed ('But I'll get lost in that, Mr Power!'), and kicked off her sensible navy-blue court shoes. Padding across the shag pile carpet ('Honestly, so luxurious!') in her stockinged feet, she opened her fitted wardrobe and drew out a pair of shoe horns. She stretched them in her court shoes and tidied them away in her shoe cupboard. Then she wandered into her en suite rose-pink bathroom and turned on the gold taps of her outsize bath ('I'll drown in that if I'm not careful!'). She picked up her Boots Oil of Evening Primrose bath foam and measured half a capful into the running water.

Outside her bedroom, along the plush, red-carpeted corridor, down the sweeping spiral staircase to the grand chandeliered entrance hall of Power's residence, the faint tinkle of female laughter could be heard, even from the mansion's west wing.

On the opposite side of the mansion, Victor Power was also readying himself for bed. A pair of red-taloned hands were unbuttoning his shirt for him in the purple suite of his bedroom quarters as he lay back on a leopardskin-draped couch. Silk cushions propped up his head, and across the room, a huge black marble jacuzzi was already bubbling away in readiness, the oils poured into its waters filling the room with a heady scent. Power savoured the last few puffs on his Cohiba as he allowed himself to be made ready for his bath.

Winifred crossed from the bed into her bathroom once again and tested the water in the bath. Perfect. She turned off the taps and began to unbutton the tight fastenings on her tweed skirt. Dear, dear, she seemed to have put on a little weight recently, she admonished herself quietly, and thought how she really must cut out her afternoon cream bun. Then she undid the zip, and with some difficulty stepped out of it, she was beginning to detect a little stiffness in her hips in her old age. Shrugging off her shirt she revealed a terrifyingly complicated set of underwear: a wartime series of hooks and eyes, straps and girdles, belts and buckles that even the most ardent of lovers might have balked at. Corsets, girdles, brassieres and control pants, all in a particularly unattractive shade of faded 'nude' kept the shape of her body in check. Reaching under her sink she pulled out a bag of rollers and deftly began to roll them into her hair with expert fingers.

Thirty metres away her husband was having his scalp massaged with hair oil, his skin lathered in cocoa butter and every muscle in his toned body was being gently squeezed and pummelled by the soothing fingers of his attendant.

'What time is it?' asked Power of his 'maid'.

'It's exactly ten to eleven, sir,' she replied huskily.

'Time for me to phone my wife, then. Please pass the telephone.'

On the other side of the mansion, Mrs Power's extension began to buzz. She glanced across at her bedside alarm clock and noted it was exactly ten to eleven. A little smile of contentment spread across her face. He was so reliable, her husband, so thoughtful in his little rituals.

Shuffling across the room, a trail of yellowing pantyhose falling behind her, she picked up the receiver of the phone.

'Yes?' she asked with thrilled expectancy.

'Mrs Power? It's Mr Power wishing you good night.'

'Oh,' she exclaimed, as if pleasantly taken aback by the intrusion. 'Mr Power. A very good night to you too.'

'Sleep well, my dear.'

'Thank you, and you.'

With that Winifred placed the receiver back in its cradle, allowed herself a smug feeling of security and flattery, and returned to the bathroom for her final ablutions before bed.

To suggest that Winifred Power did not know there were other women present in her husband's bedchamber was ridiculous: of course she knew her husband had attendants. If you could afford them, then they were a wonderful help in life. She had three herself, that Power had provided her with when they married: a chauffeur, a butler and a hairdresser. Such luxury!

And of course Mrs Power also knew that their marriage was very convenient to her husband, in fact she was rather proud that she lent him an air of respectability and allowed him a share of the moral high ground. As for what he provided her with, where should she start? Her quality of life now was far beyond any expectations she might have had, even in her youth. The little nest egg she had been building for herself seemed quite redundant now, but she had had such fun building it, she didn't see any reason to stop. 'You can't be too careful!' her mother had often told her, and Winifred saw no reason not to believe her. She had been given all these blessings so suddenly and she was going to enjoy them while she could – you never knew when they were going to be taken away again.

Of course Mrs Power was aware there had been quite a lot of tittle-tattle recently about the nature of her husband's business dealings, but she was quite able to turn a blind eye to this sort of frivolous gossip. Mr Power had warned her that the newspaper business was pretty ruthless, but it was nothing she wasn't strong enough to deal with.

After all, in her years of working for Mr Power she had seen a lot worse. All that nonsense in his magazines – why, it was just ridiculous 'boys' things' that she occasionally had the misfortune to glance at. Male sexuality had always been a mystery to Winifred, and she was quite determined that it should remain so. Different strokes for different folks. it certainly wasn't anything a self-respecting woman of her standing needed to understand.

Winifred pulled a stiff, starched nightie over her head, rubbed a little talcum powder on to her arms, and screwed two pieces of cotton wool tightly into her ears (the habit of a lifetime spent enduring her mother's snoring) then pulled back the cover of her bed. No, thought Mrs Power, there was nothing she could possibly question in this arrangement with her husband: in fact she could only congratulate herself on its marvels.

# chapter nineteen

Toby sat quietly on his bed with the windows closed and the curtains drawn, in complete darkness but for the sliver of grey light that squeezed itself through the gap in the curtains from outside. He was perfectly still except for his fingers that worked themselves over the shape in front of him, feeling urgently for the turns and the folds of the metal. It didn't matter that he couldn't see, he could feel and in his hands it seemed the piece was finally coming together. A twist here, something smoother there, maybe some more volume on this curve: his woman was beginning to take shape. Except now she was Woman with Child. The piece was bigger than he had originally conceived, in fact she was growing by the day, but her form, moulded by his mind, his spirit and his hands, had an organic shape to it. It was almost as if Toby had no control over it. He was excited; he knew already that it was going to be the finest work he had yet managed to complete. He didn't need to see it, he could feel it, and he liked to be able to visualize it in this half light and imagine its shape throwing strange shadows out across the room. It was extraordinary to at last be part of that instinctive creative process he had been taught about, had read about in the biographies of the masters. The process had quite suddenly seized him and his work, had reduced him to a fever of creativity. He was now sleeping with the piece by his bed and working on it in every waking moment; living with it.

His mother had given up knocking only to be ignored, and now she just left a tray of food outside his door that he sometimes ate, sometimes not. He would not take phone calls either, Emily just took down messages which she left on his tray and which he didn't return. Cas had called a few times, but Toby, it seemed, wasn't interested in talking to anyone at the moment, not even to her.

In his hands the metal felt so soft, hot even, to his touch. The material seemed to be responding so well to his handling, it was almost as if he didn't need his tools. It was because he was listening to it, he knew, trying to anticipate which direction it wanted to go, which direction the 'grain' of the metal flowed. All he cared about now was this piece – in this room it was just him and his work, which was all he wanted. Too much lay beyond his bedroom door. The only thing he knew for certain any more was that he had to finish this piece, until that was done he need not address anything of the horrors so recently related to him. All his emotional energy was being channelled into his work right now, and that suited him fine.

\*

Outside, his mother's heart was breaking, but she had known this moment would come. As she waited patiently for her son to appear, to grapple with the truth he had just been told, she consoled herself that even if he never forgave her, then at least this emancipation of her secret was a relief. At last it was out, the burden that had weighed on her and her marriage for all of Toby's life.

She waited. Toby needed time whereas she had had too much time waiting for this moment.

Toby was not to know, but back in London Cosima Beane had been rather successful on his behalf. Following his phone call when he had told her, rather sheepishly, that he would be happy for her to represent him, Cosima had managed to strike it lucky for him. She had touted his name and his story about, dangled it in front of a few buyers, slipped it in over lunch, surreptitiously dropped it among a few collectors, and now she felt she had enough of a buzz going to make their first sale. But to who? Whoever it was, they had to be high profile. The first buyer was always crucial.

Then one day the Actress Model Whatever, Cosima's favourite type of person, Charlotte Want, dropped into her showroom, just when Cosima had been musing on this particular subject and Cosima could not help thinking that Charlotte would be just right. She would be bound to boast about any piece she bought to *Hiya!* magazine, generating some crucial publicity. Cosima immediately resolved to woo her with a charm offensive, but she need not have worried because the two women hit it off immediately. Both had read about the other in the gossip columns for months now, so within seconds of clapping eyes on each other they felt they understood each other perfectly, sharing the rapport of fame that only true celebrities know about.

'Oh! Fantastic coat, darling! Is it Marc Jacobs? Or Vuitton? It looks quite sensational on you!'

'Love the blindfold, Cosima. I think I might have to steal that look for my video. Do you mind?'

Charlotte's progress in the recording studio had been halted altogether when it was decided that her voice was probably not quite up to carrying the song that had been written for her. Once they had streamed her warblings through various tuning machines it was almost unrecognizable as her own, so the record company had decided to cut their losses and just produce her voice electronically. As far as Charlotte was concerned, image was all, and just as long as she was consulted on her 'look' for her return as a pop star, then that was fine by her. She wouldn't be the first pop star to make it who couldn't sing.

And so all that remained for Charlotte to do was choose her outfit and learn the dance routine. The former was providing her with much diversion (and the stylists for the record company with quite an ordeal as she kept changing her mind, 'That's because fashion moves so quickly, darling.'), and the latter was providing her with much frustration. She was now being forced into five-hour rehearsals every day in the hope that she might just remember the moves in the right order in time for her song's debut. The video, it had been decided behind Charlotte's back, was not going to contain any dancing – at least by Charlotte. Pouting, it had been decided, was what Charlotte was best at, and this was all the video director was prepared to work with her on.

Luckily, her rehearsals still afforded her just enough time in the day to go shopping. While out perusing the goodies of New Bond Street one day, looking for further inspiration for her image or for something arresting to join the spectrum of outfits she was planning for Power's forthcoming party, Charlotte had passed the Beane Gallery and had decided to pop in to see what all the fuss was about. She had not been disappointed, even if she had been slightly miffed to have missed the last penis (sold to Sting only an hour ago) because Cosima, dressed in a Lacroix velour jumpsuit and lace eye mask, had been there herself and had seemed more than delighted to personally show her around the gallery. She had been particularly effusive about a set of canvases that she told Charlotte she was the first to view. Charlotte felt very pleased about this, which went some way to making up for missing the celebrated phalli. She was not, however, as taken with them as Cosima appeared to be, as far as she could see they were completely empty. According to Cosima however, each had taken months to produce. Vast, white rectangles ('Obviously they'll only hang in your home if it's enormous, so they're not for everyone – just those who can afford the wall space.') they were supposedly imprinted with the genuine footprints of one of the last remaining nomadic Namibian desert tribes. Apparently it had been hell keeping the sand out of the wet paint, but the artist, Nobodishu Mbubu, had managed it, and for this feat the prospective owner could expect to pay £325,000 a pop. Charlotte nodded reverentially at such wonderfully conspicuous consumption, but not even she could stretch that far. Yet.

She had already spent too long hearing about the talents of this other artist, so she wasted no further time in sharing with Cosima the release date of her forthcoming single, and was most insistent Cosima come along to the launch party ('perhaps we could display some of your work on the set?'). She was to perform (well, mime) the song for the first time at the *Hiya!/Daily News* party, and had telephoned Victor to put Cosima on the invitation list right there and then.

'Darling, it's absolutely going to be *the* place to be seen that night – Madonna and Guy have confirmed, Nicole and Liam are a definite and Charlie Dimmock is doing the plants.'

'Oh, what a ball!' replied Cosima, 'I'd lurve to come!'

After several sips of some very strange imported herbal tea concoction ('It's ayurvedic, darling. Believe me its tremendous for us pitta-kappas.') and some ostentatious gossip swapping, Charlotte had been utterly convinced by Cosima that she needed to invest in some art immediately if she had any hope of being taken seriously in London.

'I mean, you've gotta have something to talk about at all these drinks parties.'

'Well as it happens I'm actually in the process of buying

a flat – I mean house – in London. It is going to be very minimalist, with big, white walls, but I need something of a centrepiece. Have you seen my Manchester penthouse in *Hiya!*? I really want to copy that look, you know, but as this place is going to be bigger, it will need some sort of focus. That's what my feng shui master says, anyway.'

Cosima tried every single piece in the gallery on her, but after two hours of hard sell, nothing had seemed to quite grab Charlotte.

'Listen, honey,' persevered Cosima, who absolutely would not countenance letting a customer who she had invested this much time and gossip in to leave without depositing a sizeable cheque in her till, 'I've got a great idea: why don't you commission something?'

'Commission something?' replied Charlotte blankly.

'Yeah, you know, get someone to make something especially for you,' she explained. She paused, looked conspiratorially around her, and leaned closer to Charlotte and employed the tried and tested technique of the most successful salespersons. 'Can you keep a secret?' she stage-whispered.

'Of course!' replied Charlotte in matching conspiratorial manner.

'Well, I've got this great young artist up my sleeve. He is *very* up and coming, and very, ah, attractive, if you know what I mean.' Cosima let a lewd expression pass across her face, fully aware of Charlotte's reputation as something of a man-eater. 'By the time I've launched him, I'm telling you, he's gonna be huge. HUGE! You know what I'm saying?'

Cosima was now talking exactly the language Charlotte understood. 'Really? What does he look like? How huge?'

'Cute, real cute, kind of tall and dark and English, very English. He's got this great story behind him: he's aristocratic, you see, got a double-barrelled surname and a great big stately home in the country, but his grandmother had it away with all the maharajas during the Raj so he's got all this regal Indian blood in him. Considered to be something of an embarrassment, obviously, for these English types, but you've gotta admit: the story's mesmerizing!' Charlotte, at least, was mesmerized by now. 'Really shows in his work and also gives him *the* most exquisitely beautiful aquiline nose. You – everyone – will die for him when you see him. He's such a hunk. But he's my little secret for the moment.'

'Oh!' squealed Charlotte, who immediately saw a way out of the Silvio problem. 'Can I meet him?'

'I've got a better idea than that.' Cosima grinned, she definitely had the size of her subject by now, 'why don't you sit for him?'

'Sit for him?'

'Sure, he's a sculptor. He could do your bust.'

And that absolutely swung it for Charlotte Want.

## chapter twenty

Cas sat alone in the newspaper library. The lights had been turned off for the night and, but for the illumination of the screen in front of her casting a bluish haze over her face, she was in complete darkness. The librarians had long since gone home and the night cleaners had emptied all the bins and wiped all the desks, only the lingering scent of their enthusiastic chain smoking remained.

The clock in the corner ticked on noisily to half past ten, the progress of its second hand the only movement in the room. It would be almost eight in the morning now in Nauru, thought Cas idly, and Sam would be just arriving. She prayed he would find something, and that she too would be able to find something tonight as well. If anything Cas's task was more risky than Sam's, at least he wasn't working undercover. It had been a long time since Cas had done anything like this and she was understandably nervous. Victor Power did not look like the sort of man you would want to be caught with in a dark room alone, late at night. Cas shuddered involuntarily at the thought, and tried to calm herself.

Jerry, the security guard Cas knew best, was taking this evening's shift, but he knocked off at midnight. She had to do it soon or she would have to risk the surveillance of a night porter she did not know. Breathing deeply, she ran through her plan once again, nodded to herself, then logged off the computer and walked down the stairs to the lobby.

Fortunately, when working late she had quite often joined Jerry in his tiny office for a cup of tea, and it was this ritual she was now going to take advantage of. She paused outside the lift to buy two cups from the vending machine. Good – her hands weren't shaking. Calmly, she made her way over to Jerry's desk and greeted him with what she hoped was her usual breeziness. As the words fell from her lips her voice sounded distended, as if it was coming from someone else's mouth, but Jerry did not seem to notice. He looked up from his crossword and smiled.

'Aw, working late again, love?' he said sympathetically.

''Fraid so – brought you a cuppa though.'

'Lovely! You *are* a good girl.' Jerry relished the ministrations Cas bestowed on him. His job could be lonely at the best of times, and in the still hours of the night, with no interruptions, the time could pass painfully slowly. But it was work, as he had said, over and over again for years, and you couldn't complain about that.

Cas pushed open the door to his office and tried not to

let her eyes linger on the sets of keys above his head. 'I'm such an idiot, Jerry,' she heard herself say. 'I've left my bag in Tamara's office – I couldn't borrow the spare key could I?'

'Sure, love. Here you go.'

She watched Jerry reach behind him to find the key and used the moment his back was turned to scan the labels above the hooks – there it was, 'Penthouse Office', bottom right. He turned back to her with Tamara's key and she put one cup down on the desk to take it, smiling her thanks. Carefully, she positioned herself next to him, under the rack of keys and made to perch on the counter. As she did so she let the other cup slip from her fingers and watched as it spilled its contents all over the floor.

'Damn!' she exclaimed, 'I'm so clumsy!' and in the ensuing confusion, as poor, arthritic Jerry bent down to tut tut over the upended tea, Cas swiftly switched Tamara's key for Power's. Struggling with his stiff knees as he retrieved the empty cup, Jerry saw nothing.

With Power's key now in the palm of her hand, the adrenaline surged through Cas's body. Her success was tinged with guilt at the way she had duped her friend Jerry, but she consoled herself by reasoning that he would be none the wiser – no one would notice the keys were on the wrong hooks until a spare was next needed, and that might not be for several weeks. And, after all, she told herself, the deception was all in a good cause, wasn't it?

Apologizing profusely Cas mopped up the rest of the tea and went off to 'get another cup and retrieve her bag'.

Round the corner she let the mask slip from her face and breathed deeply. Her heart was pounding against her chest in excitement, fear and triumph. The lift doors opened and she pressed the button for the top floor. As the cabin made its progress up the lift shaft she told her heart to be still, she needed a clear mind for this. The doors opened: all was quiet and dark. Before she got out, she sent the lift back down to Tamara's floor, just in case Jerry, or anyone else, should notice.

Quietly, she made her way along the corridor, past the executive suites and boardrooms to the far end and the large office that overlooked the river. Shafts of light came through the windows, casting long shadows from the furniture. As her eyes grew accustomed to the light she could see the torch in her pocket was not going to be necessary. In London it was never truly dark.

Outside Power's office sat Mrs Power's desk, a sentry guard to the secrets of her husband's workplace. Cas looked around her, unnecessarily checking she was still alone, then drew out the key, fitted it into the lock and turned it. The catch gave way excruciatingly noisily and Cas winced, then she pushed down the handle and slipped inside. Suddenly the full realization of what she was doing came home to her: trespassing, snooping, breaking and entering. It was illegal, she could be sacked and, worse, arrested for this. What was she doing? Calm, she told herself, calm: it's for the right reasons. Just pretend it's school, this is the headmistress's office, you are just poking around, having fun. She swallowed and efficiency took over. Cas wanted to be out of there as soon as possible, and she made her way over to Power's desk to begin the search.

On top of the desk there was nothing but his computer, a blotter and a cup of pens; it was pointless trying to log on to his computer, she had decided beforehand, he would have a password. So she tried the drawers on his desks: the top one was full of stationery, she shut it and moved down. The next contained what looked like accounts for each of his magazines: she scanned the names of creditors and debtors, looking everywhere for the word Rapture. Leaf after leaf of paper she looked through, replacing each carefully where she had found it. Nothing. The next drawer contained sheafs of itemized bills, the next memos and personal letters. She had to read quickly but nowhere could she see a familiar reference. Shutting the bottom drawer, she looked up at the filing cabinet in the corner of the office. She pulled out the top drawer and read the tags: names of the magazines, of employees, photo files of models, invoices. The next appeared to be dedicated to *Hiya!*: each celebrity had a file and in each were copies of correspondence. Fascinating reading, thought Cas, but not what she was looking for. In this sea of paper, it was like looking for a Smith in the phone directory.

She swore at herself. She had no idea how long she had been in the office but it seemed an eternity. She glanced up at the clock above Power's desk – nearly eleven. She had to find something, she hadn't risked this much to come away empty handed. She looked around, scanning the tops of the surfaces, the bookshelves and the magazine racks. If he had some sort of illegal business going, he wouldn't leave papers lying around the office, would he? What about his secretary?

Cas moved out of the office and inspected Mrs Power's immaculate desk. A row of newly sharpened pencils, In and Out filing trays: she flicked through the contents, it was mostly correspondence, but no mention of Rapture. She opened the top drawer. More paper, then tried the ones underneath it: the same. But the bottom drawer, she noticed, was unusually cluttered, not neat and tidy like the others. Spare batteries, a tape machine, some handkerchiefs. The drawer was deeper than the others, and feeling to the back, she touched something. It was a video tape. Pulling it out, she turned it over in her hand. Scribbled on the side was a reference number and next to it the word 'edengirls'. Cas's heart skipped a beat. She could hardly believe what she was holding. If this had anything to do with the eden-girls website then she had the evidence, it had to be.

Her elation was short lived. Within seconds of her finding the tape the lift at the bottom of the corridor pinged and she heard the unmistakable heave of the doors opening. Quickly, Cas replaced the video tape and silently slid the drawer shut. Power's office door was still open, she grabbed the handle, pulled it shut as quietly as she could, but she fumbled the key and there was no time to lock it. Where was she going to hide? Opposite Power's office was a waiting room, the door was open and she dived inside, just as she heard the soft pad of steps making their way down the corridor carpet.

Inside, she pressed her back against the wall behind the door, her heart was in her mouth, the key in her hand. Slowly she turned her head and through the crack in the hinge of the door she glanced out. Had she given her presence away? What had she left unstraightened? Someone flicked on the lights and the sudden illumination made Cas squint. The scene of her crime was now bathed in light. She looked again through the hinge but could not see who it was. She could hear someone moving around: the movements were measured, gentle. They didn't sound like those of a man. Who could possibly be up here at this time of night? If it was Power he would find his office unlocked. Then what? Cas didn't even want to imagine it. It could be a cleaner, or perhaps Jerry. All she could see was the cheese plant in the corner of the room. Carefully she pushed the door open a fraction, revealing Winifred Power's desk – and its owner sitting in the chair. With her head bent down and her half moon glasses balanced on the end of her nose Mrs Power appeared to be looking through some papers. She switched on her computer and began to type. Something was printing out now, Cas could hear the whirr of the printer, and Mrs Power got up to collect the paper from it.

Cas was curious. What was she doing in the office so late? Had she forgotten something? Had she and her husband been out entertaining and she had stopped on the way home? Cas watched her sit down again in her chair. She opened the bottom drawer of her desk and drew out the tape, Cas held her breath. To her horror, Winifred Power slipped the tape into her handbag, picked up the papers from her desk, shut the drawer and turned her computer off. She stood up. Please don't go into your husband's office, Cas willed her, don't find it unlocked! But the elderly lady had moved towards the light switch, for suddenly darkness prevailed again and Cas heard her walking back down the corridor.

Cas remained pressed against the wall in the waiting room breathing hard, for what seemed like an eternity. She could not risk Winifred Power coming back and she wanted her well clear of the building before she tried to move. But beyond the nervousness and the relief at not being caught, Cas was furious. She had possibly had the evidence they needed in her hand and now it was gone. But at least, she consoled herself, there appeared to be a link. For the first time Cas had seen the firmest piece of evidence yet that Power Publishing was involved in something it shouldn't be. As she left the building, her bag swinging on her shoulder and the keys returned to Jerry, she finally felt her investigation was justified.

The next morning Cas sat at her desk as if butter wouldn't melt in her mouth. She felt vindicated: she had been right all along, Power was a man entirely unsuited to running a national newspaper. But with this knowledge on board, she also realized the supreme danger of being employed by the man while working against him. It was imperative then, that he did not suspect a thing. So, she arrived neither early nor late, dressed as nondescriptly as she could, changing out of her black polo neck and black trousers after she looked in the mirror and decided she looked like a burglar.

She had phoned Sam in Nauru the night before, almost as soon as she had left the building. Like her, he had been devastated she hadn't managed to keep the tape. But, they consoled themselves: five minutes earlier and she would have run into Winifred Power in the lift, five minutes later and she would not have found the tape at all.

Now they knew they weren't looking in the wrong place, they just had to find the proof. Sam was busy tracking down every company with the name Rapture in the title to see if any had links to Power Publishing. It would just take time, thought Cas, before they found it.

Tamara, she noticed, had made a special sartorial effort this morning: her suit looked expensive and the neckline of her blouse was low, the lipstick bright, the heels agonizingly high. It didn't take long to work out why: today was the day of the Want/Ravelli visit.

Most of the newspaper staff faked boredom, but there was a palpable air of excitement about the office. No matter how insignificant a couple they were, there was always something god-like in the anticipation of meeting the famous. Sally, Tamara's PA, could hardly contain herself – she had pictures of Silvio Ravelli stuck all over her computer and had spent the morning carefully dismantling them to save herself embarrassment, but she did have her United shirt at the ready for him to sign. Cas flicked through a magazine until she found a picture of Charlotte in a Wella advert and gave it to Sally for

Charlotte to sign as well, thinking it might be politic to make Charlotte feel famous too. As for Cas herself, she caught herself applying a little more make-up in the ladies'. Was she really looking forward to the attentions of Silvio Ravelli again?

Needless to say, the couple turned up at the paper with more pomp and circumstance than even Victor Power. Dressed in a tiny neckerchief tied around her chest, skintight Dolce and Gabbana jeans and a pair of wrap-around sunglasses despite the pouring rain outside, Charlotte stalked in majestically, a weary-looking Ravelli trailing behind her, still in his tracksuit. Power greeted them as if they were his long-lost children (although Cas saw Silvio wince at Power's touch), then began to guide them around the office, showing off his paper and introducing them to department heads who were expected to bow and scrape. He asked the sports editor in front of Ravelli why he had savaged Ravelli's play on Saturday.

'Because it was not good,' quietly cut in Ravelli, saving the sports editor a gruesome moment.

Charlotte smiled down beatifically on those she met, while Ravelli looked at his shoes and mumbled. It was clear he was finding the experience excruciating. They were finally brought round to the magazine, and handed over to Tamara, who fell over herself with unctuousness.

'Soo fantastic you are going to write for us . . . highly privileged . . . dying to hear what you are going to say . . . ' etc. etc.

Cas thought she was going to be sick, then remembered

the picture of Ravelli throwing up as he left the Cosmo bar a couple of weeks ago and smiled to herself.

'What's so funny, Caris?' Tamara asked sweetly for the benefit of her guests, an innocent smile puncturing her normally shrew-like face as she led Charlotte and Silvio round her empire.

'Oh, nothing,' said Cas. 'Just something I was reading.' She stood up and stretched out her hand. 'Hi, Charlotte, nice to see you again. Silvio, hello.'

Cas tried not to look directly at Silvio but the freezing glower she was getting from Charlotte forced her to redirect her gaze towards him. For the first time, Silvio looked as if he didn't want to be a million miles away and, beaming at her, he wished Cas a very pleasant hello. Tamara looked somewhat put out at the overt friendliness of the up till now sullen Ravelli, and Charlotte looked like she wanted to stick pins in Cas's eyes. Thankfully, Silvio did not say any more and Cas swiftly sat down and returned to her work. Silvio, she reminded herself, was the one other person in this building who knew what she was up to and she did not want to risk him giving anything away.

As they walked on, Tamara laughing a little too much and a little too loudly, Cas peered after them, and found Silvio looking back at her too. She smiled and he smiled back. Rather a cute smile, really.

At that moment an email popped up on her screen. She opened it. Christ! It was from Power! Or rather, Mrs Power, asking her to go upstairs to Power's office immediately. Cas went hot then cold then hot again – what was this about? She couldn't have been spotted last night could she? Wildly, she tried to imagine another reason for the summons but as she had barely exchanged two words with the man since he had arrived, she found it difficult. It couldn't be about last night though, she had definitely not been seen.

Her heart beating loudly, and in a state of panic and confusion, Cas tried to persuade herself it was something to do with work. Trembling, she picked up a pen and a notepad, and hurried upstairs. Mrs Power was in her seat, exactly as she had been last night, but this time she was looking very stern.

'Hi!' began Cas nervously, trying to be casual.

'Go straight in, please,' Mrs Power ordered her curtly.

Power was scribbling something on a bit of paper as she entered his office, the very same one she had been nosing around in last night. This was far too close for comfort, she thought. Power ignored her knock so she shuffled across the room and stood in front of his desk. He continued to ignore her. His oiled head was bent over his blotter, his manicured hands gripped a fountain pen. Cas could smell his aftershave, pomade, whatever it was, and she felt nauseous and dizzy. Her heart was thumping so loudly in her chest she thought he must hear it, but still he didn't look up. She kept repeating to herself: he cannot know, he cannot know, stay calm, but already her knees were beginning to go weak. In front of her all she could see was the slicked-back dark hair, the broad shoulders of his dark-grey jacket harbouring the odd fleck of dandruff (despite

Fagge's best efforts) and his great hairy wrists struggling to burst out of the arms of his suit.

Finally he looked up. Cas nearly gasped out loud. His face was twisted into a snarl, his eyes were full of contempt and by the flushed colour of his skin Cas realized that he was very angry indeed. He must know, she thought. Then: I'll deny everything. The thought that Silvio may have said something to him crossed her mind and she kicked herself for telling him anything. Power continued to glare at her, taking in every detail but saying nothing.

'Er . . .' mumbled Cas, trying to break the terrible silence.

'Don't you speak until I've spoken to you!' he hissed, his voice quiet, but with a terrifying glacial edge to it. Cas shifted uncomfortably in front of him. Her legs were now trembling, the blood was pounding in her ears. Suddenly she just wanted him to put her out of her misery and get on with it – if not she thought she might faint.

He continued to stare at her to the point where Cas did not know where to look. Finally, after what seemed like hours, he opened the top drawer of his desk, the same one she herself had opened last night, and drew out a piece of paper and placed it between them on the blotter.

He sat back in his chair and gestured at the paper. Slowly, Cas bent over and picked it up from his desk. It was a print-out of an email. It was a print-out of one of her own emails: the email she had received with the eden website address which she had forwarded to the *Guardian*. A lump gathered in Cas's throat so big she thought she would choke. Panic surged through her body, and for a moment she felt light-headed. How had Power managed to track this down?

'Well? What the fuck do you think you're playing at, you stupid little girl?' began Power, his voice quiet, but the menace undeniable.

He waited, but there was nothing she could say. She re-read the email. All she could hope was that this was all he had, at least then he would not know the extent of her disloyalty.

'What kind of behaviour is this? Fuelling a rival newspaper with malicious lies about me?' His voice was getting louder, as if a lid over boiling liquid was about to explode. 'I knew someone had been informing on me from this building, so I had all the telephone lines and emails checked. But I hardly thought someone would want to finger me with this. Do you have any idea what this website does? It's some sort of illegal sex trade. That is a highly serious allegation. And you, whom I pay, out of my own pocket, are tipping off the *Guardian* news desk that it is something I am involved in.'

'It was just an email sent to me –'

'Who from?'

'I don't know, it was anonymous. Look it says no.one@ –'

'I know what it fucking well says. What the fuck do you take me for? Now, who sent it?'

'I honestly don't know!' cried Cas, her voice now pitched high with fear.

'Not good enough!' roared Power, leaping out of his

seat and stalking round the room until he stood directly behind her. 'Try and guess,' he whispered into her ear, the smell of his pomade now overpowering.

Did he really think she would tell him?

'Look, honestly, I really don't know, I'm sorry. If I did know, I would tell you,' lied Cas, stammering, blushing and trembling, hot and cold flushes racing up and down her body. Punishment was coming, she could feel it, but what would it be?

Power stared at her, trying to take her in, incredulous that someone would betray him like this. Seconds passed. He walked round in front of her, standing in the narrow space between her and his desk. He was so close that she could feel his breath on her face. He stared at her, and all Cas could do was shrug her shoulders and open her mouth – but she had no voice to speak with.

Then Power reached out and snatched the email out of her hands, so that she jumped back, startled. He screwed the piece of paper into a ball and threw it across the room.

'Why would you do this?' he asked, his voice now with an uncontrolled tone of madness about it. Cas felt another wave of fear wash over her body.

'I'm . . . I'm sorry. A friend on the *Guardian*, I knew he was doing something so I just passed it –' began Cas, her tongue rushing in panic.

'Not good enough! Thanks to the fucking *Guardian* I have been portrayed in the press as a pornographer rather than a businessman. In order to regain some kind of credibility I am having to sell off half my fucking company!

What do you think that makes me feel about you? It's stupid, malicious gossip like this that makes people think I am some kind of monster and stops me from doing what I want – which is building this paper into some sort of profitable organization!'

Strangely, Cas thought she could hear a hint of pain in his voice at this. Was he faking it?

'Thanks to people like you!' he roared. 'One of my own staff!'

'Oh God!' Cas thought she was about to cry. His voice was filling the room and the air around her seemed thick with violence.

'Wrong! Not even He can help you now! You are sacked, Brown. Out of here. No notice. You have broken your contract by supplying news to a rival paper.' Power pressed a buzzer on his desk. 'Get me security!'

All Cas could think of was that she had to stand in this office for the minutes it would take security to arrive. Power's bulk and anger were filling the room and she started to become afraid that he might attack her, or that she might faint, and she began to look about for somewhere she could run, or for something to hold on to.

'You know, you are very lucky,' he continued, his voice unsteady, 'because if this wasn't a newspaper, I'd do more than sack you – I'd destroy you! In fact, I might do that anyway. Because believe me, Brown, I can – I know people!'

Cas was crying now. She could feel the tears burning on her hot cheeks. She heard a sob and she realized it was hers.

'So if I were you, I would get the fuck out of my life as quickly as possible. Get your fucking coat and if you have any sense you'll make sure I never hear from you and never see you again!' Power was stalking round the room again, his face flushed, working himself up into an even worse rage. 'I can't believe it's you – an idiot girl, who has contributed to the loss of half my business. Thanks to the fucking *Guardian* and its insistence that there is something immoral about some of the more entertaining magazine titles we own. And it's all your fault. Do you hear me? Your fault!'

Behind her Cas heard someone coming in the door. She felt a hand on her arm and turned to see Terry, the day security guard who she said hello to every morning. She looked at him imploringly. Terry looked uncomfortable.

'Now get out of my fucking office, out of my fucking life and take your snivelling, interfering little face a long way from mine. Preferably to another country. And don't think you are going to find other work if I can help it: I will be telling everyone I know in the business about your untrustworthiness and dishonesty. You will never work for anybody who owes me a favour – and believe me there are lots of them!'

Cas was floating down the corridor on Terry's arm as Power was shouting behind her. Terry marched her into the lift where she turned to face the raging animal behind her.

'You have betrayed me!' he shouted shaking his fist, 'and I will not forget it!'

Then the doors closed, and Cas collapsed in tears on Terry's shoulder.

'There, there,' he said kindly, patting her shoulder awkwardly.

Terry took her swiftly down to the magazine office, 'I'm sorry about this, love,' he muttered under his breath. 'But you've got to get your bag and your coat and then I'm under instructions to escort you straight out of the building.'

They marched down the corridor and into the magazine office. The whole room went quiet, and everyone turned to look at Cas's stricken face. Blindly, she stumbled towards her desk and picked up her bag.

'Cas, what's the matter?' asked Chris, who was sitting at the desk next to hers. 'What's going on?'

'I've been sacked,' she said, her voice coming from somewhere distant.

Quick as a flash, Tamara was at the door of her office, Silvio and Charlotte behind her.

'What?' the PBfH exclaimed with undisguised glee.

'I've been sacked,' Cas repeated stunned. Cas couldn't bear to look up but she couldn't help herself. Instead of seeing the triumph all over Tamara's face, she only noticed the shock in Silvio Ravelli's.

'Oh,' said Tamara lightly. 'What for?'

Cas saw Charlotte staring at her and Silvio looking horrified. The words came out: 'For passing information on about Power.'

'What information?'

Cas shook her head and Terry took her by the arm. But this was too interesting for Tamara to let lie. 'Caris!' she shrilled, stomping down the corridor after her, 'what information?'

Cas suddenly felt all her panic and shock turn to anger. This woman, whom she had worked exceedingly hard for for nearly a year now, was so obviously pleased about what had just happened and was making no effort to hide it. She stopped, spun round, looked Tamara straight in the eye, and said, 'Ask your friend, Power.'

Time collapsed. The next thing Cas knew was that she was in the lobby going through the doors, then she was standing in front of the building, leaning on one of its pillars trying to get her breath back. The thought of Power terrified her and she realized she had to get away, so she started to walk. She felt very shaken – light-headed almost, and she stopped for a second to try and gather herself together and take in what had just happened. Looking behind her she saw that she was still in the shadow of the office, if Power looked out of his window, he might even see her, so she started to walk away again – quickly this time.

Pulling her mobile out of her bag, all she could think of doing was phoning Sam, but he was in Nauru and it would be the middle of the night there. But then strangely, at that moment the phone rang.

'Hello?'

'Cas? It's Toby.'

'Oh, Toby!' Cas had never been more pleased to hear his voice. 'Where have you been?'

'Busy. Listen, Cas, I need to talk. Something's happened.' His voice sounded different to Cas, thicker, muffled.

'Oh my God, not you too!'

'What?'

'Nothing – oh, something . . . I mean . . . You're not going to believe this, but I've just been sacked.' As Cas stuttered her way through the story, a long black limousine pulled up to the pavement beside her. She leapt back, thinking it might be Power, but as the window came down, she saw it was Silvio Ravelli.

'Can I talk to you?' he asked, leaning out of the window, the expression on his face unmistakably kind and concerned.

'Um, yeah,' said Cas, completely taken aback. 'Just one moment. Toby? I've got to call you back. I'm so sorry, something's happening here.' Cas hung up her phone. Silvio began to get out of the car. Next to him Charlotte Want was looking like thunder and trying to pull him back by the seat of his trousers. Cas glanced up at the building, they were still in sight of Power's offices.

'Are you all right?' he asked, touching her arm.

'Yes, I think so,' she replied, surprised at his touch. But it was gentle, reassuring.

'I want to help you!'

'Look, you work for Victor Power,' she replied, 'who has just threatened me. I don't think I should even be talking to you.'

'No, listen. I don't work for zis Power. I don't like him. He likes Charlotte. You said somesing about information. What information? Please, tell me.'

Was this a trap? thought Cas.

'I don't know anything for sure, but I'd be careful if I were you. And your girlfriend,' she replied.

'Tell me. Zis man – he has me trapped too, with Charlotte.' Behind Silvio, Charlotte was now hissing his name. Silvio was ignoring her. 'What do you know?'

Cas glanced up and down the road. Silvio did not look like the sort of person to trap her. 'Silvio, I can't help you. The man has built his business on a porn empire, he's got a serious amount of money from somewhere to buy the *News*, and it's not accounted for. You do the maths. Look, you've got my mobile phone number, which will still work. You call me if you want to talk.'

Silvio smiled. 'OK,' he said. 'Thank you. Good luck,' he added, and touched her hair on the side of her face. Despite everything, as his fingers brushed against her cheek, Cas felt her heart do a little skip.

Back up in the *Daily News* offices, Victor Power had stalked off in a fury. Mrs Power had just about got the measure of what had gone on, but Mr Power did not always share everything with her. She gathered there had been some sort of offending email, and she gathered that the content had been on the piece of paper she had watched her husband screw up into a ball and hurl across the office. Well, Mrs Power was ashamed to say, she was rather curious about this email, and consequently was rather tempted to go and retrieve the piece of paper to see what it said. Very tempted. So tempted, in fact, that all of a sudden she found herself wandering into her husband's office, and retrieving the offending ball of paper from the floor. As she unravelled it and read its contents, her lips pursed together until all the blood had drained from them. She looked up and out of the building where she saw the girl who had been sacked talking to Silvio Ravelli outside. Mrs Power was not happy at all about any of this, and a strange look of determination passed across her face.

# chapter twenty-one

Cosima Beane shuffled briskly up the street towards Toby's house. She had had her chauffeur drop her round the corner so she could experience some of the real urban angst such an area had to offer, although she was aware she had better not remain unaccompanied in such a 'risqué' area for longer than was absolutely necessary. Hoxton Street was certainly a far cry from Mayfair. Nevertheless, she was very struck by the rich spectrum of greys such an area had to offer: from saucepan-lid silver to decaying goat's cheese white. It was quite remarkable, she thought, the whole of a colour chart in just one scene. What a juxtaposition that was: the inner city estate Toby now lived on with the Englishman's castle that had once been his home: Old Harold Sweet at the Slade had thought it more than likely that Toby's family had once had a 'seat', as he had called it. Cosima didn't doubt it.

Today, she was dressed in an Issey Miyake architectural tent, in tangerine, cerise and lime green. It was a quite sensational piece, but it was somewhat difficult to walk in. Her hat was also impeding her progress – a sculptural cerise swan she had had custom-made by a rather fashionable New York designer. It kept catching in the breeze and twisting on her head, which was proving very irritating. Cosima generally made it a rule not to venture outside at all, except to step from limousine to red carpet, and that was how she had come always to wear hats. Wind was never usually a factor to be considered, unlike this morning – but then, one had to suffer for one's art.

Unlike Toby Hartley-Brewer, she thought, who was hardly going to suffer for his art at all. After trumpeting his, and Charlotte's, name around the various clubs and bars of London's style crowd, she had now picked up quite a few potential commissions. If Charlotte Want was buying into him, then there were plenty of other people with more money than sense who thought that recommendation enough to follow suit. Besides, the idea of getting him to sculpt a bust of them had gone down very well indeed. She was rather pleased with her idea of using Toby as a tool to appeal to their vanity. As long as he didn't mind knocking up the celebrity busts (she had not yet had a chance to discuss this with him), she could see he was going to make rather a lot of money – as was she. Twenty per cent commission on a £25,000 bust was £5,000. She had Charlotte Want's commission signed and all ready to go. The contract was nestling in her matching Miyake handbag, glowing hot as a name on a Donatella VIP list. All Toby had to do was sign it and then – the income could begin! Oh, was he going to be pleased to see her today: he had, after all, made it quite clear to her he was only doing it for the money.

She knocked on the door. She was somewhat annoyed he had not returned her phone calls since she had been working terribly hard on his behalf. But then, she supposed, he was an artist, and it was not unheard of for artists to behave with eccentricity – many of them refused to use the telephone at all. Cosima, being a resourceful sort of woman, had decided to make the most of it and use the opportunity to admire the sheer gorgeousness of his physical form again.

Unfortunately, the door was opened by an annoyingly attractive girl, rather than the vision of divine masculinity she had been expecting.

'Hello,' the girl said after she had recovered herself from the neon glare of Cosima's clothes. 'Can I help you?'

'Sure. I'm looking for Toby. Is he home?' replied Cosima in a rather clipped manner. She did not like talking to pretty girls if they weren't famous. It upset her chakras.

'No, I'm afraid, he's not. Can I give him a message?'

'You can, I'm sure, but I'd rather give it to him myself. Do you know when he's due back?'

The girl looked uncertain – embarrassed, even. Was that a blush? 'Um, no actually. I'm not sure of that. Sorry, you are . . .?'

'I am Cosima Beane.'

'Oh. *You're* Cosima Beane.'

Cosima was not entirely sure she liked the way the girl had said that. 'And you are?'

'Caris Brown. Toby's, um . . .' why was she hesitating? 'Girlfriend.' She said the last word so very quietly, Cosima almost could not hear.

'Oh. He's gotta girlfriend has he? That's a shame,' answered Cosima brashly. 'Well, be sure to tell him that he has got a commission and that he needs to phone me right away.'

A commission? Cas decided to ignore the woman's rudeness in order to extract the information she needed. 'He's got a commission? You mean, he's working for you?'

'Yeah,' said Cosima Beane, as if Cas was the only person left on earth to know. 'Some girlfriend,' she muttered under her breath.

Cas stared at her. 'I beg your pardon?'

'Nothing, honey. Anyway, he needs to call me because he has to meet with the client right away. The meeting's set for Wednesday at a *very* glamorous event,' said Cosima haughtily, while looking Cas up and down disapprovingly. Cas was aware that in her tracksuit bottoms and T-shirt she did not look very glamorous at all. 'I am going to take him as my date. Tell him to meet me in the Cosmo bar at seven.' And with that Cosima Beane spun on her heel and left.

What a nasty piece of work, thought Cas as she watched the crimped luminous ball make its way back from where it had come. And what a ridiculous spectacle she made of herself, with a bright-pink swan on her head. Toby was right, she was absolutely inexcusably rude, no wonder he had been hesitant about working with her. But – and Cas could see that it was quite a big but – she said he had a commission. In the light of her sacking, this was definitely good news.

Since she had been sacked, she and Toby had been enjoying an awkward exchange. She had to admit it had been rude of her to hang up on him the day that he had called, but as she had tried to explain, the circumstances had been exceptional: she had just been sacked and the premiership's golden boy had stopped to ask her if she was all right. Still, Cas felt guilty, but her apology had not seemed to mean much to Toby. He had been monosyllabic when she had phoned him back, and would not tell her what it was he had so urgently wanted to speak to her about. She begged him to come home, but he said that he wanted to spend some time with his mother.

Great, thought Cas, I am having a huge career and personal crisis and the man with whom I am in love would rather be with his mum. Apart from anything else there were practical things they needed to discuss – after the end of this month Cas would not be able to afford the rent on the flat, they would need to give notice, or Toby would have to get a job. She could freelance, but she had no idea how successful she would be, especially as Power had said he would make it difficult for her. It probably wasn't going to be enough without Toby's help. The two of them needed to make a decision, but Toby wasn't interested in talking about it. Cas had not been able to keep the annoyance out of her voice.

Now she was not working, Cas also had plenty more time to think. It was almost as if she and Toby had had their roles reversed: she was the provider, the pragmatic half of the relationship, he was the creative intuitive half. Perhaps all she needed to do was accept that.

Feeling his absence acutely, Cas picked up the phone and tried again.

'Emily, is that you? It's Cas here.'

'Oh Caris, hello. Have you spoken to Toby yet?' She sounded flustered, out of sorts, thought Cas. Probably being bullied by her God-awful husband.

'Yes, but not properly, if you know what I mean,' said Cas shamefully. 'Is he there now Emily? Can I have a word? I think I've got some good news.'

'No. He has gone out for a walk. He's quite upset.'

'Upset about what?'

'I think I'll leave it to him to tell you.'

Now Cas was really worried – Emily sounded just as shaken herself. She hadn't had a proper conversation with Toby since he left. No, scrub that, since weeks before that, and suddenly she had no idea what was going on in his world. No idea at all.

'Emily, when you see him, please can you tell him to come home,' pleaded Cas desperately. 'Tell him, please, that I love him very much.'

Emily smiled to herself, glad there was something in her son's life that made sense. 'I will.'

Cas swallowed the lump in her throat. 'Do you think I should come up and see him?'

'I don't know. I'll tell him you suggested it, but he wants to be on his own at the moment, I think. And he may be planning to come up to London quite soon.'

'Well, listen, you better pass onto him that his agent, Cosima Beane, has been round here to see him. She says she has a commission for him, and that he needs to meet the client on Wednesday evening. She said she would meet him in the Cosmo bar at seven. Maybe he should give her a call.'

'I'll tell him.'

Emily put down the phone and sighed. Toby had been like this for days now – not talking to anyone, avoiding her eyes, shutting himself up in his room. Strangely, the only person he seemed to be comfortable round was St John. He could sit in the same room as him, just watching him, looking as if he finally understood. He had joined him in his whisky drinking and the two of them would sit there, not talking, staring into the fire, for hours on end.

Emily had not told St John that she had shared their secret with Toby: St John was not altogether mentally there any more and it made no sense to burden him further. Besides, it was too painful. They hadn't spoken about it between them since Toby was a baby and she failed to see what it would achieve now. Emily had little desire to have it out with him for her own sake – she had long ago reconciled herself to the fact that the quieter St John was, the easier it was for her.

But Toby was not helping her. One night, after several glasses of whisky, Emily had bumped into him as he was staggering to bed.

'I forgive him everything now, Mum. At least I know

now why he hated me so much,' he had said in a choked voice, before falling into his room.

Emily had cried and cried. He didn't forgive her. Bitterly, she had sat in the kitchen, twisting her apron and fighting back the tears. Why not? It was St John's fault that all this had happened and not hers, but she knew she was the one who had to bear it all, she was the strong one in all of this and she had to give Toby time.

He was working hard on a piece he had said, and that was why he had been shut in his room for so long. Yesterday, though, he had come out and announced that he had finished it. In something of an advance in their relations, she had asked him if she could see it and he had shown it to her. Emily had been amazed. It was beautiful and powerful, and she had had to look away to begin with, to stop herself from breaking down again. He had watched her closely as she had traced the bold curves of the metal, it was bronze but the material had some kind of greenish tinge, which gave it a natural, almost organic look. About half the size of her, it depicted a woman kneeling down, pregnant, with her arms wrapped around her swollen stomach. But it was the expression on the woman's face Emily had found so painful. It was love, absolute love, but there was something unbelievably sad there too.

'I'm going to sell it,' he had said suddenly.

'Are you?'

'Yes. I just wanted to make it. And now it's made I feel better, but I don't want it any more. I want something back from it. I'm going to take it down to London and sell it.'

Cas was worried about how upset Emily had sounded. Emily was normally a very calm, grounded sort of woman, and the last thing Cas would have descibed her as was emotional. This just made Cas more anxious for Toby's state of mind. She knew she had been caught up in 'her moment' for a long time now. Her encounter with Cosima Beane made her think exactly as Toby had – that he shouldn't be involved with her. Why hadn't she listened to him? He was right – the Beane woman was loathsome.

The days were slipping by. It was amazing how quickly time went when there was nothing to fill it. She spent them idly, reading and just thinking, or watching the mindless display of images on the television.

She sat down on the sofa and idly flicked on the television again – it was *Richard and Judy*. Absurd daytime television, but she found herself hypnotized by it – a sure sign she was unemployed. She couldn't help thinking that if things hadn't broken down between her and Toby then he would be here right now and they would be spending some precious time together. Suddenly, that seemed much more important. Much more important than her job and her wage slip. She realized, now she was out of a job, that it did not seem very important at all any more. She had been so terrified of losing it when she had it, but now she had lost it she almost didn't care. When she was working, going to that office every day had seemed vital, now it was a relief not to have to deal with Tamara Yearbank. Toby had been right about that too. And now she felt lonely, afraid, insecure and upset, and the person she needed at a time like this was not around.

She had not nurtured Toby because she had been too busy thinking about herself, and, miserably, she hated herself for that. She wished Toby was here so that she could tell him, have the chance to apologize, then they could give notice on the flat, tell Cosima Beane to take a running jump and just get out. Alone together.

Except, there was Victor Power. After she had got over her initial shock of being sacked, she had become angry – angry that she had been spoken to in the way she had, and she had been more determined than ever to push this investigation forward. Now, she felt distracted, and ambivalent towards Power. As Bentley had said, there were always going to be people like Power in the world, and if they got rid of him, then someone else would just replace him. Was it really worth carrying on? Sam could pick up where Cas had left off.

When he had come round for dinner before he had left for Nauru he had asked her about Toby, because, of course, Toby had not been there. As the evening wore on and he hadn't returned, she had eventually been forced to tell Sam that he had left her – temporarily. Sam had been sweet, had even put his arms around her, so Cas had missed the longing in his eyes. By the time they'd finished talking it was late, and Sam had been inclined to stay, he'd said he would be fine on the sofa, but Cas had wanted to be alone, and had called him a cab. She had felt mean doing it, but some-how it had felt right. She finally noticed there was something in Sam's eyes that shouldn't have been there.

Judy looked quite flushed today, thought Cas. She was talking about the menopause and Richard was looking nervy and jumpy – more wired than ever. But when they looked at each other across the sofa, there was genuine affection in their eyes and Cas suddenly felt admiration for them. Years of their relationship in the public eye, years of working together and still there was love. She stopped herself, shocked at her own train of thought – if she was envious of Richard and Judy, then things must be really bad.

Judy's hot tips on how to deal with the menopause and Richard's considerate frown were interrupted by the flop of the post on the doormat. Such are the great daily excite-ments of the unemployed, Cas made her way downstairs to retrieve it. Bills, unwanted catalogues, direct mail from dig-ital TV companies, a postcard for Toby from a friend, a notice of the Whistles sale for her – something she defi-nitely would not be going to any more – and a package addressed to her, postmarked central London. The package was a padded gold envelope, the script on the front in silver calligraphy. Whatever it was it looked lavish – the kind of thing only a PR company with too much money to spend could come up with. Cas wondered if it wasn't advertising the launch of some new breakfast cereal, or the arrival in London of the latest, most fashionable Antipodean chef. But why would a PR company have her home address? She turned the envelope over and ripped open the seal. Inside, padded in red rose petals that fell on the floor when she pulled it out, was a large rectangular mirror. On the mirror was etched the following:

*Victor Power and Power Publishing*
*request the pleasure of your company at*
*The Party of the Millennium*

*held in honour of*
*The re-launch of the Daily News and*
*To celebrate the third anniversary of*
*Hiya! magazine*
*on Friday, 30th November*

*7 p.m., 101 The Embankment, SW1*
*Dress: Ambitious*

Cas checked the postmark – Friday afternoon last week – after she had been sacked. There must have been some dreadful mistake, she thought, they had forgotten to take her off the invitation list. But then why would she have been invited in the first place? She was only a journalist, not A Person Who Mattered. She looked again in the envelope, and saw there was still a piece of paper inside. She unfolded it. It was a sheet of A4 and typed in the middle was one sentence:

Come to the party and you will get all the evidence you need.

Cas's hands began to tremble. Even if she wanted to give the Power investigation up she couldn't now, it was pursuing her. Someone had her name and home address. Who? Someone was luring her, but who? If Power wanted to set her up, he knew where to find her, but why would he want her at his party? She fingered the invitation. Should she go? She needed to talk to Sam but he was still in Nauru – disappointingly, he had still not come up with anything, but he didn't want to leave until he had checked everything. She prayed he would be back by next Wednesday. She couldn't make any decision until she had spoken to him.

Finally, Cas propped the invitation up on the mantlepiece and stared at it. As she walked round the room it caught the light, no matter where she was in the flat it seemed to be beckoning her, taunting her. She knew, in her heart that she had to go. She thought about telling the police but then rejected the idea. Without admitting to breaking into Power's office she had nothing to tell them.

On Monday, Sam phoned. It was late at night for him, but he was excited – he had the news they needed. Winifred Power and a character called Mike Pitts had stayed at one of the island's more isolated hotels several times. The hotel had a record of their stay, including signatures in their guest books. It was not evidence which would convict anyone, it was still circumstantial, but the net was closing. Cas told Sam about the invitation. He thought the letter must have been sent by Power.

'It's a trap, definitely, Cas. But you've got to go, hard evidence is something we still need. We can't afford to pass this one up.'

'Thanks, Sam. And then what happens? I get dumped in a canal?'

'No. I'll come with you. I'll get an invitation somehow, schmooze the PR or something. I'll make some calls now, it's too dangerous for you to go on your own.'

'It might be Silvio Ravelli's doing.'

'Silvio Ravelli?'

'Yeah. I'm afraid he knows that I've been doing some investigating on Power.'

'How does he know?'

'Well, apart from the fact that he was there when I was sacked, I told him beforehand – he's close to Power but seems to loathe him, and I thought he might be able to help us.'

'Or shop us. Well done, Cas.'

'No, I don't think so. Anyway he is definitely not a bad man – he wouldn't try and hurt me. To be honest, I think he fancies me.'

'Cas!'

'I know. It was just something he said. I get the impression he is the sort of person that fancies anything in a skirt, so it's no great flattery. Anyway, I have no idea. So I guess we'll just have to go along to this party and see.'

## chapter twenty-two

It had to be said that even the inimitable Adrian Fagge had excelled himself on this occasion. As a succession of chauffeur-driven limousines pulled up outside the grand, glittering gates ('The gates of heaven, darling – it's got to have a theme!' – Adrian Fagge), their passengers, most of them highly seasoned party goers, could see just from the outside that tonight was going to be something very special.

The twelve-foot-high gates were lit by ten flaming torches, five each side, and each one was held in the unfaltering grip of a silver-suited acrobat. Somehow the acrobats had managed to weave themselves into the ironwork of the gates, and there they stayed, like the living statues in city squares around the world, absolutely frozen, their presence required to shed the light of their flaming torches over the two metres of pavement the party guests had to negotiate between their cars and the entrance.

The path through the gates was a thickly sprinkled carpet of individually glittered red and pink rose petals, a path that wove along the floor of a muslin-draped tunnel. As the guests made their way across this bed of floral decadence, more silver-suited angelic assistants appeared from nowhere to relieve them of their coats. A sweet, heady smell of rose oil, sourced from the finest plants and pumped into the air in discreet wafts, completed the ambience.

The tunnel led into a huge, purpose-built perspex marquee, its transparent walls displaying the lights of London as they were reflected in the surface of the Thames, and through its domed roof the stars could be seen in the clear, winter sky. Inside the tent, a specially commissioned and grown biosphere had been set up ('Eden, darlings, I want them to walk in and think: Ah! Paradise regained!' – Adrian Fagge). Various tropical plants whose normal habitat would be the lush jungles of Brazil or the tangled rainforests of Madagascar, hung down from the tent's forty-foot-high roof, and sprung up from its four thousand square feet of floor. Flying from frond to frond were bright macaws and birds of paradise on loan from London zoo, who were making delighted use of an environment they had only previously dreamt of ('Don't give them any food beforehand, I don't want them crapping on any of the guests!' – Adrian Fagge). Their squawks and calls blended in beautifully with the tinkling of the silver fountains ('I want them running with vodka, but it must be Silver Label, anything less simply will not do.' – Adrian Fagge) and the drum beats of a band of South American dancers. Up in the trees more acrobats, dressed in the pinks, blues, yellows and greens of tropical plumage, swung on suspended silver swings from branch to branch, tossing each other with practised ease from hoop to hoop. Handsome girls in silver tutus sat in branches combing their hair and strumming on harps, while stilt walkers dressed as lions, tigers, elephants and giraffes prowled the floor beneath.

Among them swept a fleet of cherubic waitresses bearing tray after tray of bite-sized delicacies: chocolate-dipped Polynesian strawberries; syruped kiwi fruit inserted in fans into rosehip-soaked watermelon balls; tiny little puff pastries containing every savoury delicacy from quails' eggs to Avignon's finest foie gras; miniature Vietnamese rice pancakes enveloping chopped crevettes and squid; chunks of lobster carefully balled and skewered with silver cocktail sticks; small heaps of the finest golden Iranian caviar mounded on to sour cream and potato blinis; tiny morsels of flash-barbecued Aberdeen Angus steak – and a hundred more newly invented canape innovations ('Frankly the menu list was so long I just didn't have the time to get to the end of it. As ever, I had very little notice to pull off this feat.' – Adrian Fagge).

Drinks were cocktails and bubbly, freshly squeezed and pulped, iced and un-iced, in short or long, sugar-dusted or non sugar-dusted glasses, with silver straws to sip through and tiny cocktail brollies with the *Hiya!* logo on them, ('I'm really not sure about those, Mr Power.' – Adrian Fagge). Over a hundred mixologists operated with mechanical precision along the length and breadth of a mirror-surfaced bar that stretched down one side of the tent. Their mission:

to keep every guest as well irrigated as possible. No guest was able to take a sip of their drink without it being immediately refilled, no one was able to turn round without being in swiping distance of a banana-leaf decorated tray of canapes. Opposite the bar, the bottom panels of the dome had been rolled up to reveal a huge, floating platform over the Thames, lit up by more acrobat-borne torches and on which more food and drink was being served to the milling guests, who were being kept warm by lamp heaters. Lighting, engineered to reflect off the surrounding water, gave the guests the impression they were floating on a sea of silver and gold. Moored to the platform were several state of the art Sunseeker powerboats, from which floated bunches of helium-filled silver balloons, ready to transport guests out on the water for a river's eye view of the proceedings.

London, it was generally agreed, had never seen an event like it. Unmatched for lavishness, unparalleled for ostentation, the city's most celebrated hostesses wondered how they would ever be able throw a party again. Victor Power had spared nothing: Adrian Fagge had been given a blank cheque, and had gone on a shopping trip the like of which even Elton John would have been proud.

The host himself was naturally delighted with the party. But even more delightful for Power was the turnout of the guest list: anybody who had ever appeared within the pages of *Hiya!* magazine had been invited, and plenty more who had yet to take his cheque. All, it seemed, had come. They could no longer afford not to, for the *Hiya!* shoots were fast becoming an important second income for celebrities, as well as a pensionable activity once working became too tedious. Any celebrated player of the fame game lived their life in terror of the time when they slipped down a grade, from A to B, B to C, or – horrors! – C to D. *Hiya!* was there to counteract such an eventuality, and each member of Adrian Fagge's comprehensive guest list had looked on the mirrored invitation to The Party of the Millennium as an insurance policy to a wealthy and famous future. The celebrities were beginning to need Victor Power.

Amid such generous luxury, the quality of the guests could obviously be relied upon to supply the frosting on Adrian Fagge's lavish decoration. As the three special-edition souvenir issues of *Hiya!* magazine portrayed, in the weeks following the event, the assembled throng contained every recognizable face from every facet of celebrity imaginable: rock stars in their toe to neck leather; supermodels in the outlandish creations of their best-friend designers; actresses of varying success in dresses of more or less diaphanous material; TV personalities; authors; film directors; singers; agents; Hollywood producers; athletes; sports stars; explorers; minor royals; aristocrats; curators; artists; photographers; politicians ('Only the well dressed though.' – Adrian Fagge); soap heroes; dance troupes; pop tarts; reality TV contestants; prima ballerinas; opera divas; classical actors; racing drivers; boutique owners ('Yes, you can definitely be famous for owning a shop.' – Adrian Fagge); entertainers; pier-show artists; game-show hosts ('Mr Power operates a broad church in his inclusion policy.' – Adrian Fagge); in short anyone who was anyone, was there. And quite a few who were not anyone at all, but who used to be someone, or who hoped to be someone in the near future. There was no one who was judged not quite famous enough for entry, for who knew when their star would rise, or when it fell, how cheap they would come?

Of course, the party wasn't much fun. People did not go to such public preening fests as this to enjoy themselves – no, they went to be photographed, to be seen, to mingle with those more glamorous than themselves in order to be judged more famous than they were, and because it was a necessary part of their business. In much the same way as the rest of the world went to their offices, this industry went to parties. Besides, they had nothing much to say to each other, they all saw each other every night anyway at various other launches, openings and commemorations. Their purpose for attendance was quite easy to see: they clamoured around the few A-listers as soon as a photographer was in sight, and spent the rest of the time surreptitiously checking their appearances in the mirrored bar. Only the reality TV contestants, poor naive young things, were under the mistaken impression that this was a 'party' rather than an 'event' (an impression reinforced by their rather drunken antics on the dance floor).

As king of all he surveyed, Victor Power congratulated himself. With such people-pulling power, no one could ignore him now. His plan to become the country's greatest fixer, an indispensable networker who could put you in touch with, whisper a kindly word in the ear of, ask a favour of, get you an audience with whomever you wanted, was gathering apace. And this party proved it. Plus, if anything was destined to give his takeover of the *Daily News* maximum publicity, then this was it. Those who mattered would *have* to take notice of him now.

The newspaper industry had never seen anything like it. The most glamorous a newspaper shindig had ever got before was warm white wine and cheese balls in a Fleet Street pub. Other newspaper proprietors (all of whom had been invited so that Power could show them exactly how to do it), were left feeling rather uncomfortable at the standards which had been set.

The paparazzi were gathered outside like flies round a dung heap. The constant flash, flash, flash of their cameras, heralding the picture opportunity of yet another arriving star, ensured that all these photos would be syndicated around the world, and in the caption for each one published would be the name of *Hiya!* and the *Daily News*. Invaluable global publicity, which, as far as Power was concerned, came cheap at the price. Inside the event, copies of the *News* lay scattered around the tent and every time someone posed for a *Hiya!* photographer, they were handed a commemorative issue of the paper to pose with. These photographs would be blown up into huge adverts which were to be plastered on billboards around the country. In the coming weeks Power was to see his circulation rise quite considerably as a result.

Winifred Power played the silent, smiling presence on

her husband's arm to perfection. Dressed in a rather under-stated black number she had, nevertheless, given in to just the tiniest touch of rouge. The couple paraded majestically around the tent where they were charmed and charming to as many people as possible. Behind them, trailed Power's trusty bulldog Pitts, one meaty arm folded behind his cylindrical torso, the other pressed to his earpiece. As the man in charge of security, and of the Powers' own personal safety, he lent the couple an air of importance that separated them from all others present. (Personal bodyguards had been strictly disallowed. 'If you let them get away with it, celebs these days will turn up with an entourage of up to twenty people. And frankly, security is not who we are catering for!' – Adrian Fagge). Power could have been imagining it, but as he made his way around the room, it seemed every person he met had something congratulatory and respectful to say to him. With a certain satisfaction, he could not help wondering whether he was at last being accorded just that little bit more respect because he was now a newspaper proprietor.

Outside, across the road from the edge of the embankment where the tent had been erected, Cas surveyed the scene. There were security men everywhere, huge, bulky beasts, dressed head to toe in black with earpieces that appeared to be directing them in some sort of co-ordinated movement. Cas noticed a journalist from the *News*'s rival paper try to talk her way in. After being refused entry she was physically picked up by two of the guards and carried down the street.

Cas fingered her invitation nervously. All invitations were being scanned under an ultra-violet light. Suppose hers was not genuine? By her side was Sam, lightly tanned from his Pacific jaunt, doing his best to calm her down. He was rather proud of the invitation he had secured from the *Guardian*'s celebrity fashion editor who was in Snowdonia shooting a story on 'Sheepskin, it's the new wool'. Sam's invitation, at least, was genuine. He had gallantly suggested to Cas that they swap invitations, in case hers was marked in some way, but she wouldn't hear of it, she just made him promise that he would not leave her side from the moment they entered the gates.

Cas had taken further precautions. Not wishing to be recognized by Power or any of his cohorts, she had donned a blonde bobbed wig and heavy make-up. If someone was hoping to meet her there then they would have to find her. She had also chosen the sort of spangled, figure-hugging dress which she knew every female guest would be wearing – the sort of dress that would render any normal group of people absolutely dumbstruck, but which tonight would allow her to blend in. As she had left the flat, she had taken a long look at herself in the mirror, and had been impressed by her own transformation. She looked so much the starlet that she hardly recognized herself. When he had come to pick her up, Sam's jaw had hit the floor.

This was just as well, she now thought as she surveyed the army of men in black, because if she was recognized, then Power would probably have his team of heavies bind her hand and foot and throw her directly in the Thames. Taking a deep breath, she and Sam marched across the road, Cas's emerald-green dress swishing between her legs, and presented their invitations at the gates. Both were scanned, and the couple were admitted. As they disappeared up the tunnel, Cas breathed a sigh of relief. Had she known that behind her, the head of door security, her invitation in his hand, was whispering fervently into his earpiece she would not have felt so secure.

In the midst of the party throng, Pitts, one of his large digits pressing his earpiece further into his lughole as he strained to listen above the noise, was nodding. While Power was in the middle of persuading a particularly well-known hairdresser to share the secrets of his gay marriage for the Christmas issue of *Hiya!*, Pitts whispered something quietly in Winifred Power's ear. Winifred's mouth tightened, her eyes gleamed, and she craned her neck towards the entrance of the tent.

Not long after Cas and Sam's entrance, a vintage silver Rolls Royce rolled up at the gates, bearing the unmistakable headgear of Cosima Beane. Tonight, it seemed, nothing short of a burkha would do. Except, rather than the dour brown or dirty-blue versions that Muslim women of extremist states sported, Cosima's was bright scarlet and had her name embroidered in gold across her forehead. Toby thought she looked like an extra from a Flash Gordon cartoon. Did people really take this woman seriously? he wondered. The art world were disturbingly credulous if they did.

'It's designed by Hussein, sweetie, Hussein Chalayan,' Cosima explained. 'Back from bankruptcy with a vengeance! Don't you think it says something wonderful about womanhood today?'

No, Toby did not, and sitting beside Cosima in the Rolls Royce doing his best to look invisible, he resolved to flee from her the moment he got inside. His agenda for the evening was very different from that intended for him by Cosima. As he turned his invitation over in his lap, he saw his hands were shaking. A nervous sweat had enveloped his body, and he pulled at his wing collar to try and breathe a little more easily. Tonight Toby had no intention of seducing Charlotte Want, or charming the well-known and touting for commissions. Tonight, Toby intended to find his father.

Charlotte, for her part, had been at the venue all day rehearsing and re-rehearsing her performance. Her inability to remember more than five of her dance steps in sequence, despite the weeks of practising her record company had paid for, had driven her choreographer to distraction. Victor Power was already nervous about giving her the stage at his most extravagant and important event, but he also knew, as she did, that it was the perfect platform for her launch. If she could pull this one off, then she was definitely off the C list and onto the B – with A well within her sights. And, she was all Power's. So he had decided to risk it (which did not do much for Doug's blood pressure). At the last minute, then, it had been decided that Charlotte's dance routine should be radically changed to minimize her chances of messing it up. Her backing dancers were now to undertake most of the work, while Charlotte mimed the singing and only joined in with their steps for the chorus. It had been something of a stressful day for all concerned.

Charlotte had finally been allowed to leave at five o' clock in order to get herself ready, but was in such a foul temper that she informed Doug she could not possibly endure having to sit beside 'the ghastly Silvio Ravelli'.

'Just one more night, Princess, just one more night. Once your single's released you'll be famous enough in your own right. Just for the launch of the single, come on now, darlin'!'

A compromise had eventually been reached whereby Charlotte's limousine was to meet Silvio's somewhere in Belgravia, ensuring the couple would only have to endure each other's company for two minutes prior to arriving, when they would extract the required photo opportunity from the waiting paparazzi.

Silvio, whose disappearances up to London on behalf of the demands of Charlotte Want had become all too frequent, had finally been forced to admit to his boss the hold she had over him. Ferguson had been speechless, but had eventually agreed that it was better for all concerned that her antics with Ravelli in the Old Trafford shower room were not plastered all over the nation's tabloids for the delight and delectation of the club's shareholders. He had allowed Silvio this one final outing, just as long as it was the last. Ravelli earnestly promised his boss it would be and

Ferguson could tell by his face he meant it – Ravelli's 400 one-arm press-ups at six in the morning had failed to produce an expression anything like as pained as the one he wore when he talked about Charlotte Want. Ferguson could see his player had been quite punished enough. Nevertheless, he acted swiftly, placing a ban on Want even so much as applying for a match ticket and making it a club rule, to be inscribed in the statutes, that any player caught so much as talking to her, would be immediately expelled from the club for the rest of their lives.

Bentley Rhythm was also present at the party, decorated in the spangled bikini and tail feathers of a golden pheasant. Her Amazonian figure was truly breathtaking in such regal plumage and, as she swung from trapeze to trapeze in the rooftop of the tent, her long limbs stretching and bending their graceful progress through the air, she far outshone any of the other birds present. She, unlike any of the guests, was having a fine time at the party, having at last persuaded Rocky to try her out on something other than pole dancing. Tonight she was performing without having to peel her clothes off. The trapeze work was very demanding though, and the artists were having to work in teams, taking it in turns to work. As she finished her second performance, Bentley slid down the trunk of a Himalayan sal tree, and came to rest on the ground behind a blonde girl in a green dress who was doing her best to blend in with the vegetation.

'All right, Cas, what you up to?'

The girl in the green dress jumped out of her skin and whipped round.

'Bentley! How the hell did you know it was me?' she gasped.

Bentley tapped her earpiece. 'Got myself tuned into the security channel. Much more interesting than the choreography one. Someone's got your card marked, girl. What you up to, then? Nice barnet by the way.'

'Shit!' cursed Cas. 'This is bad. How do they know it's me?'

'Must have known you from the moment you walked in. Wouldn't underestimate this lot, they're professionals, I tell you. Why don't you lose the wig and throw 'em off the scent for a bit? Nip into the ladies', at least they can't follow you in there. Here, I'll get you into the staff ones, just don't follow me too closely. Then you can fill me in on what you're up to, you minx.'

Bentley was breathless with excitement at performing at such a party, and the added bonus of Cas's intrigue only heightened it. Cas, however, realized she was in serious trouble. If security knew she was here, then Power would too. Her invitation must have been labelled in some way, and now she had to be walking into some kind of trap.

'Bentley, I think I'm in real trouble. I've got to get back to Sam.'

'Calm down, girl. Here, give us your wig. You're identified on the security channel as a blonde in a green dress, so if you go back to brunette it'll take them a while to catch up.'

Cas handed over her wig and teased out her hair. At

Bentley's insistence, she explained briefly what she had found out, and thanked Bentley for her help.

Bentley grinned at her. 'Anything for a bit of excitement, I tell you.' Then she paused, and added more seriously, 'I thought about what you said after you came by the club that night. I thought: Good on you. No one's ever stood up to him like that before. Just cause I wouldn't let him sleep with me, he took me off the payroll. It's hard starting out in this game. When you need the money you'll do anything – almost.' Bentley gritted her teeth. 'And I've seen some girls forced into bad stuff.'

Cas nodded. 'Bentley, was it you that sent me that email?'

'What email?' she replied innocently, but there was a twinkle in her eye and a smile on her face. 'Now, more importantly Cas, who's Sam? Is he that boy with you? He's a bit tasty. He the fella you told me about?'

'No. Sam's my friend, not my fella,' replied Cas. 'I'm afraid there's little progress on that front. My fella has gone AWOL and seems to be in some sort of trouble, which is also what can be said for his girlfriend. Here, come and meet Sam. I need to stick with him in case something happens to me.'

The two girls appeared from the wings from behind the frond of a Polynesian fern, not too far from where Cas had originally been standing. She quickly spotted Sam craning his neck around the room looking for her. He looked very relieved to see her, if somewhat puzzled by her new hair, but nothing like as amazed as he was when he clapped eyes on the body behind her that was Bentley. Cas introduced her and explained what was happening, but Sam did not seem to be hearing a word – the sight of Bentley appeared to be taking up all his concentration.

'Sam! This is important! Are you listening?'

'Sure,' he said. Bentley gave him the benefit of one of her stunning smiles before bending over coquettishly to kiss him on both cheeks and whispering in his ear, 'You're gorgeous!' Then she said a little louder so Cas could hear, 'Right, I've got to get back up there, but I'll keep an ear out for security. Sam, you look after this girl and I'll come back down and find you later.' With this she tipped him a naughty wink and was gone.

Charlotte Want, after the trials and tribulations of the day, was now finally getting down to business. Positioned right in the middle of the room, wearing little more than a pair of pants and a piece of netting that in combination was what could only be described as an economic attempt at a dress, she was making an unashamed exhibition of herself with the photographers. Charlotte had half an hour before she was due to perform, and she wanted to make sure she got as many photos of herself in beforehand as possible. Behind her stood Silvio Ravelli, his dark features smouldering with a mixture of boredom and fury. As the cameramen took a step back from Charlotte, she turned round, flung her arms round his neck, and planted a huge kiss on his lips. The photographers' flashlights went into a frenzy. Silvio had no time to register anything other than surprise.

Cas and Sam found themselves inexplicably drawn to

this performance, and wondered what to do next. Was somebody going to come and present them with the dream evidence, or was it all just a trap? Aware that she was the talk of the security men, Cas was becoming increasingly nervous and suggested to Sam that they should leave soon, but Sam thought they should stay a little longer. But then Sam had his head in the clouds watching Bentley Rhythm swing from branch to branch.

Useless, thought Cas, and turned back to watch Charlotte Want. Perhaps she should have a word with Silvio and see if he knew anything about what was going on. She tried to keep herself pressed up against people so no one could see her dress, and as far from security as possible. Once Charlotte had done with the cameras, Cas saw her being introduced to someone, but couldn't see who as he had his back to her. He was being held in a very firm arm-lock by a woman dressed in head to toe scarlet, and now her companion was shaking hands with Silvio too. Cas was about to look away when the man coughed, and turning his face to the side she caught a glimpse of his profile. The man, thought Cas, looked strangely like Toby. Curious to get a better look, he even seemed to be the same height and shape, Cas worked her way a little further through the crowd so she could see his face. She stared. It *was* Toby. What the hell was Toby doing at the party in the midst of all those celebrities? But surprise aside, Cas's heart leapt – at last, Toby was in the same room as her. She wanted to run up to him, but maddeningly, she knew she couldn't. Instead she took the opportunity to observe him unnoticed. She found herself thinking once again how handsome he was, how gentle were his gestures, how appealing was his demeanour of slight embarrassment.

Toby had never been to a public launch like this before. Cas was quite at a loss to explain his presence until she realized the ridiculous vision in scarlet at his shoulder was in fact Cosima Beane. The witch had her claws into him now, thought Cas jealously, dragging him along to parties like this, introducing him to the likes of Charlotte Want. Why had he agreed to come? She could see from his face that he was in some kind of excruciating agony.

Desperately, Cas wanted to make herself known to him, share a joke with him, flash him a knowing smile. Perhaps she could get a little closer, just to be that much nearer to him. She pushed through the crowd towards him, instinctively drawn to him, wanting to touch him, feel him, smell him – closer and closer until she found herself standing right next to him. Then he saw her. She saw his eyes flick past her, then return, staring. He was puzzled, someone who looked like her, but didn't. She watched his brain go through the motions, but Cas couldn't afford to be recognized, not for one moment, not even by Toby. Quickly, she put a finger to her lips, shook her head, mouthed, 'No, no, no', – but it was too late.

'Cas? Is that you?' he asked.

Charlotte Want, who had been in the middle of addressing Toby, whipped round furiously to see who her competition was. When she saw it was Cas she looked as if she would happily walk all over her in her best stilettoes.

Toby, unaware of their previous acquaintance, politely introduced her, 'Charlotte, this is Caris Brown,' he supplied dutifully. Cas wondered where the explanation of 'my girlfriend' was, but could see by the reproachful look on Toby's face that it was not going to be forthcoming.

'I know,' replied Charlotte icily.

However, Silvio, on hearing her name, had none of these qualms, and whipping round he beamed at her admiringly. Now Cas was completely exposed, recognized on all sides. Panicking, she looked round for approaching security guards, and was about to flee when Charlotte let out a shriek. Her pinched face lit up, and the words that Cas had dreaded most rung out across the floor, 'Victor! Hi! How are you?' and Charlotte flung herself into the waiting arms of Victor Power.

Without a second's thought or a glance backward, Cas started to make her way straight ahead, desperately hoping not to be seen by Power. But as she broke away from the group she walked straight into Winifred Power.

'Ooops, excuse me,' she mumbled, catching a breath of the old woman's intoxicating lavender perfume. When she tried to move on she felt Winifred's hand close tight around her arm. She looked into her face and saw a steely gleam in her eyes. Suddenly Winifred Power looked far from the defenceless old woman Cas had suspected she was.

'And where do you think you are going, young lady? Didn't you come here to get something?' she hissed.

Cas froze – so the invitation had been from her. Behind Winifred, Cas saw the fast-approaching bulk of Power's sidekick, Mike Pitts, the second name that Sam had found at the hotel. His punch-drunk face was twisted into a snarl of satisfaction now he had Cas in his sights. He was muttering furiously into his microphone as he charged towards her. Cas turned to escape but Winifred had her firmly by the arm now, her fingernails digging in to Cas's naked flesh. She was surprisingly strong for an old woman, and Cas was unable to twist herself free. As she writhed in her grip, Cas found herself face to face with Victor Power.

'What the fuck are you –' began Power furiously, but then something strange happened. Just as Cas thought she was trapped on all sides, she felt a firm grasping sensation underneath each of her shoulders, and suddenly Mrs Power's grip was wrenched from her arm and the crowd of people who had surrounded her began to disappear beneath her feet. Toby's amazed upturned face, Charlotte's expression of incredulity, Silvio's disappointment, Power's blank expression of puzzlement and the fury on the face of Winifred Power – all these were below her now and getting smaller by the second. Pitts made a last ditch lunge for her feet but Cas was moving upwards too quickly for him and as he propelled himself towards her he landed flat on his face at his boss's feet. Cas looked up to see how this was happening, wondering if she had fainted and this was some kind of surreal dream landscape, but there was the smiling face of Bentley Rhythm, her legs suspended from the arms of another wildly plumed bird, all three of them swinging through the air from the ropes of a trapeze.

Beneath Cas, all hell had broken loose. The guests were

admiring the snatch as some kind of party stunt and soon every pair of eyes in the tent was fixed on Cas's progress over the crowd.

Victor Power, however, wanted answers. 'Why is that fucking girl here?' he shouted, 'and what is she doing up there?!' Turning to Charlotte he roared, 'Get up on that fucking stage and do your song – Now! Distract them for Chrissakes!' Charlotte fled, and Power turned to Pitts. 'Get that journalist and that bitch Bentley out of this building!' Pitts did not need telling twice. Already his men were moving across the floor, their heads turned skywards, watching as Bentley deposited Cas at the top of a large cypress tree.

With a face like thunder, Power turned to his wife.

'What, exactly, was all that about?' he asked her through clenched teeth.

'Well, I saw her come in, dear,' replied Mrs Power with customary insouciance, 'so I had Mr Pitts do something. She was the one who you fired the other day, wasn't she? Well, I hardly thought you would have wanted her at your party. It appears she knows this gentleman here,' she explained, deftly switching the blame to Toby. Power turned to face Toby.

'And who the fuck are you?'

'I am Toby Hartley-Brewer,' Toby replied slowly and calmly.

Victor Power turned sheet-white.

Up in the trees, Cas turned to Bentley. 'Christ, Bentley, you just saved my life!'

'Not yet, I haven't. We've got to get you out of here. Shit!' she swore, pressing her earpiece. 'These boys are going mad. They want you badly!' Both girls looked around, but the only way down was the tree, and already a black-clad security guard was shinning his way up it.

'Well, if we can't go down,' said Bentley, and both girls watched as a violet-adorned bird of paradise made her way through the air towards them. She landed lightly on their platform, beaming.

'You in trouble, Ben?'

'Think so, Em. Can we borrow your trapeze?'

'No problem,' the bird of paradise replied, and grabbing Bentley, who grabbed Cas, the girls took off again, this time making their way across to another side of the tent. But even before they had landed on the platform, another guard was clambering up a tree towards them. The girls swung again, but it was hopeless, every tree was now being climbed by a heavy security guard. The girls came to a stop, just above the stage, to catch their breath. As soon as they alighted, the lights began to dim.

'What's going on now?' gasped Bentley, panting from the effort of swinging Cas around the room. As pitch blackness enveloped the tent, the opening chords of a song could be heard. A single spotlight highlighted a golden cage suspended from the rafters a few metres below the girls. Inside was Charlotte Want, writhing around the gold bars in various sultry poses, while wrapped around the top of the cage was what appeared to be a large white python, its forked tongue slithering out from between its jaws in a manner that indicated it was not entirely happy to be there.

'Are you thinking what I'm thinking?' asked Bentley. Cas feared she was. Both girls had spotted a rope leading from their rafter down to the hydraulic pulley system that was operating Charlotte's cage. Looking down, they saw that the guards were already clambering towards them and would reach them in a matter of moments. Before either of them could think of the consequences, Bentley had wrapped the trapeze wire around the rope, and they were both sliding down and heading straight for Charlotte's cage. Bentley had just enough time to shout, 'But I can't stand snakes!' before she landed them both on top of the cage, knocking the python off its perch and landing it right on the top of Charlotte Want's head.

The ensuing havoc was the talk of party circles for weeks afterwards. Charlotte's shriek could be heard as far away as Canary Wharf, drowning out the opening bars of the electronically produced voice she was supposed to be miming to. As the crowd collectively gasped to see the starlet's neck being swiftly circled by the snake, while her supposed voice started singing over the speakers, humiliatingly revealing her mime, Bentley and Cas jumped the last few feet to the floor and fled backstage. Unfortunately, by the time her backing dancers had disentangled the python, Charlotte had not recovered herself enough to pick up the words or the dance steps. By halfway through the first verse she was in so much confusion she burst into tears. The crowd were delighted – their sympathy for the singer and her tussle with the serpent was far outweighed by its comic spectacle, and all the unfortunate Charlotte could hear was their roars of laughter as she stumbled, lost, among her dance troupe. It was all too much for her, and she turned, defeated, for her last glimpse of what it looked like to see an audience from the stage.

Silvio, meanwhile, was delighted that the object initially of his passion but latterly of his unqualified disgust had at last been foiled. The latest target of his affections – Cas – had unfortunately been pretty much unreachable all night. He had also detected that she seemed fairly immune to his charms, not something a hot-blooded Latin male found too attractive in a partner. However, the affection of the Brazilian groupie, Floriana, had not proved half so difficult to crack. Out of the corner of his eye, Silvio had been aware of her stalking him all evening, and the moment Charlotte left his side she had appeared right behind him.

Now Floriana, like every good Carioca, knew just what to tell a Brazilian man: that he was gorgeous, that he was handsome, that he looked so much a man and that he was undoubtedly the most irresistible person in the room.

Flicking his hair back and preening a little, Silvio found it hard not to be tempted by Floriana's syrupy voice pouring honey in his ear, particularly when, as the lights dimmed for Charlotte's song, her hands were driving home her point as they ran the lengths of Silvio's thighs. Silvio eventually turned round to face her and found himself pressed up against Floriana's admirable cleavage.

He had quite forgotten about her undeniably fabulous breasts (their last meeting, after all, had been somewhat blurred by alcohol). After the pointy little mounds of Charlotte's figure, the large bowls of flesh in front of him felt very inviting indeed. By now Floriana, for whom the art of seduction was a well-practised technique, had her hand down the back of Silvio's trousers, and Silvio found his hand down the back of hers. Oh! and his lips on hers too, and those breasts on his chest, and . . . goodness, the pair were going to have to repair to the Cosmopolitan Hotel right away.

Cosima, who had managed to lose Toby in the throng, damn him, was not long without a new project. Like all good agents, she had spotted a marvellous opportunity. The disastrous debacle of Charlotte and the snake appeared to her to be a very modern parable on the Eve of our times. She had just had a quite brilliant idea about a piece of installation art for her next window display and was already rushing to secure the deal. Shuffling through the crowds as quickly as her burkha would allow, she hoped to catch Charlotte Want backstage before she disappeared. If she could just get her to agree, then Cosima could already see the headlines: 'Want girl finds paradise is not lost after all.' She broke into a light sweat just at the thought of it.

# chapter twenty-three

Cas bolted out of the back of the tent, through the back exit Bentley had shown her. Once they had landed on the stage, Bentley had whisked them through the wings and out through a stage door. 'Run, girl!' she had shouted after her, but Cas's path was not clear, ten-foot-high metal barriers formed a circumference around the back of the tent. They would be impossible to scale, thought Cas, not least in her kitten heels and cocktail dress. Adrenaline and fear were now pounding through her body, as she pressed herself flat back against the tent and crept forward around to the front. Ahead of her lay the main entrance, and the only way out from behind the fences. Thronging in front of the entrance were the photographers, if she could just make it as far as them she had a chance of picking up a taxi on the road before she was caught, or at least escaping down a side street.

Breathing deeply, she steeled herself for the dash. She waited until the men on the door had turned to attend to guests appearing from the inside of the tent and then darted out. And she would have made it, but for the couple who were so engrossed in each other, with their mouths glued together that, as they emerged from the tent, they stumbled straight into Cas, knocking her flying.

'Silvio!' cried Cas, as she tried to pick herself up off the floor.

Beside him stood a rather buxom woman who looked more than a little surprised to have had her man knocked from her lips in such a dramatic fashion. Floriana was used to competition, but this was ridiculous. But for Cas it was too late, security had seen her and were descending on her fast.

'Help me!' Cas pleaded with Silvio as she tried to get to her feet.

Silvio turned and saw, with a gulp, that he was all that stood between Cas and her black-clad aggressors. Mustering all the Latin manhood he could, he gallantly drew back his arm, balled his fist and hurled himself at the approaching men.

It was useless, the wiry footballer was small fry for the body building security guards and they swept him out of their way as if he were no more than a loose sequin on a starlet's frock. To the strobe-like flashing of the photographers' cameras, for whom the sight of an attractive young lady sprawled all over the floor and a premiership footballer brawling in the street was as if all their Christmases had come at once, Cas watched as the security men bore down on her. First she felt them on her arms, then her legs, then she felt herself lifted up and carried round the side of the tent.

From the back of the tent, Bentley had seen it all. Before anyone could see her too, she had fled back through the secret exit and into the party, thinking she had to find Sam and alert him. Deftly scaling a tree to a trapeze platform, she scanned the room. To her horror, she spied him in conversation with Victor Power and a tall dark-haired young man. What was Sam doing talking to Power?

Sam, of course, had not intended to have anything directly to do with Power, but he had heard Cas address the tall dark guy as Toby. Knowing a little about Cas's recent problems, Sam considered that as her friend, it was his duty to Cas to try and explain to Toby what was going on. It also occurred to him that now Cas had been discovered, Toby might be in very real danger from Power's henchmen and should be warned. Sam had gestured behind Power's back for Toby's attention, and Toby had eventually excused himself and come over. Sam quickly introduced himself and explained the danger Cas could be in and warned Toby not to return to his flat that night. He apologized for being alarmist, but said he had reason to believe they were in trouble.

'Anyway,' he asked Toby curiously, 'how do you know Power?'

Toby had smiled and, putting an arm on Sam's shaken shoulder, explained he thought it unlikely Power would harm him. Victor Power, he told him calmly, was actually his father, and although they were just getting acquainted, it did not, so far, appear Power wanted him out of the way.

'On the contrary,' Toby remarked, 'he seems quite relieved to meet me finally.'

Sam was shocked: Cas had never mentioned her boyfriend was in any way related to the object of their investigation, let alone his son and heir. 'Toby, does, er, Cas know about this?'

'No.' Toby grimaced. 'But it is not for lack of trying, I can tell you. So what is all this about Cas being chased?'

Sam explained and, frowning, Toby suggested they both go and talk to Power. Sam was already beginning to be suspicious of just how much Power himself actually knew about what was going on in his company.

Power, for whom the night still held many more revelations than those he had already been stunned with, was now informed that the girl he had recently sacked for, as he believed, single-handedly discrediting his entire business, was in fact the lover of his newly found son. He insisted to Toby and Sam that he was completely unaware of anyone pursuing Cas, he had merely asked for her to be removed from the party.

At that point Bentley appeared and breathlessly explained Cas was being abducted at the back of the tent. Power looked around for Pitts to find out what was going on but noticed that not only had he disappeared, but his wife had as well. A look of thunder came over his face. 'Where did they go?' he demanded briskly of Bentley.

'They picked her up and carried her round the back, I'm not sure where they were taking her!'

'Was Pitts with them?'

'Yes,' replied Bentley, who had noticed him directing proceedings.

'Then they've made for the boats,' responded Power. 'Come on!' and the four of them set off for the floating platform that was still filled with milling guests. Pushing celebrities, canapes and drinks trays aside, Power led the way, Toby, Sam and Bentley following behind him.

Sure enough, there was something of a commotion going on in front of the boats where a mass of security men, led by Pitts and the grey-haired Winifred Power, were struggling with something in front of them.

'Wattle!' shouted Power menacingly at his wife, who spun round to see them approaching, revealing Cas with her hands bound, being thrown into one of the boats. At the sight of her approaching husband, Winifred scrambled into the boat with Cas, just as Pitts started the engine.

Power roared his anger and bolted towards the departing craft.

'Toby!' screamed Cas, as she caught sight of him on the platform. Without thinking, Toby charged the security men lining the path to Cas's boat. All of the security seemed to be following orders from Wattle and Pitts now – Power's authority was useless. Still, Toby managed to knock two of them into the river, clearing his path to leap into another boat. Sam followed, his charge making a space for Power to leap in beside his son but, as Sam struggled with the muscle men, he was knocked flat by a stray punch. Bentley shrieked and ran over to help him. But Sam's valiant efforts had created enough of a diversion for Power to start the engine of the boat and he and Toby now set off in pursuit of Cas, Pitts and Wattle.

On board the speeding boat Cas was petrified with fear. She had been badly knocked about by Pitts, but the rope they had used to tie her wrists with was coming loose.

'Where are you taking me?' she shouted at them, struggling to make herself heard above the scream of the wind and the roar of the engine. Wattle and Pitts ignored her. Pitts, at the helm, was concentrating on their getaway.

To her relief, Cas saw another boat was pursuing them now, and thought she could make out Power and Toby at the helm. But behind them came other craft driven by the black henchmen, and they did not look very friendly. Cas realized who the enemy really was, and unfortunately she was on their boat. Somehow, she had to get off. She struggled with the rope tying her wrists, and to her delight discovered she could loosen it enough to wriggle her hands free. Discreetly, she wrapped the rope back round to make it look as if her hands were still tied up.

Underneath Waterloo bridge they sped, and the great tower of the *Daily News* offices hove into view on the south bank. Lit up from inside in the dark it suddenly seemed a very safe place compared to being on board a speedboat with a crazed elderly lady and a guffawing bulldog.

\*

On board Toby's thoughts were only for Cas: what the hell had she got herself into that she was being abducted by henchmen and spirited away on a speedboat?

'Who are those people?' he shouted at Power, struggling to balance as the boat thumped over the waves on the water.

'They were my wife and my right-hand man,' shouted back Power, a cold desire for revenge overtaking his fury. 'But they're not any more,' and with that he drove the boat even faster into the wake. Behind him the other boats roared faster too.

By now Pitts and Wattle had noticed they were being hotly pursued and the laughing had stopped. Pitts was barking instructions into his radio. Presumably instructions for the other boats, thought Cas. She looked around on deck for something – anything – that would help and saw underneath the seat she was being tossed around on a large wooden paddle. The two at the wheel were now so engrossed in the movements of the boat behind and with dodging oncoming obstacles that they didn't notice her crouch down to pick it up. It was heavy and about four foot long. Cas calculated it was going to take all her strength to swing it round her head and wield it with any effectiveness. She waited for her moment. Toby was so close now he could see what she was doing and began shouting at Pitts and Wattle. Both turned to look at him and Cas took her opportunity. Throwing the rope from her hands, she heaved the paddle up from the floor of the boat, swung it behind her, then, with all the strength she could muster, she brought it crashing round into Wattle's waist. With a shriek, the old lady was knocked sideways and tumbled over the side of the boat. With an almighty splash, she landed in the water, her dress billowing up over her perm-set.

Pitts looked in alarm at what had happened and, turning round, saw Cas was free. With one hand on the wheel he grasped at the paddle, just as Cas was thrown to the floor by the lurching of the boat. They narrowly missed an oncoming tug by inches.

Cas felt ringing in her head and something warm and sticky gliding down her cheek. She blinked and her vision restored itself, but for a split second she did not know where she was.

'Cas! Jump off! Cas? Are you all right?' She could hear her name being called by a voice that was familiar and comforting. It was Toby. Forcing herself into consciousness, she scrambled to her knees. Pitts was now pushing the gear stick into full throttle and they were going faster up the river than ever before. Cas looked back. Wattle was now just a small dot in the river, being picked up by one of the pursuing boats. About thirty metres behind them were Toby and Power, but they seemed to be losing ground.

'Jump!' shouted Toby, and Cas threw herself overboard into the river. For a few seconds she was confused, but the bite of the cold water brought her to her senses. Her head bobbed above the surface and she looked up to see Toby's boat circling around her. Other boats were coming too looking as if they were going to try and run her over. She tried to swim, but the current was too strong and she felt herself being swept downstream. Suddenly Toby's arm was in front of her and she grabbed hold of it and with a little effort he pulled her on board.

'Put her off here!' she heard Toby shout to Power, as he wrapped his jacket round her shoulders. The boat slowed, and they pulled up to a jetty. 'There's money in the pocket Cas – get out of here!' Toby shouted at her, and the next thing she knew she was being pushed up a ladder onto a pier. Power was already driving the boat away, and Cas turned round to see the disappearing figure of Toby as he and Power made after Pitts. Toby turned back to glance at Cas – he knew she would be all right now. And he had other matters to attend to: his father. Whatever Cas had been doing with Power over the past weeks, she had managed it without him. As much as it pained him to abandon her, he still wasn't sure what their relationship was, or how much she needed or wanted him.

Toby had gone, had rescued her, then left her dripping on a jetty. The roar of the speedboats had decreased to a buzz as they made their way up river. Cas was soaked through, but had on Toby's large jacket which covered up most of her ridiculous state. She was on the north bank, on a pier near Tower Bridge, she realized slowly, not very far from their flat. She felt in Toby's pockets. Yes! Keys to their flat and, she noticed as she pulled her hand out, a twenty pound note. She could get a taxi back home and change, but she couldn't stay there, it wasn't safe. Whatever happened on the boats, Pitts's henchmen would come looking for her. Whatever she was going to do, she had to do it fast.

Running down the pier, she made it to The Highway until, miraculously, a cab appeared and the driver, taking pity on her bedraggled state, pulled over.

'You all right, love? What happened?'

'I fell in the river. Look, I've got money, will you take me to Old Street?' she stammered, fighting for breath through her exhaustion.

'Jump in!'

Cas tried to recover herself. She opened her mouth, but no words would come out. She looked at her hands and saw they were shaking. Then she realized she was trembling all over. She was frozen.

'How d'you fall in the river then, love?' asked the cabbie.

Cas shook her head. 'Long story,' she managed to say.

'That's a nasty cut you got. How d'you come by that then? Hit your head when you fell in, did you?'

Cas felt her forehead with her fingers and found they were covered in blood. Her head was ringing.

'Please. Just get me to Old Street,' she pleaded – the last thing she wanted now was a conversation with a nosy cab driver.

'Please yourself,' he replied huffily.

Cas tried to think, where could she go? Where would she be safe? Her mother's? No, they might have her address and the last thing she wanted to do was explain everything to her mum. A hotel? She could do, but London suddenly seemed very hostile.

Then she thought of the answer – Toby's mother's. Suddenly she wanted to go there more than anything else.

If she couldn't be with Toby tonight then she wanted to be as close to him as possible and find out what had happened to him while he'd been staying there. She looked at her watch, nearly 10.30. She would easily make the last train.

When they arrived at the flat she checked the windows. They were dark, so hopefully no one inside. The door was intact. It looked safe. Asking the driver to wait for her, she stole across the road, quietly unlocked the door and let herself in. She stood still, listening – no sound. She changed into dry clothes, grabbed her credit card and crept up to the living room.

She reached for the phone and dialled Emily's number. It was an emergency, she told her, could she come and stay? Emily sounded alarmed, but relieved to hear Cas was all right.

Cas got the driver to drop her at Euston Station. She had twenty minutes till the train left and she locked herself in a cubicle of the ladies' loo in case anyone had followed her. Once on the train, Cas tried to calm down but it was impossible. The adrenaline rush of her escape was still making her nervous – every time the carriage door opened she jumped in case it was another man in black. She tried to piece together the events of the evening. Power, it seemed, had been genuinely surprised to see her at the party, but Mrs Power had clearly been expecting her. When she had gone through Power's office she had found nothing; it was Mrs Power who had come back and picked up the incriminating evidence. Slowly it was dawning on Cas that maybe Power was not quite as in control of his empire as he imagined.

But all the time her thoughts kept coming back to Toby. How had he become involved in this sorry mess, and, chillingly, what would have happened to her if he had not been there? And where was he now?

# chapter twenty-four

It was past one in the morning when Cas's train finally drew into Shrewsbury station. Still fearful she was being followed, she checked for black-clad security men, but could see none. She loitered in the shadows until the taxi queue had gone, paranoia still haunting her, then waited another fifteen minutes in the sleet for another taxi to turn up.

When she arrived at the cottage, Emily was waiting for her, sitting in the kitchen. Cas walked in the kitchen door and just the sight of Emily, in a kitchen, by a fire, triggered something in her. She ran over to her, hugged her hard, and the tears began to course down her cheeks. Only now did she feel completely safe.

Emily sat Cas down, inspected her carefully, then went to fetch a warm, damp cloth with which she began to swab the cut on her face. She made her a mug of strong, sweet tea, and gave her some warm, dry clothes to change into. By the time Cas had the mug in her hand, she had managed to stop shaking and her sobbing had receded to the odd hiccup.

Emily took her chair opposite Cas and smiled at her. Her grey hair was pulled back from her face into a bun, and she wore a long skirt that had seen better days. She was only in her fifties but her face was weathered and tired, she had fought all her life against her husband and his moods and every conflict was etched in the lines on her face. Toby had once painted her, describing every line as testament to one horrific incident after another. Her face, he said, was like a map of her marriage. She was still beautiful, though, thought Cas, she still had her strong features, her dewy eyes. She could see Toby's cheekbones and it gave her a feeling of intimacy with him. She missed him now more than ever. How she would have loved to have felt his arms around her, his reassuring strength enveloping her. She wondered where he was, and closed her eyes on the last image she had of him chasing Mrs Power and Pitts down the river. Had he caught them? Was he safe?

Emily remained quiet. She was not a demonstrative person, but Cas sensed she was angry with her. Because of Toby. Of course she was.

'Emily,' she began, 'I'm so sorry, I am desperate to talk to him. But there has not been a moment, things have been a bit hairy in London. I've got myself involved in a story that has turned quite nasty.'

Emily looked down at her lap, her lips pursed ever so slightly. 'So I see.'

Cas made a decision not to go into the events of the evening with Emily, half because she was slightly ashamed, and half because she did not want her to be anxious about

Toby. There was nothing either of them could do until morning. All she could do now was try and convince his mother that she really loved him.

'I want him back Emily, I really do – I love him so much. This time, if he lets me, I will look after him, I promise.'

'It's not your fault, Caris,' said Emily softly.

Cas paused. Emily's eyes did not move from her lap.

Eventually she glanced up. 'He hasn't told you, has he?'

'Emily, we haven't had a chance . . .'

Emily drew in a deep breath. 'What I am going to tell you now, I will only tell you tonight. I would be grateful if you never refer to it again. There is a secret in this family that has been kept too long. I told Toby the other day. I think it's what he wanted to talk to you about, but seeing he hasn't had a chance, I might as well tell you myself.

'When Toby's brother, Stephen was born, St John and I were already very poor. St John took to gambling as a way to get us out of our hole, but of course he lost all the remaining money we had. It was not a good time. I wanted to get a job, to keep us alive and feed us but St John could not bear what he called the "ignominy" of me working in the local village – goodness, all I could do was clean, I had no other qualifications. I had been sent to finishing school, and all I learned there was how to arrange a bowl of flowers.'

Emily stopped and took a sip of her tea. She breathed deeply, as if trying to compose herself. Cas remained completely still. An atmosphere had settled on the kitchen that told Cas she was about to hear something horrific.

'But you must understand, St John came from a different time in this country, his family were still in a pre-war time warp. In his experience women didn't work and, frankly, neither did the men – they just managed their estates. My parents helped us out as much as they could, but they had their three other daughters to think about as well. They thought I had made what they called "a good marriage", and at eighteen I thought it was a good marriage too. St John was the lord of the manor, his father sat in the House of Lords, everybody talked about his name as if it was very grand. He was much older than me, fifteen years, and his father was putting pressure on him to find a wife. St John was his only child, and he needed to secure the line before he died. I suppose I was the nearest unattached female. After a summer of courting he asked me to be his wife, and I could not have been more thrilled.'

Emily's voice was deep, sonorous and full of regret. She could not have sounded less thrilled.

'But very early on it became clear St John's gambling habits were a problem. After I had Stephen, I found myself with no housekeeping money to buy food, no money to pay the gas bill for the heating. It was a nightmare.'

Emily's lip quivered, and she waited until she had regained control. She concentrated on the floor in front of her feet and continued. 'Then one evening St John had a particularly bad night. I waited up for him, knowing that he was sitting at a green table somewhere, gambling with god knows what. I waited and I waited and he still did not return. But I didn't go to bed, it was too cold in our bedroom. I sat by the Aga in the kitchen, waiting. By first light there was still no sign.' Emily's eyes were staring into the middle distance now, Cas could see she was in another place, had gone right back to that day over thirty years ago.

'He came back, eventually. I can still see him now, staggering across the lawn, emerging from the early morning fog. The grass was covered in dew, so by the time he arrived at the Hall he was soaked from his ankles to his knees. As he walked into the kitchen, Stephen, who had been sleeping all night, woke up and started to cry. He looked at the boy, then he looked at me and his face was . . . was awful. Hollow, white, distraught. That night broke him, and he has not been fixed since.'

Emily was quiet for a little while. The fire had died down, Cas shivered and put on another log. Emily's mouth was twitching, and Cas waited. Still she said nothing – it was as if she couldn't, as if the words were stuck in her throat underneath a lifetime's worth of suppression.

Gently, Cas prompted her. 'What had he done?'

Emily looked grateful, and continued. 'He had gambled away everything. Hartley Hall, the house that had been in the family for seven generations; the contents and every single one of our possessions. He told me this, while he stood in the doorway, but somehow I had been expecting it. I was waiting for it to happen. What I had not expected was that in a last desperate attempt to win it all back, on one hand he had gambled me. If he won the hand, then the loser could have me instead of our home and all that we owned. Unfortunately, he won the hand.'

'Oh my God,' breathed Cas. But an air of serenity and strength had settled around Emily, she had lived with this for too long to need sympathy for it now. 'I had to go to this man, in London, for three days, after which I could return and the debt would be settled. The man who St John lost his hand of poker to had wanted to see how desperate he would get, how far he would go, how low he would sink. He had waited until St John was absolutely desperate – absolutely mind – then he asked him about his wife. St John showed him my picture. The man said he would take me for three days in return for all that he had lost. St John passed the test. He sank as low as he could.'

'Emily!' Cas was horrified. She'd known St John was bad, but this was appalling.

'What could I do?' asked Emily, looking Cas in the eye. 'My husband had lost me in a bet.'

'You could have refused to go,' said Cas simply.

'I did. Obviously I did. Stephen was a small baby, my husband was a disappointment and you must understand I had not been brought up to live like this. But then I looked at Stephen, my son, and I looked at St John, my husband, and I knew this was something that I could do to save the family. It was within my power. Ultimately it was my choice: the man I had been gambled to had left an address and then gone. No threats were issued, nothing. And St John rather hoped that this was one debt he could skip honouring. But as time passed I became so angry about what he had done that I wanted to punish him – I wanted to go. I did not know what would happen to me when I got to London, but then I thought we could spend the rest of our lives waiting for this man to return to collect his debt. So one day I packed my bag, took Stephen and went.'

'My God,' whispered Cas.

'Frankly, I was so fed up with my husband by then that I was quite happy to leave. I thought, I need never come back if I didn't want to.'

'The man at the address seemed surprised to see me. To be honest, I don't think he had expected me, and I certainly don't think he had expected me to turn up with a baby. I offered to cook for him, clean, do any chores, whatever it took to pay off my husband's debts.

'He was a fair man, a kind man. He fed me, he tolerated Stephen's crying and he treated me with respect. He understood my position and he was good to me. Because of the months of St John's alcoholic rages and the fact that he had gambled me – sold me off – I was susceptible to the kindnesses of this man. I was young and I had not known anything of kindness or of affection, let alone love.

'I am not going to go into the details of my time with this man, but I will tell you that everything that happened was of my own choosing. After a while, I knew I could not carry on as we were and he knew he could not continue to keep me on the terms under which I had arrived. I wanted to stay, desperately, but I was married and I had borne my husband's son. Eventually, he told me I had to return to St John and try to pick up the pieces of my life. He also told me that if I ever needed help ever again then all I had to do was call him.

'But I was too proud for that. I had been away a long time but when I returned St John knew he could not reproach me, and he knew that I had known a better time without him. Instead of rising to this challenge he was crushed by it. Of course, it did not help matters when I discovered a few months later that I was pregnant. I prayed that it was St John's, it would have been so much easier if it had been. But of course Toby was born looking like he does. St John went into denial and the family made up some story about a past indiscretion. No one wanted the truth.'

'Did you tell Toby's father?'

'Eventually, yes. A few years later. I thought about keeping it from him but I knew the truth would out in the end and also that Toby had a right to know. He was good about it, asked me if I wanted him to support Toby. I didn't – it would have been too difficult with Stephen, but he sent me money every now and then which helped a great deal.'

Cas was horror-stricken, but Emily was strangely calm.

'As you can imagine, telling Toby this was difficult.'

'But after all of this, you lost the Hall anyway?' asked Cas.

'Yes, yes, St John did,' replied Emily with a snort of contempt. 'After all that. Once a gambler, always a gambler I'm afraid. It's an addiction and you cannot beat it. Ten years later he was sitting at the same poker table and he lost it all again. But that time he had the decency not to gamble his wife.'

'Emily, can I ask you a question . . . why did you stay with him?'

Emily looked at her as if she was strange for asking. 'For the boys, of course.'

Cas bit her lip. She wanted to say that St John had been an appalling father and Emily would have been better off leaving him anyway, but she didn't.

'You think I should have left him, don't you?' she said looking at Cas with half a smile on her face. 'Well, maybe, if I was a twenty-year-old girl now, that is what I would have done. But things were different then. There was no choice for women – our marriage was our career. If I had left him, the truth would have come out and the scandal would have enveloped the boys. I took a decision based on the best interests of my sons, and what was most realistic for me. I stayed with him, within the bounds of respectability, and no one was any the wiser.'

'And now? What about now?' asked Cas gently.

'Now, Caris, I am ground down by the years and change does not suit me. In a few years time St John will be so deranged I will be able to put him in a home and live out the rest of my life in peace.' She paused and looked straight at Cas. Cas felt her gaze go all the way through her, challenging her with the secret she had just unloaded.

'And do you know what my one hope is, before I die?'

Cas shook her head.

'That Toby should find someone who loves him, marry her and have children by that woman, and the family life that he has always been denied. Because, Cas, he deserves it.' Then Emily smiled at Cas. 'But don't worry, I'm not about to die yet!'

Cas smiled back. In the light of Emily's story, Cas's own decision and choices seemed suddenly very simple.

That night, Cas could not rest for worrying about Toby. She had no idea where he was, or how he was. What had happened to Pitts and Mrs Power? Cas shuddered at the thought of them. Unable to sleep, she rang the flat several times during the night, but there was no answer. She tried Sam's flat, but there was no one there either. Eventually, unable to sleep, in the early hours of the morning she tried the numbers again. Strangely, it was Toby who answered the phone in Sam's flat, but at least he was safe. Cas closed her eyes in relief and silently said thank you.

Toby sounded surprised when she told him she was at Emily's, but slightly pleased, too. Then he asked her if they had talked. Cas bit her lip.

'Yes.'

'So you know then?'

'Yes, I know,' she replied.

'Then there is one more thing you need to know.'

'What?'

'The man St John lost his hand to – his name was Victor Power.'

Cas dropped the phone.

## chapter twenty-five

Sam's night had continued in similar dramatic vein. Once he had come round on the floating platform to the tender ministrations of Bentley, the two had acted quickly. He had phoned the police straight away and let them know what was happening. They had arrived and, although somewhat surprised to find him accompanied by a six-foot golden pheasant, they had not been entirely averse to allowing Bentley to come down to the station with him. As far as Sam was concerned there was no argument: he was certainly not going to let such a specimen of womanhood go, and Bentley, it appeared, was highly reluctant to leave his side too. The two sat in the interrogation room, hand in hand, while Sam explained everything he knew about Power Publishing and what he suspected – that in fact Power knew very little of Power Publishing's interests in Rapture or edengirls. He told them about his trip to Nauru too, and the complicated set of financial hurdles that had been set up to protect the company from exposure – even from its founder. Sam suspected that with the purchase of the *Daily News* Wattle and Pitts had known their scam would soon be found out and so had got greedy in a last attempt to milk the company for all it was worth, and then they planned to disappear.

By now the river police had managed to catch up with the fleet of power boats, and very soon a bedraggled Wattle, several disconcerted-looking security men and Toby and Power trooped into the station. Only Pitts was missing.

Wattle and the security men were swiftly locked up – Power, it seemed, was going to be in for a long night of questioning. The police took a brief statement from Toby, then sent him outside to wait next to his father.

Victor Power had known this moment would come when his son would come and find him. And as much as he was shocked at the timing – the moment he discovered his two most loyal employees, one of whom was his wife, had bitterly betrayed him – he was also delighted. Among all the confusion of the evening, Power could only stare, admiringly, at the man before him who was so much his flesh and blood.

Toby looked like a good, brave man to him, handsome too, of which he was particularly proud. The fact that Toby had deliberately come and sought him out seemed to indicate that at last they might try and establish some kind of relationship. Power had never settled down with anyone long enough to have children, and his nonchalance in this area of his life was always aided by the knowledge that, somewhere, he already had a son.

Toby could see this pleasure in Power, and it warmed him to know that his father, his real father, was glad to be called that. It felt strange, very strange seeing him, but then the events of the entire evening had been surreal too. Eventually Power was called in to the interview room, and Toby was told he was free to go. Power turned and looked at him, shook him by the hand, then with a heavy heart, turned to face the reality of his hideous betrayal.

Meanwhile, Toby had rung the flat several times looking for Cas, but there had been no answer. Sam said there was no way Cas would go back there that night, and said it was far more likely she would be staying at a friend's.

'You sure she was all right when you dropped her off?' he asked.

'Well, she had quite a nasty cut on her head,' replied Toby. 'Perhaps I shouldn't have left her.' Toby regretted it now, and he knew that part of the reason he had left her was because he was still angry.

'Oh, don't worry, mate. She'll be fine. You know what Cas is like. Never more capable than in a crisis.'

Toby allowed himself to be comforted by Sam's breezy assumption, but he was still anxious to find her. Sam insisted Toby return to his flat and spend the night there, along with Bentley. But Bentley gave his hand a squeeze.

'It wouldn't look very good me leaving your place in the

morning in nothing but a spangly leotard and a head dress, would it?'

'I don't know,' replied Sam. 'I reckon my neighbours would be rather impressed.'

'No, Sam. I'm an old-fashioned girl. Give me a call tomorrow,' and with that she scribbled her number down on a bit of paper and Sam went to hail her a cab.

Cas watched the houses, roads and cars of the north rush past her as the train sped south. Sam had related to her the events of the night before on the phone: Pitts had eventually been apprehended at a ferry port trying to make a crossing to Amsterdam. This, it turned out, was where his and Mrs Power's centre of operations was based. The profits of their efforts, which Victor Power was beginning to discover went back for several years, were also apprehended. Power Publishing, it seemed, had been nothing less than an unwitting shell for the foul business scams of his closest and most trusted employees.

'What are you doing in Shropshire you nincompoop?' Sam had said on the phone to her that morning. 'It's perfectly safe down here – I've sorted it all out. The Wattle woman is going down, the *Guardian* has a scoop, and will madam be requiring a front page byline in tomorrow's paper?'

'Hmmm. Actually, Sam, I don't think so, in the light of my newly discovered relationship to Power.'

'Are you sure, Cas?' Sam sounded slightly incredulous. Wasn't this what Cas had been doing the whole thing for all along: the glory?

'Yes, I am sure,' replied Cas firmly.

'Okay then,' teased Sam, 'I shall keep all the glory to myself.'

'As you should do,' replied Cas seriously. 'I hope they are all very pleased with you down there.'

'I should say so. In fact, I have just been called into the editor's office where the great man himself has congratulated me warmly, clearly gleeful about tomorrow's impending sales, and has offered me the LA correspondent's job! Can you believe it? I'm off to La-La Land next month.'

'Sam, that's fantastic!' Cas congratulated him, really pleased that after all her bullying this whole debacle had been worthwhile. He sounded triumphant, she thought to herself. She had not heard this kind of joy in his voice for years.

'And at eight o'clock this evening,' he continued cockily, 'I shall be persuading a certain young lady to come with me.'

Ah, thought Cas, well that will be why then.

'I don't suppose by any chance that this young lady would be over six foot, blonde and sensational on an aerial trapeze, would she?'

'The very same!'

'Well, if you bag both Bentley and LA then I think you can consider yourself justly rewarded!'

'Damn right. I think she would go down a storm in LA, don't you?'

The two laughed, then, Sam said seriously 'It's been good working with you again Ms Brown.'

'Yeah, good job, Sam. Thanks for everything.'

'No. I should thank you. The paper's got a huge scoop tomorrow thanks to you, and I get the glory.'

'Hey, that's how it should be.'

'You sure you don't want a byline?'

'Yes. Somehow it doesn't seem very important any more.' Cas sounded sad as she said this.

Sam paused, thinking what to say. He and Toby had spent most of the night talking. 'Look, Cas, if it's worth anything, I think Toby's a great bloke.'

Cas smiled. 'I know that.'

'And if I am not being too presumptuous, I think he thinks the same about you too.'

'I hope so,' mumbled Cas.


Cas's taxi pulled up outside the Old Street flat. Inside Toby was waiting, and Cas's heart was pounding hard as she tried to control her nerves. The two had not sat down and talked together for so long, she almost had no idea what to say.

Toby opened the door of the flat as she got out of the taxi, he must have been waiting and watching for her. She turned and smiled at him, but he looked different: he was hunched over and his forehead was creased into a frown. With a pang, Cas realized how much he had been, and was, going through.

The two moved clumsily around each other, pecking each other on the cheek in greeting, bumping into each other as they went up the stairs. The absence of the easy familiarity they had once known was all too strongly felt.

In the kitchen they made tea, eager for something to do that was natural, organized. Finally, they sat down at the table together.

'Toby, I owe you an apology,' began Cas, 'I have not been there for you when you really needed me, and I am so sorry.'

'Well, I can see you've been busy.' Cas looked away, guilty. 'Look, it's not been easy finding out about my father,' Toby continued eventually. 'But I am dealing with it: I've met him now, which is something, and he's not the monster he's made out to be. We are going to write to each other for a bit to start with. We talked for a while, but it's a lot to take in at once, so we decided writing was better.' Cas nodded encouragingly. 'He has also offered to pay for Dad – I mean St John – to go into a home which is nice of him. I think Mum is going to accept.'

'That's great.'

'Yeah, I think it'll make her happier in the end.'

'She deserves it. You know, I learnt something from your mum last night. Learnt how lucky I am, or was. She never had the choices I had, but I don't think I have appreciated what I had until now, when, maybe, it might be too late . . .'

Cas let her voice trail off, and looked questioningly at Toby. The sentence hung in the air. Toby looked uncomfortable.

'Look, Cas, maybe you thought all the time you were in the office I was sitting around the flat doing nothing – not washing your clothes, not cleaning the floor, not working on my art. But maybe I *was* doing something, just in a different way from you. I don't have to be plugged in to a phone and an email and a tight schedule. I don't feel I have to be doing several things all at once for it to be a worthwhile day.'

Cas frowned, mortified, and hung her head in shame. 'I know Toby, I was wrong.'

'And just because you are "going out and getting", that does not make you the provider and me the receiver. I was providing, you just weren't here to take it, not paying any attention. If you are going to be the one who takes responsibility and plays the man then you are also going to have to accept you are a woman too. You need nurturing and caring for, as do I. I want you to be the best person you can be Cas, but you have to let me help. What, exactly, is it that you want?'

Cas paused. 'I've thought a lot about this recently, Toby,' she mumbled, 'and I think I know what the answer is.' Cas looked up from the circles she was drawing on the table with her finger. Looking him straight in the eye, she said earnestly, 'I want you. I want you back. But I also want the time to enjoy having you back.'

Toby smiled at her and for the first time the frown on his forehead dissolved. 'Well, we've done everything your way and it hasn't exactly worked out, so what do you say to trying it my way for a bit? I have made a bit of money. Enough for us to go and live somewhere beautiful for a while, a good long while, and you can do some writing and I am going to do some sculpting. And we are going to be together and every day we will watch the sun set. And then when our money has run out we will see how it is we want to make some more.'

Cas nodded slowly.

'But it is going to mean leaving here, this town, all your security. This morning the landlord came round wanting to know where his rent cheque was. I paid him, but I said that we would be leaving by the end of the month. Are you in?'

Cas looked up into the face of the man she loved and smiled. Without hesitation, she replied: 'Oh baby, I'm in.'

# chapter twenty-six

A few days later, Cas found herself sitting on the tube once again, undertaking the well-trodden journey from her flat to the offices of the *Daily News*. On her lap were a pile of newspapers she was flicking through – the fallout from the Power case was still dominating the headlines.

Power had gone public with his condemnation of his recent bride, and the fact that his very own wife had actually managed to fool Britain's most notorious porn baron seemed to convince everyone that Power had known nothing about the treachery beforehand. He was also doing his best to absolve the company from any of the business dealings Wattle and Pitts had been channelling through it. With a hefty charity donation to the NSPCC and several stories he ran in his own paper protesting his innocence, his public profile appeared to have been done nothing but good. Already he was organizing another *Hiya!/Daily News* party, which he announced would be a charity event with the proceeds split between various immigration and children's organizations. The prospect had apparently driven Adrian Fagge to the Priory where he was frustrating therapists by making 'To Do' lists in the middle of his sessions.

On the back pages the talk was all of premiership pin-up Silvio Ravelli. His ongoing and very public relationship with Floriana Dos Santos appeared to be causing his manager such consternation that Ferguson had announced Silvio was being sold back to Brazil 'where he belongs'. The premier Rio club, Flamengo, had apparently made a record offer for the young striker, who stood to become even richer from the transfer. There were excerpts from an interview with his mother which had been published in Rio's *O Globo* newspaper, where she praised the Lord for the return of her son, and the many riches that were being bestowed on her family. She was already commissioning architect's plans for a huge mansion to be built on a hill above the city, which was to house the entire family as well as Silvio and his new fiancée Floriana. Silvio had, apparently, greatly enjoyed himself in England but had been rather depressed by the weather and the girls. He was therefore much looking forward to returning to his home city and playing for 'the greatest club in the world'.

'That girl Charlotte Want used my son and broke his heart,' were his mother's thoughts on the subject. 'I am only praising the Almighty God that at last he has found true love with a proper Brazilian woman.'

*

As for Charlotte, she was still drawing headlines herself, although perhaps not in the manner she had expected. After the debacle of her stage performance, Cosima Beane had persuaded her to take part in a 'Living Art Installation' in the front window of her now notorious gallery. Clad only in a couple of fig leaves, Charlotte spent the hours of daylight posing with a drugged snake wrapped around her, while a strapline across the window read 'The Real Eden Girl'. Desperate not to be forgotten by the fame game, Charlotte was enduring her new role, but Doug was trying to get her other work at Gloria and Charlotte's hourly request. All he had come up with so far was Victor Power's offer to have her posing as the lottery girl for the masthead of the *Daily News*.

'Who do you think I am? F***ing Anthea Turner?' had been Charlotte's response to that. 'And get me out of the company of this bloody snake – fast!'.

Cas folded the papers into her bag and got off at her stop. How wonderful, she thought, that I no longer have to do this journey every day. She walked across the bridge and revelled in the fact it was now nearly noon and not the morning rush hour. In the lobby of the *Daily News* building Terry waved a quick hello but was occupied with unwrapping a large object that was being winched onto a podium in the centre of the lobby.

Cas took the lift to the magazine floor where she was met like some kind of returning heroine. Although her involvement in the *Guardian* story had not been publicly acknowledged, it was well-known in the bars of Fleet Street that much of the story had been 'an inside job'. The staff on the magazine were genuinely thrilled to see her and among their hugs and kisses, some even cried – although they explained this was because Tamara had been so evil in her absence and had been bullying everyone else mercilessly, particularly since the magazine had started to fall apart. Then Tamara herself appeared at the door of her office. She was wearing her regulation spike heels, a micro-mini skirt, a huge power jacket and, disconcertingly, a welcoming smile. Tamara had never once, in all the time that Cas had known her, smiled at her.

'Cas!' She beamed delightedly. 'How wonderful to see you again. Welcome back!'

Cas felt nauseous just at the sight of her, let alone at the insincerity of her greeting.

'Hello, Tamara,' she replied, looking forward to the ensuing conversation, and followed her inside her office. For once, Tamara shut the door behind her without slamming it.

'Do sit down, Cas,' she begged. 'Now, tell me: how are you?'

'I'm okay. It's been quite a mad couple of weeks, but I think I'm okay now.'

'Well, that's great news, Cas,' continued Tamara simperingly. 'Now, I asked you in because I had a little chat with Victor the other day. He is, as you know, incredibly grateful for all your sleuthing skills in tracking down the corruption of Wattle and Pitts. He was also rather impressed.' Tamara said this last rather conspiratorially, expecting Cas to agree with her by admitting her surprise and gratitude. Cas merely nodded. Tamara cleared her throat and continued. 'Well, anyway, he asked me to convey to you that your presence has been sorely missed on the magazine –' Tamara coughed, she was clearly finding this very difficult – 'which it has.'

Cas, however, was rather enjoying it.

'You proved yourself to be a very talented editor while you were here, he said, and he wants me to get you back. I assured him that wouldn't be a problem at all as we had had such a fantastic working relationship. Wouldn't you agree?'

Cas suppressed a smile and looked down at her feet, but refused to grant Tamara the satisfaction of a nod of agreement.

'So I would like to offer you your job back.'

Tamara waited. Cas said nothing.

'With a ten per cent raise.'

Cas continued to stare at the floor, the corners of her mouth twitching quite uncontrollably.

'I can also inform you that your title would be grander as well, you could be called editor as long as I was something like editor in chief.'

Typical, thought Cas. She couldn't stand me getting a promotion without her getting one too.

'Obviously we would like you to start again as soon as possible. Would tomorrow be okay?'

Cas looked at Tamara properly. Were those bags under her eyes? Cas recollected her own delight the other morning when she had got out of bed and and noticed that, for the first time in years, she had managed to get rid of hers.

'Naturally anything pertaining to your sacking would be swept under the carpet, Caris. I mean, under the circumstances . . .'

Cas nodded. Tamara waited. And waited.

'So,' Tamara drew in a breath sharply, 'would tomorrow be okay? Victor is most keen I persuade you to start as soon as possible.'

Cas finally allowed herself to smile. This was about to be one of the sweetest moments of her life.

'Tamara, thank you very much for your very kind offer, and for all the lovely things you, or Victor, has said about me, but I'm afraid wild horses wouldn't drag me back to this magazine. I have discovered there are much more important things in life. So I'm afraid I'm going to have to turn you down.'

Tamara's face fell, and the fake smile she had plastered on to it disappeared in an instant.

'What?' she replied rudely. 'You can't say no – I promised Victor you wouldn't!'

'I'm afraid it is a no,' confirmed Cas, enjoying every second of this revenge.

'Is it the money? Do you want more money?'

Cas shook her head.

'Or your own office? Is that what you want?'

Cas continued to shake her head, a giggle now rising fast in her throat.

'More power? Your own secretary?'

Still Cas was shaking her head.

'Well, what the hell is it you want then?' shouted Tamara, incredulous that all these luxuries had been turned down.

'Tamara, you don't seem to understand – I don't want to come back here and work for you.'

'Well, that's a very stupid decision to make, Caris!' snapped Tamara impatiently, giving Cas every reason to believe it was exactly the right one. 'Do you have any idea what a prestigious job this is? You'll never make an editor if you turn this down. This is a fantastic opportunity for you!' Tamara was spitting like an overheated frying pan.

'Well, I'm afraid I think differently, Tamara. I've already tried out this job, and I have to tell you I didn't have a very happy time here. So I'm going to freelance for a while, do some writing and live a little differently. I am moving out of London, which hopefully means I can spend more time with Toby – I do hope you understand.'

Tamara burst into tears and began to crawl under her desk in a last ditch attempt to persuade Cas to change her mind, but Cas ignored her. Gathering up her bag, she walked out of the office.

As the lift doors opened into the sunlight of the lobby, the crisp sun of a December day filled the glass room with light, and Cas knew she was doing the right thing. For the first time she felt really free. She walked across the marble floor to the door she had been so unceremoniously kicked out of last time she was here. In the centre of the lobby, the security guard had just unveiled a sculpture mounted on a plinth. It was quite beautiful, thought Cas, as she surveyed it for the first time. Abstract, yes, but still the shapely curves of the woman holding her swollen belly were quite obvious to make out.

She paused and examined it for a second. The expression on the woman's face – one of pain, but one of pride too – was one she would always carry with her.